There was something in his eyes.

A bright reflection of…a hard and ruthless warrior? Whatever it was in his eyes, it was of the angelic dominions.

He moved swif'' 'h hers. He brackete essing too roughly, re he wanted her.

It was a kiss. ...prising kiss. Rough and fast.

Pyx had not been kissed before. And it was being issued by a Fallen one. To a Sinistari. How many ways of wrong was that?

Didn't feel wrong. Felt kind of tingly and exciting.

Cooper swept his tongue across hers. A giddy sparkle radiated in Pyx's belly—until he pushed her away and stepped across the room. Hand to a hip, he turned and gazed at her.

She swiped her mouth with the back of her hand, forcing out her most pissed tone. "That's not how you disarm an opponent?"

"Oh no?" He toed the blade and kicked it across the floor toward her boot. "Looks like it worked."

Dear Reader,

Opposites do attract, and that makes writing, and thinking up new and interesting heroes and heroines so much fun. It's not always easy. The hero of Fallen has no past. He's an angel, and before he landed on earth, well, he spent a lot of time just hanging out in Heaven, imprisoned for his original Fall thousands of years ago. So where to begin with a man who has so much to learn, and the entire world before him?

One of my favorite qualities in a man is a childlike wonder—the ability to see the world as if for the first time, and Cooper is that man. I hope you'll enjoy this entry in my *Of Angels and Demons* series. And so you know, this story is a part of the overall paranormal world that I write in, and I call it Beautiful Creatures.

For more information on my books and the characters within them, do stop by my website: michelehauf.com

Love Michele

FALLEN

MICHELE HAUF

5 306 270.

All the characters in this book have no existence outside the imagination of
the author, and have no relation whatsoever to anyone bearing the same name
or names. They are not even distantly inspired by any individual known or
unknown to the author, and all the incidents are pure invention.

First published in Great Britain 2011
by Mills & Boon, an imprint of Harlequin (UK) Limited,
Eton House, 18-24 Paradise Road, Richmond, Surrey TW9 1SR

© Michele Hauf 2011

ISBN: 978 0 263 88010 6

89-0611

Harlequin (UK) policy is to use papers that are natural, renewable and
recyclable products and made from wood grown in sustainable forests. The
logging and manufacturing processes conform to the legal environmental
regulations of the country of origin.

Printed and bound in Spain
by Blackprint CPI, Barcelona

Michele Hauf has been writing for over a decade and has published historical, fantasy and paranormal romance. A good strong heroine, action and adventure, and a touch of romance make for her favorite kind of story. (And if it's set in France, all the better.) She lives with her family in Minnesota, and loves the four seasons, even if one of them lasts six months and can be colder than a deep-freeze. You can find out more about her at: www. michelehauf.com.

To any and all who like to marvel
and wonder at the world.

Prologue

Pyxion the Other had been waiting for a summons to earth too long to fathom the passage of time. Centuries had passed. Even millennia.

Now Pyx stood among the mortals on a busy street in a city that boasted the much-lauded, medieval Nôtre Dame cathedral. After a night of walking the world—for that is how the Sinistari gained knowledge and assimilated to the mortal realm—a fierce intuition had led Pyx to Paris.

Cars, trucks and two-wheeled motorbikes zoomed by dangerously fast. The air held a miasma of chemical smells and off-gases. The chatter of water in an ancient fountain seemed out of place tucked among the urban sprawl, the result of rapidly growing populations over the centuries.

Pyx had arrived from Beneath naked and in human form, and so with but a mental gesture, had adopted clothing similar to that which nearby mortals wore. Dark, slim-fitted jeans, boots with a good heel and chains, and a button-up shirt that sported a bloody skull diagonally on the shoulder. It got the looks. Mortals stopped to gawk as Pyx strode by, confident and head held high, jaw snapping at gum snatched from a vendor's stand, which proved an interesting mortal treat.

Passing a mortal female chattering with another, Pyx nicked the pink cellular phone from her back pocket, without missing a stride. The small device had a touch screen and it fascinated Pyx. The learning curve was a snap thanks to small icons on the screen. Aiming the camera lens across the street, the demon took a photograph of a couple kissing; the man's hands were hidden high beneath the woman's short leather skirt.

"Have to get me some of that," Pyx said with an agreeable nod. "Mmm, lust."

Sinistari were notorious for indulging in mortal sin. And what Pyx saw going on between the man and woman sure looked like a lot of sin.

Tucking the phone in a back pocket, Pyx strode purposefully across a busy street and aimed for the garish display of colored flash decorating the window of a tattoo shop.

A street vendor had set up outside the tattoo

shop, and Pyx leaned over to smell the fresh, sea-
soned meat turning slowly on the vertical rotisserie.
Being consigned to Beneath had stripped away all
sensations such as touch, taste and smell. It was
all Pyx could do to wait as the vendor stuffed the
savory meat into the soft gyro bread.

"Give me one with pomme frites." Pyx pointed
to the greasy fries that glistened with salt crystals.
Speaking French was easy, for while walking the
world the demon had assimilated all languages.

The vendor handed over a paper-wrapped lump
of warm gyro bread, sliced pork, and deep-fried
pomme frites. Pyx touched the vendor's forehead
with two fingers and shoved. "Keep the change,
buddy."

The vendor nodded and smiled widely at the
large tip Pyx had added along with the price of
food. Demons could put thoughts into mortal's hec-
tic minds far too easily in this day and age. It was
one more sliver of unremarkable chaos added to
the heap inside a mortal's brain.

The first bite was spectacular. Grease oozed and
bread squished. Savory and warm, it hit a wanting
spot in the demon. A deep, achy spot that wanted
more. Earth offered far and beyond the pleasure
Beneath had offered, because Beneath had offered
nothing. Nothing.

Pyx gobbled up the gyro and studied the tattoo

flash posted on the window. The skull with the worms crawling through the eye sockets appealed.

"Oh, yeah," Pyx muttered, nodding.

Or maybe, the skeletal angel with wings on fire. "That's what I'm going to do to you, Fallen one."

The demon tossed the empty food wrapper over a shoulder and it missed the trash by a long shot. "Watch out. I'm coming for you, Juphiel."

But first, a little decoration for this plain mortal costume the demon had been given.

Striding inside the tattoo shop, Pyx nodded to the beat of the loud rock music and swaggered over to the grinning skin artist. Tugging up the shirt in the back, Pyx straddled the chair and sat through two hours of pain.

Wow! It hurt like a— Pyx had nothing to compare it to. Never felt *anything* like that before. This mortal costume provided pain and sensation the demon had never felt while in its adamant demonic form. But nothing was going to make this demon flinch.

When the tattoo artist finished and rubbed a cool ointment over the elaborate design, Pyx refused a bandage.

"You should keep it covered for twenty-four hours," the artist explained in French. "It will not heal properly."

Pyx ran a finger through the ointment, and then wiped it on the artist's shirtsleeve. "It'll be healed by the time I step outside your fine establishment. Now, how much? I've got places to go, things to see, angels to slay."

The artist said it would be five hundred euros.

Pyx gazed into the artist's eyes. "Paid."

The man nodded. "Thanks. Hey, honey, you come back to Spider if you want another tat."

"Honey?"

Pyx sneered and wondered briefly if the man was one of those homosexuals. He paid the demon no mind as he went about cleaning his work area.

Swinging about to study the tattoo in the mirror on the bathroom door, the Sinistari demon hissed at the image staring back.

A tall redheaded person with hair down to the elbows cast a startled look in the mirror. Curves rounded in at torso and out at hips and stretched the shirt across the chest. The clothing fit well, but it was disconcerting because the style was made for men. And what Pyx saw…

"A female? No freakin' way."

What in all of Beneath? Was this some kind of joke? The Sinistari demon always manifested as male once summoned from Beneath. As far as Pyx knew.

Pyx turned sideways and clamped both palms over the breasts stretching the cotton shirt. The tattoo artist gave her a questioning look.

"Yep, they're real." Her lips pouted a little too

femininely when she made a face. Upon arriving, he—or rather *she*—had assumed the clothing so quickly, he—*she*—hadn't noticed the extra curves.

"Problem?" the artist asked as he cleaned his tattoo gun with an alcohol swab.

Pyx swung and hooked a hand at her hip. "You think I'm a girl?"

"You got a problem with your sexuality, pretty demoiselle?" He smirked, revealing the tip of a gold incisor. "There is a group that meets down the street every so often. They talk about how they're trapped in the wrong body."

"I am not trapped. I am…" She looked in the mirror. Pretty, as far as mortal women went, she had to admit. She wouldn't turn away from such a sexy looker, that was for sure. *She?* "…a chick?"

What, in the black sea Beneath, kind of joke was this?

Rolling her head and huffing, Pyx kicked the door open and stomped out from the small studio. The gyro vendor smiled and cocked his head toward her. She was still hungry—she'd never be full—but now her appetite waned.

She, she, *she!*

She'd been saddled with a chick body while here on earth to track a renegade Fallen who would be hot to track his muse and put a nephilim child in her belly.

Well, she wouldn't let appearance keep her from being the best Sinistari ever. She could do this. She *would* do this. Didn't want to risk being sent back Beneath because she wasn't doing the job properly.

She'd have to accept the fact she may be a female for her duration on earth.

"Ugg."

Tromping down the sidewalk in her shitkickers, Pyx now mused about the name the other Sinistari had given her while serving time Beneath: Pyxion *the Other.*

Apparently they had known something she had not.

"Joke's on you, Pyx. Deal with it."

Chapter 1

The dance floor thundered with hyped-up, sexually charged adrenaline. Cooper danced in the center, surrounded by hundreds of bodies that gave off a variety of scents from soft and powdery, to baby-can-we-do-it-right-now?

The sensory world was new to him, and he couldn't get enough of it. The women in their slithery clothing and dangly jewels tantalized him like sweet treats as they bumped and slid up next to his skin. The mortal skin he wore felt it all; sexy fabric with beads and metal, human heat, sweat, muscle and hard nipples.

Promises of a good time flashed in the women's eyes. Cooper took it in with a confident grin.

All the sensations he'd been denied for millennia were now his to dive into headfirst.

He couldn't remember when he'd unbuttoned the white dress shirt to let it hang on his shoulders and expose his abs. The kilt was freeing. The combat boots were not so easy to dance in—but he was no twinkle-toes to begin with.

Didn't matter. The women weren't eyeing his dance moves; their blatant focus was from Cooper's head to just about crotch level. *Look all you like, ladies.* He'd never been admired before. Vanity, thy name is Cooper Truhart.

The DJ had announced the song blasting over the speakers was called "Welcome to The World," and Cooper appreciated the welcome, indeed. He intended to enjoy his stay here on earth. Everything about it was amazing.

Most of all, he intended to make this stay permanent.

This mortal costume he wore served him well. It had muscles in all the right places, and put him inches in height above everyone else. His hair was dark and spiky with some bits hanging over his forehead. The women loved it, and many had run their fingers through it, sparking an erotic sensation down his spine he wanted to feel again and again.

Despite the earthbound costume, he hadn't lost all his supernatural strength. He could toss a car across the street if he found the need to do so. A fist to a mortal's jaw could tear it off, so he held back from fighting for the thrill of it. It was a difficult urge to quell. The fight ran through his blood, but he wanted to change—to gain humanity.

Since falling, he'd not lost all his angelic abilities. He could flash across the world, landing in one city or the next in an instant. He possessed sensory skills that would blow the mortals off their feet—literally, and his vision was only now beginning to take on color after a long confinement parasongs away from this vivid realm.

He never wanted to return to the Ninth Void. It had been a drag.

The beat increased and he danced closer to the blonde whose short red skirt fought to draw his eyes up from the fuck-me pumps. He knew that was the slang term for the shoes because a few weeks ago when he'd arrived on earth, he'd walked the world, taking in knowledge of it all.

That night he'd assimilated the world, the mortal society, their economy, their travails and triumphs. He could speak all languages and understood most of what he'd learned—though the mathematics and daily-life accounting stuff gave him problems. It was a good thing he didn't need to keep a checkbook.

He had experienced women across the world, in all shapes, sizes, colors and ages—and levels of sexual desire. Women wanted him, and he was no man to deny them.

Kissing. Ah, kissing! Was there anything finer? He'd kissed dozens in his fortnight upon earth, and had no intention of slowing down his quest for sensory exploration and fulfillment. There were so many varieties of kisses that he felt sure he'd never tire of trying new ways to make a woman squirm and giggle with delight.

He liked the blonde ones with the big breasts. But he also preferred the smart ones who could hold a conversation about something beyond the color of their nail polish or which celebrity was screwing whom.

This one shaking her red-spangled skirt before him looked a bit vacuous and maybe…stoned. He couldn't understand those who chose to dull the sensory experience with drugs or alcohol. Life was meant to be lived fully and with a clear mind.

He turned and dance-walked his way to the center of the dance floor where he paired up with a redhead whose smile touched his innate desire to flirt. With a shake of her head she tossed her loose hair over a shoulder and curved her body against his to give him a hip-bump.

Nice. But not dressed like the others. She wore masculine clothes, jeans and a long-sleeved shirt and boots. Yet her sinuous movements told Cooper she was all woman.

And she smelled, hmm…like lunch. He'd noticed the same scent wafting from street vendors parked along the main tourist streets edging the river.

Cooper had eaten little since coming to earth. His interest swayed more toward the sensual delights than the succulent. Though the two experiences combined did have their appeal. This woman's allure and savory scent captivated his desire. Cooper danced as close as he could get to her.

She tipped a smile over her shoulder at him. Wide blue eyes were surrounded by deep ruby hair that glittered under the flashing club lights.

Man, he loved seeing in color now. When he'd served the angelic dominions, earth and all its inhabitants and elements had appeared to him in black and white.

And the woman's mouth. More rubies there, but he didn't detect cosmetics on her pale, flawless skin. Her lips were naturally red, as if they'd been kissed soundly.

Tonight, he'd take this one home with him and learn exactly what style of kissing would have her begging him to do more than simply kiss.

"You're lovely," he said over the raucous music and shouts to "Rock it!"

She merely smiled and dipped a hip against his, while drawing her fingers down his bare chest.

Cooper could feel her touch all the way through to his spine. Sparkles of energy radiated through him. Life. Damn, it was so good!

With a flirtatious wink, the woman slipped away. Now she danced between two women, their breasts brushing and fingers teasing across exposed skin. Now there was a fascinating touch. Mmm…

Cooper let out a wanting moan, and dipped his head to maintain sight on the redhead until a couple danced before him. He scanned the crowd, but couldn't spy her lustrous hair or those pouting lips.

Lost her. But he'd find her again. Women liked to tease. The night was young and he was in no hurry. The world was his and he wanted to hug it, suck it all in, and keep it forever.

And drink it. Time for a whiskey break.

Easing his way off the dance floor, Cooper strutted up the nightclub's open staircase. Each step flashed red as his boot tripped the motion sensors. Twisting a glance over the dance floor below, he slapped a palm to his sweaty abs and nodded, satisfied.

Oh, yes, he'd find the redhead later.

"Whiskey?" the bartender prompted, recognizing Cooper from the last three nights.

"Three shots," he said. "Line 'em up."

When he found a place he liked he returned. But most important, Cooper didn't feel *compelled* to be in this particular city. That was a key point. Because the one annoying aspect about the Fallen was that once their feet had touched earth, they were compelled to find their muse.

A muse was a human female, descended from the Merovingian bloodline, whom the Fallen one sought to mate with to then produce a nephilim child, a hideous monster, that once unleashed, would spread chaos across the earth.

Cooper wasn't into chaos or becoming some baby's daddy right now. He just wanted to enjoy this exciting and intriguing realm.

How he'd come to earth from his imprisonment in the Ninth Void he had no clue. Someone had summoned him from his many millennia of seclusion.

He appreciated the summons. But he knew only danger waited for him.

Millennia ago, he had agreed to a pact, along with dozens more angels, to fall to earth and mate with its human females. After unfathomable time serving Puriel, the war master of the Power ranks, Cooper had been so ready to fall. Actually, it had been the angel Kadesch who had opened his eyes to humanity.

Juphiel (his angelic name, which he had no intention of using on earth) had fallen from the heavens, but had never seen Kadesch again. He'd only begun to teach mortals on earth his craft—a manner of creating beauty that Cooper still retained, thank the heavens—a short time before a great flood had swept him to the Ninth Void, a silent, cold prison where he'd existed in utter darkness awaiting final judgment for betraying Him.

"No more imprisonment or warring," he said with a tilt of the shot glass. The whiskey burned down his throat. "I'll never go back." He slammed the glass on the bar and gripped the next shot glass. "All I have to do is find my halo and I'll be home free."

During an angel's fall to earth, their halo fell away. Cooper knew if he could find the thing, he could cease this ridiculous quest he'd originally agreed to—a quest to find a muse.

So not going to happen. Because it had all been a lie.

And if what he'd learned the first time he'd walked earth were true, what usually happened to a Fallen immediately following mating with a muse was death. Death delivered by the one creature forged specifically to track the Fallen and slay them—the Sinistari demon.

He'd encountered a Sinistari since arriving on earth. The demons were a difficult kill, but not impossible. Now, Cooper kept one eye over his shoulder.

He would not go out without a fight.

"Not on my watch," Cooper said, and tilted back the second round.

He growled with satisfaction at the drink's toffee-malt bite, and eyed the back of the bar where the pool tables queued along the wall. He was familiar with the rules and techniques, but hadn't attempted the game. He'd win. No sense in trying when he knew the outcome.

Just as he reached for the third shot a feminine hand grabbed the glass and tipped it back in a quick swallow. "Another!" she called, and the bartender appeared with the whiskey bottle. "Man, that stuff is good."

It was the redhead who wore men's clothing. She slapped the bar in thanks as the bartender topped off her shot, then tilted it back with more gusto than Cooper had performed.

She winked at him, then sauntered off into the crowd.

Crossing his arms and leaning against the bar, Cooper followed the sexy siren's journey through the crush of dancing bodies. She stood as tall as him so it was easy to spot her in the crowd. She carried her head high and segued into a group that matched the music's rhythm.

She caught him staring and blew him a kiss, her red lips puckering sexily.

Man, did he love the women.

* * *

The guy with the mousse-slicked white hair and silver hoop earrings was definitely not human. Vampire, Pyx decided, and in confirmation, he flashed fang when he leaned in to whisper into a mortal woman's ear.

While mortals did not believe in those creatures they labeled *paranormal,* Pyx wasn't so stupid. If angels and demons trod the earth then so did all the rest of the monsters and freaks.

Her job was to ensure a nephilim did not join the freak ranks.

"Let the games begin."

It was dark in the bar, save for the frenetic lights flashing violet and red and bouncing off the corrugated steel walls. The atmosphere was disturbing. Frantic, alive and vital. After so much time spent Beneath she craved the activity. Adrenaline coursed through her system. Yet she needed to focus. And wonder upon wonders, the first nightclub she'd chosen had turned up the Fallen she was after. Go, Sinistari!

The Fallen had not said anything to her when she'd stolen his drink. She wasn't sure how to take that. Not defending his property? A wimp? Or a gentleman who would allow a woman to do as she desired?

Either way, for some reason, said task had suddenly taken on new weight as she watched the pale-

haired vampire eye another vamp across the room.
That dude wasn't here for kicks; he was following
someone. She knew it because she was doing the
same thing.

"Vampires," she muttered. "I so don't need this
trouble."

Pyx slapped a palm across the leather sheath she
wore strapped under her left arm. The Sinistari had
the ability to allow mortals to only see what they
wanted them to see; the sheathed dagger was only
for her eyes.

And yet her eyes didn't stray from her two new
marks. The bloodsuckers sent some kind of silent
signal back and forth through the nightclub. The
one farthest away in the balcony had his eye on a
man at the rear of the room—the Fallen one. There
were so many supernatural vibrations—vampire to
vamp, angel to demon—Pyx had a hard time keeping them straight.

So she turned her focus to the prize. The Fallen
wore a green-and-blue plaid kilt, of all things, and
was currently advertising virility and sex appeal
to the woman who slobbered over him. His dark
hair was razored short and finger-combed. A white
shirt fell open to reveal muscled abs and chest
with a tease of dark hair. His legs were striking
only because Pyx had never seen a man in a skirt
wearing combat boots, and working the look so
freaking well.

Seriously? She loved the diverse range of clothing in this day and age, but even she knew the man had daring.

Pyx could understand the attraction the other women were feeling. It was a new feeling, but a good one that centered in her belly and stirred even lower.

Hmm, all that just from observing the Fallen? A bit unsettling, but she marked it off as part of the job.

Even though she hadn't had the opportunity to dabble in it yet, lust was one of her favorite sins. Sin fed her kind.

She wasn't about to starve herself.

Pyx kept one eye on the vampires and another on the angel.

"Lucky bastard got himself a nice mortal costume," she said. Her cowboy boots clomped along the narrow aisle between tables and bar. "Let's see how much he likes mine."

Cooper turned toward the redhead, startled he hadn't noticed her approach. It was the chick from the dance floor. The same chick who'd boldly tossed back his shots and had sauntered away without so much as a thank-you.

But she had blown that kiss, which meant she was interested. His charms would prove irresistible to her once he kissed her for real. And she was walking toward him all intent and licking her lips—

Cooper's Adam's apple compressed against his spine. His shoulders slammed against the wall.

The redhead's fingers squeezed about his throat. Cooper gagged. His feet left the floor. She was so strong!

"How's tricks?" she asked. Her eyelashes were so long they tangled in stray strands of her hair. She smiled, not nicely, and in fact, rather wickedly.

Cooper couldn't answer, or slip from her grip. What in Beneath? Were they making the pretty ones so strong now?

Jamming her knee into his bollocks, she managed to unleash an inner rage he'd thought long harnessed after his war days Above. He shoved her away and wrangled her arm, twisting it behind her back and slamming her chest against the wall.

"What kind of game are you playing, sweetie?" he hissed at her ear. "You shouldn't damage the merchandise. Won't make tricks any fun later on."

She chuckled and elbowed him. He took the surprise poke to his abdomen with a gasped "Buh."

Much as he enjoyed females, he wasn't about to let one treat him this way. Not in front of the other women.

He managed to shove her into a nearby booth and she landed on the padded black vinyl, but not without pulling him onto the seat behind her.

Cooper eyed the bar. If anyone saw him wrestling with this woman, they'd suspect it was all his to-do, and not the sweet woman's fault.

Sweet, his ass. She didn't look capable of the wrestling feat she'd just performed. Too sexy. Too soft. Hair he'd like to tangle his fingers into. And did she smell like bubble gum? But for the strange masculine clothing she was a walking advertisement for all the sensual delights.

"You like it rough?" he said, sliding up to her and grabbing her wrist before she could slap him. "If so, you may be able to talk me into some rough stuff. But you gotta keep your knees from my crotch, sweetheart. That's foul play."

"I don't want to have sex with you," she said.

Cooper felt the sharp sting of a blade against his throat. Another new touch sensation. He cautioned himself from swallowing. "Whoa." Not only was she tough, she was also fast.

This was his first taste of crazy since landing on earth. Interesting, yet annoying.

He wasn't sure how much of a loose cannon this one was, and what her intentions were, so he placed his hands flat on the table to show compliance.

"I want to slay you," she said. Again she granted him that wide, not-so-mirthful grin. "Where's your muse, Fallen one?"

How could she possibly know what he was? Unless...

She couldn't be. He couldn't get a good look at the blade. He'd seen a dagger forged to kill Fallen once before—about five seconds before he had reached inside the Sinistari's chest and ripped out its adamant heart. But this wasn't right. He'd thought the Sinistari were male.

"You got it," she answered his thoughts. "I'm your worst nightmare in the one form I bet you absolutely crave, eh? A pretty redhead with nice breasts?"

"Don't flatter yourself, sweetie." He thought to wrangle the blade from her, but knew it could be his death. "Sinistari?"

"Surprise," she singsonged. "You were expecting someone a bit more macho?"

"Oh, I think you've mastered macho."

And he had only to stab his fingers between her ribs and rip out the hard, metal heart that, like his, never beat.

He couldn't take her out in the club. Everyone would notice. And he guessed she'd put up a splendid fight.

"Could you put the blade away?" he asked calmly. "One thing I do know is that thing only works on me when I'm in half form."

More specifically, when he was half human, half angel, and attempting to have sex with his mortal muse. Like that was ever going to happen.

"Sorry to break this to you, Red, but I'm not going to give you what you want."

"You're a liar."

"We just met, sweetheart. And frankly, you don't know anything about me and what I want on this earth. And how are you a female?"

She kicked back in the booth and put up one snakeskin-booted foot on the table. If she weren't Sinistari, Cooper would find her attractive. Hell, he'd already been thinking about what he would do if she were naked and was allowed to unleash his arsenal of kisses upon her.

But not a Sinistari demon. No way in Beneath or Above. The Sinistari's only task was to slay the Fallen. That meant him.

The pretty redhead with the bubble-gum smile and savory scent was the last female walking this earth Cooper wanted to touch, unless it was to rip out her heart.

And yet, one always kept their enemies close if one wished to draw breath the following morning.

"This is the way I was forged," she offered, her elbow hooking over the back of the booth. She chewed the gum and snapped it loudly. "You don't like it? Tough. Now, I don't want to spoil your fun, and I am disappointed you're not sexing up your muse right now, but tell me why vampires are following you."

"Vampires?"

"You didn't notice? Figures. You're too busy picking out tonight's sheetmate. There are two bloodsuckers in the club, and they are hot on your plaid butt."

Cooper wasn't sure how vampires played into the game between Sinistari and Fallen. Nor had he noticed, or would he notice, if a couple of vampires had been eyeing him up. They blended easily with mortals, and their kind could only determine one from another by a touch called the shimmer. An angel could connect to that shimmer, but only if he were searching for such a connection.

"You're mistaken," he said.

"I'm never wrong."

"That's funny, considering you can't have been on earth more than a few days. *Never* hasn't quite the impact."

Twisting her hair about a finger, she nodded toward the balcony railing. "Look down there."

He followed her pointing finger, but was wary she had not put away the blade. The Sinistari demon wielded the only blade that could pierce his solid glass heart and kill him.

Over by the balcony a man in a dark suit with dark hair and a neatly squared red tie cast his glance over the dance floor below.

"He's not a vampire. How can you possibly know?"

"He smells like blood and I saw the fangs.

Besides, I can sense them the same way I can sense the Fallen. Vibrations, baby. He's a vamp. There's another one below. They're doing the tag team thing. But whatever. If you won't listen to me, fine. I'll follow your wake when you leave the club. Did you, um…bring your wooden stake?"

She twirled her knife, smiling mockingly as she did, then tucked it away in the leather sheath strapped under her arm. How she had gotten past security with that thing was beyond Cooper.

"Guess not." She snapped her gum and the tilt of her head dusted a swath of gorgeous hair over a shoulder. "So, Juphiel."

"That's not my name," he corrected quickly. "Not here. Not on earth."

"Yeah? Okay, I'll play. What's the name of the man I'm going to poke with my big pointy knife and rip the heart out of?"

Chapter 2

"You're kidding me, right?"

The man was ten kinds of sexy. And Pyx had been on earth such a short time even one kind of sexy was intriguing. His gray eyes featured wild spots of color. Each time she looked at them she saw a new one, azure, green, violet—or it could be the club lights. The shadow of a mustache emphasized his lips. And his square jaw advertised power and strength, a warrior.

Warriors she appreciated, and could definitely waste some time admiring. Angels were warriors, but so not her type.

It wasn't fair. He was the enemy. She existed on this earth to kill him, not admire him.

And don't forget it.

"Cooper Truhart?" she said after he'd given her his name. "What kind of name is Cooper?"

"I was conjured to earth and landed on top of a car," he said casually. A wink was followed by a dangerous melt-her-steel-heart smile. "You should be glad I didn't go with Mini."

"You don't use your angel name?"

"I have no desire to defame my divine name as I walk this earth. You don't like it, that's not my problem. What is my problem, is you. If I can't kill you—and I'm not into murdering women—then I'll need to turn my back. I'll be leaving now. Not that you're not a peach to talk to, but demons are not my thing."

"You're not my thing either, angel boy," she called as he slid from the booth and strode off.

The kilt hem hit at his knees, and revealed tight, muscled legs with dark hair. He scratched his hip and batted that same sexy wink over his shoulder at her.

Pyx nodded, but couldn't find a smile. "Idiot. He has no clue about the vampires. Guess someone better keep an eye on the poor, lost fallen angel. Because if I don't, he'll never survive to find his muse."

And why *not* kill her? Since when did angels discern the moral quandary between killing a male or female?

Curse the black sea Beneath! Why breasts and curves? If this was a joke on her for something she'd done or not done the previous round she'd been summoned to stalk the Fallen, she did not appreciate it now. Because, okay, she had slipped up then. Then, she'd not located the Fallen she'd been assigned to kill until it was too late—a nephilim had been born.

She would prove herself this go-around. Her pride—yet another necessary sin—demanded it.

Easing her way through the crowd, Pyx found Cooper standing at the top of the stairs looking over the dance floor below. She approached slowly, keeping shy of his peripheral vision.

What would an angel be doing in a dance club when he should be stalking his muse? Unless he was picking up women for practice?

Didn't make sense. Pyx knew the Fallen could have sex with mortal women, but they didn't receive pleasure unless the act was with a muse. Seemed like a waste of time to go through the motions with any old woman and for no reward.

Pyx, on the other hand, could do as she pleased. She could be with any man she desired.

"A man?" she muttered, still put off by the fact she was a she. "What the heck would I do with one of them?"

Though she had to admit she did notice the males more than the females. Good thing for her sexual assignment. But the sexiest man in the room was also her target.

Maybe the muse was in the room? The Fallen were compelled toward their muses. Hmm…

Well, if he were going to attract a hapless mortal destined to carry his monster baby, his current fashion choice did aid in his allure.

"Why a kilt?" she wondered as she stepped behind Cooper and leaned onto the railing right next to him. "It's like a skirt for guys, right?"

"It lets my dangly bits dangle," he answered. "It's a freeing feeling. You should try it—er, oops. You've no bits to dangle."

"Are you mocking me, Fallen one?"

He turned and slipped his gaze down her torso and legs. An assessing look that unsettled her.

"Do you have issues with your sexuality, then? Because it seems as if you're not overly pleased with the mortal costume you wear. Usually chicks wear dresses, or something feminine when out clubbing."

A deeper blue edged the man's gray eyes, and they pierced Pyx right through the heart. Which was strange because her heart was metal and nothing could penetrate it. The burn she felt in her chest must be residual effects from the whiskey.

He snapped his fingers before her.

"I do not have issues," she returned. "I'm perfectly fine with the bits I've got."

"They are lovely bits." Now his eyes strayed to the V in her shirt where her breasts rose in soft globes. "Plan to take those babies for a spin while you're here on earth?"

Pyx clasped the shirt opening. "Meaning?"

"Well, I know you, Sinistari. You're all about the sin. Lust, pride, greed, vanity and gluttony. If you're in the mood, I can help you with the lust."

"You'd sleep with a demon?"

He shrugged. "I find my own desires are immense. And I do like redheads. Care for a kiss?"

Pyx shoved her fingers through the hair she wasn't so sure about. It was too long and silky. It hung in her eyes. She blew at the bangs dipping over her brows. She couldn't look at Cooper. And his question put her off. What to say?

"Kidding," he said. "I'd like to keep you at arm's distance if that's all right with you."

"Fine with me. I only need to stretch to poke you with my blade. But we'll worry about that when the time has come. Back to the vamps," she said. "You going to amble on out of here without backup?"

"I don't understand your worry. And yes, I intend to amble without a care. Not even for the demon."

"Fine."

"Great."

"It'll serve me well enough."

"Why's that?" He scanned the crowd, not look-ing at her.

"You leave first, and I'll follow the vampires as they track you."

"They're not going to— Why am I arguing with a demon? Good riddance, Sinistari."

He skipped down the steps in his clunky boots and landed on the main floor with a jump. Without a glance up at her, he then danced his way along the crowd and into the darkness toward the back exit door.

"Leaving without a woman on his arm?" Pyx tapped the railing. "Interesting. He's freaked now. I'm sure of it. The angel has more than a demon on his ass. Just you wait, Fallen one, I'll be tracking vamps on your wake in no time."

Cooper went down the Metro stairs to the train. He kept one eye scanning his periphery and over his shoulder. Two dark figures followed him.

Vampires? He didn't have bloodsucker radar. The demon would know for certain. Their earthly connection to those things could sniff out any para-normal by vibration alone.

He'd allowed the sexy, sexually confused demon to put stupid thoughts into his brain. He wasn't being followed. And if he was, they sure as hell were not vampires. Maybe a couple of pissed-off mortals who'd been dumped by their women after Cooper had flirted with them.

Turning a curve in the long cement tunnel stretching underground toward the Metro station, Cooper listened as the probably-not-vampires closed in on him. He knew this was a longer stretch and made a left turn to the C line instead of walking straight toward his usual train.

Pressing his back to the wall, he waited.

On the slight chance they could be vamps, he had no wooden stake, not even a weapon, and he knew vamps weren't so easy to take down. He was stronger than mortal men, but he wasn't sure how his strength matched up with a vampire.

Earthbound or not, he still retained a few tricks up his sleeve.

The first man rounded the corner and Cooper swung out his arm, clocking the bastard across the throat. The man took it with a gasp and a growl, revealing fangs.

So the demon had been right.

Cooper tossed the vamp against his cohort, who shoved him back at Cooper. Both charged him, fangs extended.

He could flash out of here, but that wouldn't be any fun.

Cooper set his shoulders and bounced on the balls of his feet. He welcomed the fisticuffs. And if he got the chance to bash up a few vamps, that suited him fine. He carried a lot of aggression stored in his bones and since he'd been on earth he had found little opportunity to let it out, save on that one now-dead Sinistari.

Slammed against the wall, Cooper choked out his breath as one vamp pummeled him in the gut. The other vamp drew out a dagger, which was cheating, really. And didn't they know only one kind of dagger could kill an angel?

Maybe they didn't know he was an angel? Maybe they were just jonesing for some blood? Not that angel blood would do either of them any good—it would freeze them solid, and then—kablam.

Out of all the people in the nightclub, Cooper suspected he had not been the most appetizing. There had been plenty of women with soft necks and warm, adrenaline-spiked blood. This had to be because he was an angel.

He kicked his attacker, but only landed high on his thigh. Didn't move the bastard an inch. A flash of steel careened toward his shoulder, yet the blade suddenly soared backward, away from its target.

A sweep of red hair brushed Cooper's cheek.

"Oh, enough, bloody enough!" He did not need to be saved by a woman!

Cooper bashed his forehead against a vampire's skull. His brain reverberated in his head. The bloodsucker's skull was hard! A shove of his hand—he didn't touch the vamp's chest—sent the creature flying away and crashing against the ceiling. The vamp dropped hard.

Pyx gripped the other vampire by the throat and slammed him against the cement wall. "Who sent you?"

Interrogation. Good idea, Cooper thought. Glad he'd thought of it.

The fallen vamp lunged, aiming toward Cooper.

He made a tight, straight spade of his fingers and shoved them into the vampire's chest. The creature yowled. Cooper gripped the heavy mass of hot muscle. A gut kick sent the vampire stumbling backward.

Blood oozed over Cooper's fingers and dripped onto the floor. The vampire whose chest was now empty of his heart ashed, as did the heart in Cooper's hand. Slimy ash-drenched blood oozed in splats onto the cement floor near his boots.

The other vampire spat in Pyx's face. She swiped the bloody spittle away and then pounded a wooden stake into the vamp's chest. It took a lot of force to put a piece of wood through ribs and muscle. Pyx made it look as if she was spearing an olive with a toothpick.

Ash spattered into the air. The Sinistari shook off the gray dust and delivered a triumphant smile to Cooper.

"I do have a stake," she said, then glanced at Cooper's bloody hand. "Oh. That'll work, too."

Careening around the corner flew two more vamps. Or Cooper confirmed they were of the vampire persuasion when one jumped on Pyx's shoulders and sank his teeth into her skull above her ear.

Cooper gripped the wood handrail and tore it from the industrial bolts securing it to the wall. He broke it in half and caught the charging vampire in the chest with it.

Pyx spouted every oath in the book as she struggled to detach the fangs and fingers digging into her scalp and throat.

Cooper twisted the thick wooden stake and kicked the dead vampire off from it. Ash dusted Pyx. The vamp gnawing at her skull inhaled a mouthful and choked.

Pyx smashed the vamp against the wall. "Suck on that, longtooth!" It released her, and she scrambled away the direction it had come. A new vampire appeared, saw his retreating cohort, and joined him.

Wielding the stake like a spear, Cooper threw it after the vamps and caught the tip at the back of one's head. His strength had given the soaring wooden stake rocket power and it entered the vampire's skull with ease, dropping to the ground in a clatter as the vampire became dust.

Cooper caught Pyx by the shoulder, and when she struggled to race after the final vampire that had gotten away, he twisted her arm around behind her back.

"Get your bloody hands off me!" she cried.

He released her and flicked the blood from his hand against the cement wall. Taking in the surroundings, he listened, confirming no mortals within hearing or eyesight. The bloodstains would raise questions. At least the vamp had ashed and hadn't left a mangled body behind for someone to freak over.

"Let the longtooth go," he said. "It'll run to its master and tell them what a force we are to deal with."

"It'll return to its master and give him details," she hissed.

"Details of what?"

"You!"

Wiping the blood from his hand on his white shirt, Cooper smirked. "They were following you too, sweetie."

The shirt was a loss and the blood stank. He couldn't walk around mortals with it in this condition. He shrugged it off, and balled it up. "I'm out of here."

Pyx kicked the cement wall and growled in frustration. "You're welcome!" she called in his wake.

She thought she'd saved him? Poor misguided demon.

But Cooper had no intention of hanging around

to convince her of her mistake. The day had taken a very wrong turn. And he was not stupid. He needed to put as much distance between himself and the Sinistari as possible.

A *schush* and clatter signaled the arriving train. Cooper slam-dunked the bloody shirt into a trash can, and jumped onto the train, insinuating himself within the crowd.

It was after midnight. The club rush, both standing and seated, filled the train. Sure he was shirtless and sporting an ash-dusted kilt, but he didn't raise any eyebrows from those with spiked hair, elaborate makeup or high-cut skirts that dared to show more than tease.

Cooper let out a breath. He'd never run from danger. He had once been the instigator of danger and chaos, and…death.

Those were innate characteristics he wished to change. And he would. He must if he wished to belong. Walking away had been the right thing.

Focus on what can be yours.

Now that his nervous energy had begun to relax, his senses opened wide to his surroundings. He liked the close quarters and the mingling of scents and bodies. A man could fall in love with someone if he closed his eyes and breathed the exotic spice of flesh, perfume and life. Humanity was a marvel.

The doors clattered shut and the car tugged into motion.

Bye, bye, vampires.

Seriously? Vampires? They couldn't have known they pursued a Fallen one *and* a demon. Only vampires who would do that were stupid, or ash.

He noticed a smear of vamp blood down the side of his kilt, and turned so that thigh was concealed against the train wall.

A long slender body pressed along Cooper's backside. She wrapped her arms about his waist and spread her fingers up his chest. The Parisians were so friendly.

Turning, he huffed when he saw Red smiling at him.

"What the hell are you doing?" He tried to shove her off, but it was too crowded. "Don't press your bits against me," he whispered by her ear. The man next to him smiled and waggled his brows. "You're a crazy one."

"There's nothing else to hang on to. You don't want me to fall on top of the old lady sitting behind me, do you?"

"Won't happen. And don't try that pouty, innocent look with me. Where do you live? You can't possibly be going the same direction as me."

"Nowhere. Only been here a day."

He'd been here a couple weeks, but already he'd found himself a sweet little place tucked away from the world in the 16th arrondissement, yet still within Metro distance of all the hotspots. And in that time, he'd already slain one Sinistari in much the same method he'd employed against the vamp. Though Sinistari hearts did not bleed and were as strong as steel.

Much as he liked the feel of this female's body warming up against his—and making things very hard—he didn't want the trouble that accompanied her. Or the confusion over whether to slay her or to turn around and kiss her.

"They were after you," he said. "I've had no problem with vampires until you showed up."

"Says the guy who needed rescue from two vampires."

"Rescue? Are you mentally unbalanced? Oh, right, you are."

He flicked some ash from the shoulder of her men's shirt that sported a design of blood and now some of her own black demon blood. She fluttered her lashes at him.

Not going to work on him. Not even when her pupils dilated, pushing the kaleidoscope perimeter of iris to a narrow band.

He averted his attention to the wounds above her ear. "You're bleeding."

"That's the vampire blood."

"No, sweetie, that stuff is black."

She touched her head in a moment of panic. "Is it bad?"

"No," he said under his breath. "You don't feel pain?"

"A little, but it's healed. Hope you can't catch rabies from vamps. Ugg. That thing was hungry."

"It's all over your shirt. You're not being very covert."

"Didn't know that was a requirement. You want me to take my shirt off, too? That'll show 'em how covert I can be."

"I'll give you all the attention you need if you play it cool around mortals and keep your shirt on."

"Mmm…" She slid closer to him, and if he didn't know better, he'd guess she was angling for some touch and man, did his body react. The brush of her shirtsleeve across his nipple did not preach patience.

But he did know better. She was Sinistari. She had come to kill him, not snuggle with him.

His stop was next. No doubt, she would follow him out no matter where he got off. The demon was like a tick. But she wouldn't find nourishment from him because he had no intention of giving her what she wanted. If his muse were in the vicinity, Cooper intended to walk the opposite direction.

Just because a Sinistari had found him didn't mean he was close to his muse. He'd actually landed on earth in New Jersey. Upon feeling the compulsion to stay there—and seek his muse—he'd immediately flashed across the ocean.

The doors opened and he nudged the demon's hip with his. She took the signal, wrapping her arm around his back and leading him out onto the platform.

"I don't need an escort," he said as he plodded under the *sorte* sign toward the stairs.

The tick clung. At the very least, she was hanging on to him on the side of the blood smear.

Surfacing on the sidewalk in the center of the 16th arrondissement, Cooper sighted the distant lights twinkling down the always-busy Champs Elysees.

"You're not coming home with me, so shove off," he told her. "You are like one of those sad-eyed puppy dogs, aren't you?"

"Fine. I don't need to see where you go, I can track you by vibration." She leaned against a metal street post and crossed her legs at the ankle. The cowboy boots pointed toward the sky. Drawing her finger along her lower lip, she looked up through her thick ginger lashes. "Nightie night, Cooper."

That lip demanded a nibble. Or two. And those lashes. What would it feel like to brush his mouth over them?

Cooper huffed, and marched down the narrow cobblestoned street toward his building. This quarter of the city boasted homes from medieval times sandwiched between twentieth-century buildings. The eclectic mix appealed to his sense of craft and artistry.

He forgot about demons and vampires—until he thought of them—and he scanned all around him and searched the darkness in between buildings.

At the door to his building he punched the numbers into the digital security box, then jogged the three flights up to his apartment. Listening acutely before he closed the door, he reassured himself she'd not followed him. But then, before he did close the door, he heard the street-level door creak.

"You can't sleep in the foyer!" he called down.

"Says who?"

Rolling his eyes, he slammed his door and stalked through the darkness to the bedroom.

The moon was high and it shimmered through the tall window facing the distant Seine. He kicked off his boots, then landed the bed on his back, arms spread. A pillow wobbled onto his face and he punched it away.

He'd thought his existence on earth would go easy if he kept a low profile and didn't answer the compulsion to seek his muse.

Someone had different plans for him. And it wasn't the Sinistari that worried him most.

Why in Beneath were vampires after him?

* * *

Antonio del Gado strode at a quick pace through the limestone halls of his underground sanctuary. Here in Paris he owned an exquisite mansion, the Hôtel Solange, which was underlined with a network of tunnels. The medieval and rococo centuries had been a time of necessity for secret escape tunnels thanks to the political maneuvers that tested the resilience of kings and their subjects.

During evening hours he lived aboveground, but when daylight reigned, he was forced belowground.

Vampires could walk in the sun. Ninety-five percent of them. But the rare ones who had descended from an angelic race could not, only because their bloodline had not been rejuvenated with their ancestors' blood for millennia.

Antonio was going to change that, for him, and for his entire tribe Anakim. He wanted the daylight, and he would not stop at anything until he had it.

Behind him he was flanked by Bruce Westing and Stellan the Pale. Bruce was Anakim's Fallen hunter, and Stellan's expertise had uncovered half a dozen angel halos over the past year. As well, Bruce had secured the eight paintings lined along the north wall in the dungeon, each of them depicting a different Fallen angel, complete with sigil.

Yet Antonio had no names to match to those sigils.

"You're sure it was a Sinistari with the Fallen?" he asked as he entered his underground office. The cave walls were hung with medieval tapestries depicting scaled dragons and knights with bloody spears. "I thought you said he was with a female?"

Bruce shoved his hands in his front jeans pocket. He and Stellan stopped before Antonio's marble-topped desk. "It was a woman," Bruce said, "and I'm pretty sure she was Sinistari. She was strong, as strong as the angel."

"But Sinistari are male," Antonio said. Though, honestly, he hadn't a proper description for the demon breed, only that they exclusively hunted the Fallen. "And why wouldn't she have slain the angel?"

"Still missing a key ingredient," Stellan offered.

"The muse," Bruce said.

Antonio rocked backward in the richly padded office chair and put up his feet on the desktop. He eyed the painting Bruce had carried in from the dungeon weeks earlier. It featured an angel fashioned from blue glass with a sigil impressed upon its abdomen. The name to match the angel—Juphiel—had come courtesy of Zaqiel, a Fallen Bruce had encountered months earlier. Antonio had summoned Juphiel two weeks ago. It surprised him the Sinistari had only now shown on the scene. Though certainly, if the Sinistari were slacking, that would make his efforts all the easier.

"You've been following Juphiel, Bruce?"

"Yes. He hasn't run into his muse yet. Doesn't seem as if he's looking for her, actually. Spends a lot of time in nightclubs, and during the day he wanders the Louvre."

Bruce was not Anakim blood, thus, his ability to walk in daylight. Antonio trusted and needed him to be his eyes during the day.

"Stay on him."

"I will. You know I never lose a mark."

Bruce did like to go after the Fallen. Even though the angels were much stronger than a vampire, Bruce was wily and took pride in his daring. He was also warded to the hilt against angels and their associated ilk. Thanks to a blood grimoire, Antonio had all he needed to protect himself and his closest allies from the Fallen and Sinistari.

"You keep an eye on the Sinistari," he said, glancing at Stellan. "She's the greatest deterrent to our final goal."

Stellan nodded and turned to leave, always aware of when he was no longer needed.

Bruce wasn't so quick on the draw. He turned to study the painting of Juphiel. It had been painted using a computer, or so Bruce had explained to Antonio. Eden Campbell was the artist—as well as a muse. She was living with a former Sinistari now. Antonio kept her on his radar, but he didn't want to approach her with a demon standing close by, former or not.

"Why are you lingering?"

Bruce shot him a gape. "Er, sorry, monsieur. It's just the Fallen. I don't know that he is the key to what we want to accomplish."

"And what is?"

"Well, the muse."

"Tell me more."

Chapter 3

Pyx suspected the vampires were following the Fallen for a specific purpose.

When a Fallen one successfully impregnated a muse—meaning a Sinistari had not done their job—the resulting child was a nephilim. The nephilim grew to maturity in less than a week, and began to feed. On everything. Including people. The abominable creature gave new meaning to the term *blood hungry*.

It ached in her chest when she thought about it. She had been responsible for allowing a nephilim to walk this earth so many millennia ago. *You failed*.

Never again.

Could the vampires be after the resulting nephilim? What the vampires planned to do with the creature once they had it was beyond Pyx. But any creature that fed on blood must be of interest to vampires.

Flicking at the dried blood on her scalp, she dusted off the black crust. The wound had healed, but not her pride. She really wanted to lay some vampire ass flat for no other reason than that they had pissed her off. And she'd probably get a chance since they seemed very interested in Cooper.

"Cooper Truhart." She snorted and settled on the steps out front of his building. "Stupid name."

Like Pyxion was any better. The Other, even. Man, had that been a joke on her.

Beneath had been no ball of fun. An empty void of darkness run through by a mercury sea roiling with wickedness. Pyx had wandered aimlessly, never finding anything but sea and darkness. The few times she had met another of her breed they'd recognized each other by name. It was simply a knowing.

Her fellow Sinistari had sneered and berated her. They had somehow known she was different, ineffectual, though their true demonic forms were all similar and sexless.

Well, she could do the woman thing. Just watch!

Her feminine wiles seemed to have an incredible

effect on the Fallen. He hadn't been able to take his eyes off her in the club. And when she'd pressed against him on the Metro she had felt his exhale against her cheek. And though she knew an angel's glass heart did not beat, she had felt something throbbing against her thigh.

"Wiles," she muttered. "Whatever that means. I got lucky. But I'm going to start paying attention from here on out. I'll be the best damn woman demon my Sinistari brethren have ever seen. No more sneers for me."

Perhaps she could use her female status to her advantage. It was apparent Cooper was in no hurry to locate his muse.

That had to change.

She didn't look forward to tracking him all over the world until he decided when was a good time to switch into Fallen-claims-his-muse mode. She had to prove herself.

But she couldn't sleep out on the steps hoping Cooper would trip over her in the morning. Not that she needed sleep, nor did the angel.

Scanning her sight about the dark neighborhood, Pyx roamed up and down the brick-fronted three- and four-storied buildings. A residential neighborhood with narrow, cobbled streets and steel poles to prevent cars from parking on an even narrower sidewalk. It was charming, if she were to label it.

Though charm meant as little to her as experiencing touch for the first time—it was a nuisance.

Closeness to the mark meant everything.

She spied a sign with red writing, *loger disponible*. "Room available." It sat across the street and around the corner from where she had determined Cooper's apartment must be. Perfect.

Striding across the street, she approached the building. The foyer opened without a code, but she hesitated punching a button on the speaker box this late at night. Mortals were snoozing. It wasn't that she had a problem punching all the buttons and waking them up; she didn't want to interact right now.

Drawing her finger down the list of apartments, she found the one missing a name. "Third floor, apartment 12."

The inner lobby door was locked. Pointing her forefinger, she shifted enough to grow out the long adamant talon from the top of her fingertip. She slid the talon between the door and frame, toggling it against the dead bolt. Her talon slid the solid bolt to the left, and with a shove, the door opened.

Pyx blew on her talon as if blowing the smoke from a gun—something she'd seen on a movie poster pasted in a video-shop window—then resumed complete mortal costume.

She dashed up the stairs to the third floor. Naturally, the apartment door was locked. No talons necessary this time. One kick loosened the lock in the wood door frame. Pyx marched inside.

The apartment was furnished sparely with modern glass-topped counters, unbleached pine wood, and a coffee table and leather furniture. It smelled vaguely of pine air freshener. The black leather sofa looked comfy. Pyx made a jump and landed on it with her hands clasped behind her head. She crossed her legs at the ankles.

"This'll work. Furnished and everything." She dug in the pocket of her jacket and pulled out the iPod she'd nicked earlier. "Music in my hand. How cool is that?"

She played around with the small jewel-colored device. Lots of music. Movies. A pedometer? Why would anyone want to know how many steps they have walked? "Mortals are strange."

The video camera proved intriguing. Zooming it about the room she recorded…nothing.

Searching the previously recorded clips, she clicked on one. It featured a woman with a blond ponytail standing in a kitchen making deli-meat sandwiches. She looked at whoever was holding the video camera and said, "I love you."

The holder asked, "Is that all?"

"Yep. I just love you."

"Aww." Pyx flicked off the device. "Sweet as sin. But that sandwich did look good. I wonder if there's food in the fridge."

It had been hours since she'd eaten. Gluttony was definitely her favorite mortal sin.

Kicking off her boots, Pyx then wandered into the kitchen while itching at the fresh tattoo on her back. It had already scabbed and she could feel the new skin beneath. Mortal flesh was so freakin' sensitive. She felt everything, even a breeze across her cheek.

She'd never experienced such novelty. Dancing in the club had overloaded her new-experience radar. She'd shut herself off to touch, but now, alone, she connected to it again.

She grabbed a shiny apple from an elegant glass bowl. It was cool and slick. Smelled, hmm…not how she expected fruit to smell. Kind of…oily. Before she took a bite, she realized it was wood. "Tricky." She tossed it over her shoulder into the living area.

The fridge was empty, as were the cupboards. "How's a demon supposed to survive in this realm without sustenance?"

The front door banged inward and someone clattered down the parquet hallway into the kitchen. A man wearing only blue-striped pajama bottoms, his tumescent belly hanging over the waistband, and his white hair tousled upon his head, eyed her up and down.

"What are you doing here, mademoiselle? This is not your apartment?"

"Of course it is." Pyx sauntered over and laid her palm against his forehead. "And I paid you a month's rent already. Remember?"

He nodded, shrugged, then nodded again.

"I think someone tried to break in. The lock is jammed on the door." She removed her hand.

The man nodded. "I'll have a look at it first thing in the morning. Do you need a new key?"

"Darn right I do. Talk about shoddy upkeep. I wonder, should I find a better place that has a more studious custodian?"

"Oh, no, I will see to it at first light. It was surely an isolated incident. This is a lovely building and our custodian is a gem."

"All right, but if it happens again, I'm out of here."

"So sorry to have disturbed you, mademoiselle…?"

"Pyxion. I'll see you bright and early with a new lock. Good night, funny little man."

"Bon nuit." He shuffled out and tugged at the door a bit before finally getting it to click securely shut.

Pyx crossed her arms and smirked. Mortals. So easy to influence.

From this angle she could see the front of Cooper's building and would notice when he left and could even see the light on in his apart-

ment. She would keep the light off so he wouldn't
see her.

"If he goes near the muse, I'll be right there,
ready to kill him."

Cooper poured a cup of green tea and sat down
at the kitchen table before the laptop. He put his
bare feet up on another chair and leaned back,
shrugging his fingers through his hair.

He'd washed away the vampire blood. The smell
of vamps put him off, and he felt sure now he'd
sense the next one before he saw it because it was
an unmistakable scent of dust, metal and ash.

The kilt was a loss, but it didn't matter. He didn't
need a closet of clothing because if he required a
new shirt he simply imagined it on himself, and it
became so. Nice trick of the trade.

What an interesting night he'd had. Vampires
and Sinistari after him?

He'd hoped to spend more time in this world free
of such trouble. But he wasn't stupid. The Sinistari
came with the territory when one chose to Fall.
And he couldn't argue with the chance to get out
some aggression.

It had felt sweet to rip the vamp's heart from
its chest. Yet now, he felt a twinge of regret. He'd
killed far too often when serving in the angelic
ranks. Killing had been as natural as taking a

breath. Smite this village. Slay that wrongdoer. All because he had been ordered to do so.

The stench of death had reeked on him; it had never been absent. And as an angel he'd not been attuned to the senses like touch, taste and smell. So the fact he'd eventually noticed that stench had screwed with his ideas of right and wrong.

Rather, it had become the catalyst to his developing a sense of right and wrong.

Angels weren't supposed to choose sides. They were unfeeling entities that served Him without question. But Juphiel had changed. Another angel had allowed him to see that he had a choice. That is why he'd Fallen. Juphiel could no longer kill with abandon.

And yet, Cooper Truhart was still doing it.

Was it because death had been ingrained in his being?

"No, I will change. I must."

With a gesture of his fingers, the laptop slid across the table to rest at the edge before him. He tapped the keyboard, thinking to type *vampire* in the search box, but figured that wouldn't route him to any feasible answer on why the bloodsuckers were tracking him. Instead, he opened the email program and was pleased to find an answer to a message he'd sent to Eden Campbell two days ago.

He'd discovered Miss Campbell after an

afternoon of searching the internet for halos and anything at all related to the Fallen. It was all myth and religious dogma to the mortals. They hadn't a clue regarding the truth of it. Yet, he'd found a correspondence between Eden Campbell and Cassandra Stevens from months earlier that indicated both women were in the know. Eden had promised to send Cassandra a halo she had found because, as she'd written, it would give her hope. Eden definitely knew she had the real thing in hand.

Cooper had written to her, asking if he could take a look at her collection. He hadn't given details like "Hey, I'm a Fallen and need to find my halo." No, he didn't want to scare her off until he could feel her out, sense if she might be worth trusting. A mortal may believe in halos, but in *real* angels? That was a long shot.

He clicked on the email. Campbell's reply read: How did you get my email address? I don't collect halos anymore. Do not contact me further.

Cooper sat back, and blew out a breath. "That's it? No, 'Sorry, can't help you'? No, 'I think I know of someone who can help'?"

He opened the file of saved emails between Cassandra and Eden and scanned them. "There." He leaned in and began to type a reply.

What about MD?

MD were the mysterious initials Eden had

mentioned in a post to Cassandra, a man who had helped her recently with the halos.

Hitting Send, Cooper hoped this trail would lead him somewhere.

Finding a halo on earth would be like looking for the proverbial needle in a haystack. Only this needle was made of ineffable substance and had been lost on earth millennia ago. But if he could find someone who sought halos for a hobby, then he'd be ten steps closer to his goal than he was now.

By morning, starvation roiled Pyx's gut. She picked up the cell phone she'd stolen, and scanned the address list. "No pizza delivery numbers." Though a lot of spas and wine dealers were listed. She tucked the phone in a pocket and skipped down to street level.

A figure appeared in the big window on the third floor across the street. Cooper's apartment. The sun was rising and she could plainly see the man standing in the window, gesturing she should come up.

Really?

"Don't need to ask me twice."

She rushed across the street. First the angel pushes her away and now he's pulling her closer? Worked for her. Men had fallen for lesser reasons than a sexy woman.

And yet, angels had Fallen for that very reason.

Pyx smirked. "I can so work this one."

He buzzed her in, and she navigated upward, following his scent instead of the angelic vibrations he put out. It wasn't a particular odor she could compare to anything she had learned about the world, other than that it was simply and uniquely *angel*. And sexy.

"Bloody Beneath, Pyx, buck up. The angel is *not* sexy."

The door opened to reveal Cooper standing in loose, dark jeans that hugged his hips. Cut muscles veed toward his jeans, pointing in a direction she couldn't take her eyes from. Stunning, virile and—

Not sexy. Not sexy. Not...well...maybe.

"Hungry?" he asked.

"Oh, yeah, er—" She shrugged. "For food? Yes, food. Nothing else weird, or anything."

"No, nothing weird," he said with a secretive smirk.

His attire made her take stock of her own. Still wearing the same blood-smeared shirt and men's jeans and boots. She needed to do some shopping to get a feel for what women wore, and then she could assume their costume with ease.

"You inviting *me* in?" she asked, feeling a bit sheepish, and that feeling was so new, she went with it and shrugged her elbow up against the wall, hands tucked in her pockets.

"Why not? You were lurking."

"Yeah, but—" Had he been watching her? Hope not, because she was the one watching him.

Cooper strode down the hallway and called over his shoulder, "Ever hear the one about keeping one's enemies close?"

"Who said that?" Pyx wandered after him. "Some guy who took a knife in the back while his enemy was hugging him? So what's changed? Last night you were eager to put distance between us."

"Call it a change of heart."

"Didn't think an angel's hard glass heart was capable," Pyx said, entering the kitchen.

The high ceilings lent a feeling of vastness. Glass-fronted cabinets and black granite countertops gave it a modern flair. Blue and green tiles backed the counter, and gleaming appliances sat here and there.

Most significant were the stained-glass windows over the sink. The doors leading into an adjoining bedroom were also intricate stained glass; the design touted flowers, trees and peacocks.

Cooper slapped a palm over his chest where Pyx knew his heart did not beat. "You pick up a lot walking the earth. Emotions. Ideas. Humility. You'll learn soon enough."

"Oh, I picked up a great sandwich last night and a tattoo."

"A tattoo?" Cooper smirked and wandered to the stovetop where a delicious scent wafted. "I've got crepes with fresh bananas and Nutella. That's chocolate hazelnut spread, kind of like peanut butter, but...not."

"Sounds fancy. You going to kill me with kindness?"

"Perhaps. So show me the tat."

Turning and lifting the back of her shirt, Pyx displayed her artwork. Pride prickled her ego sweetly.

"A burning angel, eh?"

"You got it. Can't wait to see you burn."

Cooper redirected his attention to the cooking. "Nice."

Pyx plopped onto a kitchen chair and propped her boots up on another chair. She leaned an elbow on the table. "How's a guy who's only been around a few weeks afford something like this? You get a job as a gigolo in those nightclubs you frequent?"

He chuckled sarcastically. "Could if I wanted to. But, no. The owner of this apartment was looking for someone to watch it during the summer while she vacations in Greece with her lover."

"Good for you. Haven't had to sell your body yet. I got a place, too."

"Did you?"

"Fully furnished. Rent is paid for the month."

She took the iPod from her pocket and switched it to video. Scanning it around the room, she recorded, for the heck of it. Zooming in on Cooper standing before the griddle, she moved the screen up and down his bare back. The muscles flexed with his motions. His skin was tan too, which appealed to her in ways she couldn't quite process.

"It's in the neighborhood, actually."

"In the—" With a dripping spatula in hand, Cooper dashed into the nearby bedroom and looked out the window. "The sign is down. You didn't," he said, marching into the kitchen.

She caught video of his frustrated huff, and the splatter of crepe batter that drooled down his pant leg.

"The place across the street? But I saw you last night. How did you…? So quickly? You stole that place."

Pyx shook the iPod at his accusing shake of spatula. "Dude, it's my nature."

"Poor excuse. You want to fit in with the humans while you're here on earth? You're going to have to work on your morality."

"Look at you, all high and mighty."

His smile was neither high nor mighty. It was genuinely appealing. Pyx wondered if morals had given him that appeal. But then, she knew better.

"Cruising the clubs for booty doesn't sound so moral to me."

"It is the human condition to seek comfort in one another."

"Comfort." Pyx snorted. "So that's what they're calling it nowadays."

He set a plate before her. A folded crepe hung over the edge. "You like bananas and chocolate?"

"Don't know. I've never tried them." She accepted the proffered fork and poked the delicious-looking delicacy. Brown, sweet spread oozed out. "You learned to cook in a few weeks? I shouldn't admit it, but I am impressed. I thought the Fallen just stalked about looking for muses to bed."

He poured batter on a wide griddle, his back to her. Every movement flexed the muscles. Strength, that was the appeal. Strength wrapped in warm human flesh that Pyx suspected would feel great if she touched.

"Did you hear me? I said—"

"I heard you," he said, not turning around. "I choose not to dignify that remark with an answer."

"Oh, so you're one of those respectable angels who fell?"

"And you're one of those annoying Sinistari."

Touché. Well, if the shoe fit, she'd try it on and kick some ass with it. Thinking of which…she needed some more feminine shoes. But the high-heeled travesties she'd seen looked like a form of torture she'd rather avoid.

Pyx forked in a mouthful. Nummy. Oh, man! Chocolate rocked. And bananas, too. All oozing together. What a divine creation. Oops. Divinity had nothing to do with this meal. This was all about sinful deliciousness.

Minutes later, Cooper joined her with a folded crepe and sat down. Licking the chocolate from his thumb, he then dug in heartily. Pyx had already downed half her breakfast.

"I wouldn't think this combination could work," she commented. "Bananas and chocolate?"

"Sort of like angels and demons breaking their fast together, eh?"

"Yes, sort of." Was she seriously here, doing… this?

He didn't seem the least disturbed by her presence. The angel should be. The guy was one stab in the heart away from oblivion.

Pyx devoured another gooey, hot bite of crepe, and while she chewed, drew out her blade and placed it nonchalantly on the table beside her.

The Fallen smirked. "I don't intimidate easily."

"I'm just setting it there. It's big and gets in the way."

"I have something that's big and gets in the way."

She caught his waggling lift of brow, but didn't

understand. Angels. They thought they were so clever.

With a flick of Cooper's fingers her dagger slid across the table toward him. Pyx slapped a hand over the weapon and slid it back. "Fancy party tricks are for amateurs."

He relented.

"So I understand you demons name your blades," he prompted. "Something ominous like Angel Killer or Death Bringer. What's yours called?"

She fingered the black steel hilt of the blade. Forged from materials unknown, the blade had been made before she had and then matched to her after she had been forged Sinistari from the earth's metals.

"Joe," she said, and forked in another bite of crepe.

"Joe?" The angel laughed. It was a deep, rumbly sound that made Pyx smile around a mouthful of banana. "Oh, that's rich. I'm being pursued by the vicious demon Pixy and her faithful blade Joe."

Pyx wielded Joe in a blink. She bent before Cooper a blink later, the blade cutting into the flesh under his chin.

"It's Pyx," she said sharply. "And I'll thank you to respect my friend Joe here or he'll get sloppy and spill angel blood on your fancy pancake."

"You cut me, I will retaliate."

She remained before him, testing the blade

against his soft and easily damaged mortal flesh. His dark eyes challenged her to go for it. Draw the blade and spill blood. She could do it. She should do it to prove she wasn't about to back down, no matter his disturbing charm.

The cut wouldn't kill him; she had to pierce his heart to bring death. And the blade could not penetrate his hard glass heart unless he was shifted to half form, which usually only happened when the angel was attempting his muse.

Had she ever seen that color of blue before? It rimmed his gray eyes. When she'd been summoned she had initially only seen the world in black and white. Until she'd walked the world, taking it all in, breathing in its languages, customs and pastimes.

Wow. There was something in his eyes. A bright reflection of…a hard and ruthless warrior? Whatever it was in his eyes, it was of the angelic dominions.

He moved swiftly. The blade clattered on the hardwood floor before Pyx realized she'd dropped it. His lips connected with hers. He bracketed her head with his palms, not pressing too roughly, but keeping her exactly where he wanted her.

It was a kiss. A strange, surprising kiss. Rough and fast. But sweet from the chocolate that whispered from his mouth and into hers.

Pyx had not before been kissed. What was a kiss for? It didn't fill the belly, or provide clothes, or gain material goods. And yet, it was definitely interesting.

And it was being issued by a Fallen one. To a Sinistari. How many ways of wrong was that?

It didn't feel wrong. Felt kind of tingly and exciting.

Cooper swept his tongue across hers. A giddy sparkle radiated in Pyx's belly—until he pushed her away and stepped across the room. Hand to a hip, he turned, head tilted downward, and gazed at her.

"What the hell was that for?" She swiped her mouth with the back of her hand, forcing out her most pissed tone. "That's not how you disarm an opponent."

"Oh, no?" He toed Joe and kicked it across the floor toward her boot. "Looks like it worked. You've never been kissed before?"

"I just came to earth a day ago. What do you think?"

"I think…" He stalked over on his bare feet, his movements sensual and silent like some kind of wild cat Pyx had seen stalking the Tibetan forests during her walk of the world. Tilting up her chin, he brushed the hair from her face. "That means you are a virgin. A strange situation for a Sinistari to be in when she should be indulging in lust. Want another one?"

The sparkle still hummed in her belly. "Kiss?"

He smirked. "No, a crepe."

"Neither." Pyx jumped to stand and, arms arched out and ready to strike, she instead looked about. Not sure what to do. How to react. Joe lay against her boot. Bending for it would put her in a position not conducive to defense.

The angel had served her a move she hadn't expected. And she was still processing the delicious taste of him, and the startling sensation of his mouth upon hers. It was a hell of a lot better than the crepe, and she had loved the crepe.

And the smile on his face bothered her. He felt he'd gained advantage in this round. Had he?

"I gotta go." She swept up Joe.

"Giving up before you've cleaned your plate?" he called as she headed down the hallway.

"Not on your life. I want to make sure the vampires aren't hanging around outside."

"They're not after me."

"They're not after me!" she shouted.

"If that's what you want to believe. It's day. Vampires don't do sunlight, do they?"

Pyx didn't turn to look at him. She knew he brandished a triumphant smirk like some kind of scalp claimed in battle. "Read your Stoker. Most vampires can go out during the day. I'll be back."

"I do hope you will be."

She stalked to the front door and strode through, leaving it open behind her.

All right, one point for the Fallen. That meant she had to regroup and figure things out. Like how to play against someone who doesn't know the rules.

And what, exactly, would her defensive move be should he lay another of those delicious kisses on her?

Chapter 4

Pyx wandered aimlessly. She needed to put a plan in order. If the Fallen wasn't interested in finding his muse then she may have to find the muse and bring her to him.

How in Beneath would she recognize a woman even the Fallen wouldn't know until he got right next to her? And if what he'd said was true, he wasn't anywhere near her right now.

"Shouldn't be my job. Why is this Fallen able to resist the compulsion to his muse?"

The Sinistari were usually summoned right before the moment when the Fallen would attempt its muse. Demon arrives with sharp, pointy blade.

Shoves it in the Fallen's heart. Muse saved. No nephilim is born. Deed done.

"Do others of my breed have this same problem?"

She wasn't going to think *because I'm a woman.* But she did consider her past mishap. She'd walked the earth in complete demon form then, so that didn't apply now.

"Well, I can handle it."

She shrugged up the tight-fitting blue jean coat she'd purchased from a woman's store. The wrists were trimmed with thick fox fur. Along the sleeves the fabric was tugged together military-style with gold buttons and chains. She'd exchanged her male jeans for some skin-hugging black leather pants. The sales clerk had tried to convince her a corset would look stunning on her but Pyx had opted for a comfortable gray T-shirt. High heels had looked a bit dangerous, so she'd opted for a two-inch heel on some pointy-toed black crocodile ankle boots.

She could have easily assumed the costume with a thought, but the shopping part had been—fun. And it had given her clues to what women wore.

She wasn't sure about the makeup thing, but the sales clerk had directed her to the cosmetics department where a commando clerk had attacked her with a free makeover, brushing, spraying and stroking on various types of smelly products. Now Pyx toted a bag full of more smelly stuff with the promise it would enhance her ability to attract a man.

"As long as the man is Fallen," she muttered. "And not a bloodsucker."

She veered down a street before a grand railway station and read the name of the building. "The Gare du Nord." Hundreds of people filed in and out, destined for other cities, or returning from trips.

"Try Germany," she called to a passing family of five lugging suitcases. "The schnitzel is awesome."

The father shuffled his kids away from her as if she'd said something obscene. Pyx just smiled. She nicked a wallet from the back pocket of a man arguing with his girlfriend and inspected the contents as her path led her away from the busy area.

A hundred euros and a bunch of credit cards. She picked out the gold credit card because she liked it best, then tossed the wallet into a nearby trash can.

Eyeing a restaurant across the street that advertised wine from the Rhône river valley and fresh scallops, Pyx was distracted by a shadow moving across the street. It had been a blur, a person moving much more swiftly than mortals were capable of doing.

Feeling a twinge of instinct, Pyx decided food could wait. Striding onward, bag full of makeup banging against her hip, she angled toward the alley where she'd seen the blur go.

At the end of the alley she noticed it again. It stopped long enough so she could plainly see it was a man. He exposed fangs and chuckled, then took off to the right.

Stuffing the credit card in a back pocket, she took off after him. He moved in a zigzag pattern farther away from the city center. Eventually he blurred into a brick building where all the lower windows had been broken out.

Pyx stomped across broken glass and debris of boards into the darkness. "Here, bloody vampire. Come out, come out, wherever you are."

She shoved off her jacket and tossed it aside, dropping her bag of makeup on top. Cracking her knuckles, she strode to the center of the empty three-story room. "You wanted me to follow? Well, here I am!"

Slammed bodily from the side, Pyx took the brunt force of the vampire's hefty frame with ease. She twisted at the waist and pushed him away from her. The vampire stepped through the shove, circling toward her and chuckling maniacally. His blue eyes were bloodshot, and his thin lips curled.

Did he think a little flash of fang was going to intimidate her?

Pyx didn't have to touch him; she had a few tricks up her sleeve.

She made a shoving-away gesture through the air before her. The vampire gasped and went flying, his shoulders hitting the wall, but he landed on both feet and immediately marked a determined stride toward her.

"You're strong for a girl," he said.

"Yeah? You're an idiot for a vampire. Oh, wait. All vampires are idiots. My bad."

She waited for him to charge and took the impact full force, his shoulders barreling into her chest. Okay, that one hurt. Felt like something broke, but her insides were metal so that couldn't be. Still, this mortal flesh was too damned tender.

The two of them stumbled, Pyx backward, the vampire pushing her. They landed on the concrete floor in a grappling roll. He managed to kick her in the gut, which hurt even more. She punched his jaw, which sent spittle of crimson puddling across the floor.

"Don't you know what I am?" she demanded, furious this insolent creature dared not show her the reverence she deserved.

"Sinistari." He jumped up and brushed the dust from his leather coat sleeves. "I'm not much for demons. You do not deserve the respect you demand."

"We are the kings of the demon realm," she stated, defying him with the entitlement. She snatched Joe from the sheath under her arm—no matter the new clothing, she never went anywhere without Joe. "You will die for your insolence."

"Whatever. You look more a princess than a king. Your lipstick is smeared."

Pyx touched her mouth. Really? But the color she'd chosen was so pretty....

The vampire pulled out a gun and fired.

Pyx took the bullet in her shoulder. It burned like hell's fire, but it was not going to kill her.

And if the vampire didn't watch it, he'd piss her off. And she did not play well when pissed. She swiped at the corner of her mouth, frustrated more by the greasy smear of red.

Screw the lipstick.

"Why are you playing with me? Got an itch you need to scratch, buddy? Just to let you know, I don't do bloodsuckers."

"I wouldn't touch your damned ass with haz-mat gloves on," the vampire replied.

Pyx lifted a brow, fighting a wince from the pain. "Anyone ever tell you that charm will get you a stake in the heart?" Not that she'd remembered to bring along a stake...

"It's my business to keep an eye on you, Sinistari." He waved the gun menacingly. "Keep you away from the Fallen one."

"So it was me those idiot vamps were after last night?" And here she'd been sure it was Cooper.

"You and the Fallen. You catch sight of the muse

yet?" he asked as he paced before her. A swipe of his sleeve wiped the blood from his mouth, leaving a smear she figured resembled her mouth.

"If I had seen a muse, I wouldn't tell you. I'm tired of this conversation. You need to be gone."

She flung out her hand, directing her energy toward the vamp, but he ducked and managed to fire the gun again. This time the bullet pierced her outstretched hand.

Pyx gripped the searing pain. "Now you've pissed me off."

Letting out a throaty growl, she began to shed her mortal costume with a shake of her shoulders. The Sinistari were forged from fluid metal as sinuous as flesh but stronger than any known mortal substance. They were virtually indestructible, unless a stronger opponent faced them down.

Vampires were not stronger.

The shift complete, she stood a head higher than when in mortal costume. Her black metal body pulsed with the vicious desire to do some damage. Tightening her fists and twisting her horned head, Pyx eyed the vampire.

The bastard didn't even flinch. In fact, he smiled and tore open his shirt to reveal a tattoo emblazoned across his abdomen. From waist to under his nipples a bizarre sketch of ancient sigils covered every inch of flesh.

Demon wards. And it looked as if he wore a sigil

for every demon that stalked this realm and all the other realms.

The vampire wasn't an idiot after all.

"Points for you," Pyx growled.

She felt the ward's repulsive force scream out toward her and shiver within her metallic frame. It squealed, high-pitched and sharp. The noise was unbearable.

Clamping a hand over one ear, she struggled to face her opponent, but knew it was fruitless. Pyx turned, snatched her coat and bag with a talon, and ran. Before she reached the door, she flashed…

…and landed in her apartment living room, naked and resumed of mortal flesh.

"That vampire was not playing fair," she muttered, pressing her forehead into the soft fur edging the coat sleeves. "And he's after me."

And if properly warded, which he had been, he stood a chance at defeating her.

"Damn it. I've got to find that bloody muse, and quick, before he comes back."

Cooper wasn't sure why vampires were tracking him, but he wasn't about to stand with arms wide open and welcome them to do as they pleased. It wasn't smart to rip out their hearts when an innocent bystander may witness—not to mention the mess—but damn, it had felt good.

He had to be careful. If this realm were to

become his permanent home, he must learn to play by the rules, and respect mortals.

But that didn't mean he had to play nice with the vampires.

Elbows to the glass counter, he looked over the bowie knives as the store owner observed him. This little shop was tucked in the fifth arrondissement at the end of a street that catered to tourists with video stores and T-shirt shops.

"The handle is pure silver," the owner said. "Pretty thing, isn't she?"

Cooper stabbed the weapon into the wooden beam stretched floor to ceiling, designed for such purpose. He knew a blade wouldn't stop a vampire, but it might slow one down.

What he needed was a fancy stake like Pyx had sported. But he suspected she wasn't the type to share, unless he begged. And put chocolate and bananas on top.

He did love her appetite. But that was obviously the gluttony shining through. If the girl weren't careful she might have to let out her snug-fitting leather pants a bit.

On the other hand, eat away, pretty demon. It may slow her down if he ever did stumble across his muse.

"You have any crosses?"

The owner tilted his head quizzically. "There's

a religious shop down the street," he said, pointing. "You buying that?"

"Yes." Cooper laid the knife on the glass counter. "And give me a couple of those, too." He gestured to the four-pointed throwing stars on the wall behind the counter.

"That'll be seven-hundred-fifty," the owner said, sliding the weapons toward him.

Cooper placed his palm on the owner's forehead and put into his mind the image of him handing over a stack of euro notes. After he'd berated Pyx for stealing the apartment, he should look to his own actions and stop throwing stones. Yet he had no means to employment or an ID card or driver's license. He was off the grid and intended to remain so until he'd found his halo.

It wasn't stealing when he planned to use the weapons to destroy something that could harm or even kill humans.

Tucking the blade at the back of his jeans and the stars in the pockets of his black wool pea coat, Cooper walked out onto the sidewalk and almost tripped over a spunky redhead.

Pyx hooked her arm in his and together they went down the sidewalk. Perky ponytails sprang out at either side of her head. Rouge brightened her cheeks and gloss shimmered on her lips. She smelled…fruity.

"Is this a date?" he asked.

"No, it's a walkby kidnapping. I'm taking you to find your muse."

"Ain't gonna happen, Pretty in Pink. I haven't sensed her at all in Paris. That's why I'm here. What's with the fur?"

"I like this jacket. It's fun. And so is the pink T-shirt. It's a girl color, isn't it?" she asked with strange hope.

"You trying to be feminine? Why is it so difficult for you?"

"I don't know. It's just…weird. How would you feel if you suddenly had these?" She cupped her breasts.

Cooper whistled. "I think they'd feel pretty good. Can I touch?"

"No. I mean, it's taking time to adjust. But I thought the lipstick a good move." She pursed her lips and puckered like a fish. "You think?"

"Watch who you make that face at, Pyx, you just may find a boyfriend."

"No time for that stuff."

"There's always time for letting others into your heart."

"Didn't you used to be some kind of warrior?"

He felt the dig all the way to his gut. Yes, a warrior on a path of righteous glory. Such glory is never pretty.

"You've softened, buddy," Pyx continued.

"Letting people into your heart? Our hearts are adamant and they don't beat."

"Just because the blood doesn't flow in and out doesn't mean we can't feel."

"Says the guy who ripped out a vampire's heart without a second thought last night."

"That was different. You don't want to go and fall in love with a bloodsucker."

And he suspected Pyx could feel emotion too, because right now she was uncertain about his mention of boyfriends and hearts. She was experiencing the same emotions all mortals felt. It was impossible not to when treading earth. Compassion and empathy and love and admiration were weird though, he had to admit.

Violence had always come easily to him. Still did. Only now he must take a second to think it through before doing something rash, and usually that second changed his mind. It never would have before, when he'd served the angelic ranks.

That had been his past. Violence and aggression was the one part of humanity he despised. If he wanted to move ahead, he had to embrace a new mindset.

Maybe he could use Pyx's emotional confusion to his advantage. He knew he'd never get a demon to trust him, but perhaps he could interest her in the sensual delights, maybe a little seduction. If it changed her mind about slaying him, he'd give it a go.

It was either that or rip out her heart. And right now, he kind of liked where it was, inside and behind those gorgeous breasts.

"So did you kill many when you were a real angel?" she asked suddenly.

"A real angel?" It was difficult not to take offense at every other word that came out of her mouth, and yet, Cooper found he preferred Pyx's rough edges to someone who would speak only to please him. Humans did that a lot. "I served in Puriel's ranks. I guess you could say we participated in much smiting."

"And you chose to fall because you weren't into the smiting?"

"I can smite with the best of them," he said defensively. But his anger cooled quickly. The need to *not* smite had surfaced thanks to an angel friend who'd made him see more than just the holy light. "Smiting serves no purpose now."

He wouldn't tell her it had taken a Fallen one to point that out to him. He wondered what had become of Kadesch. When they'd Fallen, each of the two hundred angels had touched earth in different areas of the world, some—because of the length and velocity of the fall—even in different time periods.

She stepped off the curb. Cooper tugged Pyx's

arm, stopping them at the street corner where the light flashed red. She would walk against the light if he let her, but if she were going to hang with him, the woman had better start learning the law, if only not to draw attention to the demon and angel standing on the street corner.

"What are you doing?" Cooper swept a long look down her bopping figure.

She shifted her hips from side to side and snapped a finger near her ear. "Jiving."

"To what?" He now noticed she wore something in her ears. The small devices that played music were everywhere. Cooper popped one of them out and put it in his ear. He liked the funky tune. "Nice."

She nodded, working her shoulders into her impromptu shimmy. The demon had no grasp on her sexuality. Men walking by stretched their necks watching her movements.

Casting a sneer at one man who stared far too long, Cooper then clasped Pyx's hands.

"May I have this dance?" Instead of waiting for her reply, he led her in a mock waltz, there on the street corner. Their steps were not on the beat at all. Didn't matter. Holding Pyx close to him was all the music he needed.

"That's not the way to dance to this music," she said, but followed his steps. One of her ponytails bonked him on the forehead. She laughed and popped a big pink bubble of gum. "Street waltz-ing. I can dig it!"

Cooper twisted her under his arm, spinning her once. The move tore out the earbuds as he hooked her over his arm into a dramatic dip. Pyx stretched one arm high over her head in a ballroom-worthy finale and kicked up one leg.

Behind them, clapping erupted from a singular source.

Drawing his partner up to stand, Cooper turned to find an older woman with gray hair and sensible shoes performing enthusiastic applause. He and Pyx exchanged winks.

He bowed grandly, then offered for the woman's hand. "May I have this dance, madame?"

The old woman giggled and allowed him to dance her side to side with only the rhythm of traf-fic to guide their steps. He moved slowly, allowing her careful steps, then ended in a grand-yet-pain-fully-slow twirl. The woman pealed out a bright giggle as she spun up to his chest where her eyes were level to his diaphragm.

Cooper could feel her delight deep in his chest. It felt damn good. Humanity was all he'd expected it to be. He kissed her cheek and thanked her.

When Cooper turned to Pyx the demon stood with arms clasped before her, a smile softening her tilted face.

"Sorry," he said, splaying out his hands in surrender. "I like to dance."

"Apparently." Though her tone sounded more appreciative than blaming. "This world has gotten under your mortal skin, Fallen one. That can't be a good thing."

"It's not good. It's awesome."

"To each his own."

"You liked the dance. Admit it."

"I've a plan," she said, ignoring his ribbing. "Let's go to your place."

"My place?" he offered. "I'd rather hunt vampires. I need to test my new weapons."

"So would I. More action." She snapped into a fighter stance and punched the air between them a couple times. "But what you don't understand about me is that I have a goal. And that goal won't be met until you've found your muse."

"Let me guess. Your goal is to kill me."

"You got it, buddy."

The light changed and they began to walk, arm in arm, a strange couple if only the world were aware.

Cooper couldn't fault her for wanting to do her job. But she was going to have a tough time of it trying to convince him to do his job. It wasn't even a job, it was some kind of freaky innate compulsion.

"Why does a demon have to prove herself to her fellow Sinistari?"

A shrug of her shoulder and her pace moved faster. "Maybe it's a girl thing. Just never felt I fit in," she called back. "Always."

He joined her and grabbed her hand again to hold her closer. "Always?"

"Never felt as though I've been *in place,* if that makes sense. Look at me. I'm a chick who thinks she should be a guy. And Beneath! Don't get me started on that place."

He could only imagine Beneath was as dismal and menacing as the Ninth Void. Had he not been summoned to earth he would still be there, awaiting final judgment.

Why *had* he been summoned? The question niggled, but not enough to worry about it. He was free. He was not going to question that.

"So your goal on earth is to prove yourself to the Sinistari," he guessed.

"Yep. What's your goal?" she asked.

"Finding my halo." He strode up the street. His apartment was ahead. As was hers.

"Your halo? I've never heard of a Fallen looking for his halo. You need it because it's a mighty weapon in your hands?"

"Something like that." Sure, it was a weapon, but Cooper wanted to find his halo for reasons he could never explain to a demon who'd marked him as a target. "Got a means to track an angel's halo?"

"Maybe."

He smirked and slowed to allow her to catch up. "You have no idea how to track a halo."

"I didn't say that. I'm just not willing to do something for you until you do something for me."

"Sweetie, the something you want me to do involves my death. My halo won't hold much importance after that."

"Yeah well, life is tough."

Cooper stopped before his building and gripped her by the upper arm. She didn't struggle, because his sudden move made her barge into him, and she tried to hold her balance. He preferred her unsure and not so cocky. "Let's make a bargain, shall we?"

"If you think you can trade sex for favors..."

"I didn't say a thing about sex."

"You were giving me that look."

"What look?"

"That hungry look. The same look you were giving every woman in the club. The same look you had on your face after kissing me. You have no shame."

"I like kissing, is all. Kissing is an art form. It is a pleasurable means of exploring touch, taste and smell. Aren't you indulging in the senses, Pyx?

After my imprisonment I can't get enough of it all."

"Don't have time for silly stuff."

"You like to eat."

"Food keeps my energy up."

"You like clothing." He stroked a palm down her arm, his fingers clicking the gold buttons. "Tell me what it feels like, the fur about your wrists. Is it soft? Sensual?"

"You are the strangest angel I've known." She moved around to his right.

Cooper dodged to block her escape. "Know a lot of angels, then?"

"Actually, no."

"Well, then. I think you need to let your freak flag fly."

"My what?"

"You should be indulging in *all* the mortal sins," he said. "That is what the Sinistari do."

"I have been. I steal. I eat. I...put art on my body. I take great pride in the vanity of looking good. I haven't stopped chewing this delicious gum since I got here. It's full of sugar and I'm sure it'll rot my teeth."

"Ohh, you are a rebellious one. But no interest in sex?"

"Is sex a sin?"

"Yes. No. It's a beautiful act between a man and a woman in love. But lust can be sinful."

"Oh, I've been lusting."

"Have you?"

About who, he wanted to know. But he'd hit a nerve in the demon. A nerve so new to her she couldn't process the uncomfortable sensation. He liked that she wasn't so sure of everything. That meant she was learning, becoming more human.

And, that she wasn't on top of her game.

"It's because I'm a girl, right? You think I can't be tough and all in your face like a Sinistari should be? Well, try this one on for size."

When he felt the prick of a blade at his spine, Cooper put up his hands in surrender.

She was tough. Tougher than she realized. And he did have a healthy fear for what she and her blade, Joe, could do to him. But she was new to this world. He had at least two weeks on her. And he must use that to his advantage to stay alive.

Even if it meant seducing the enemy.

Chapter 5

Pyx followed Cooper into his living room. He snapped his fingers to turn on a lamp. "You got salt?" she asked.

The angel lifted a brow.

"I want to perform a spell that will help you locate your muse."

"Hey now, let's not get overzealous."

"It won't bring her to you, it'll just open your senses to her. That's my plan I was talking about."

"If you do that what do I get out of it? I know a bargain was mentioned. You going to help me hunt for my halo?"

She shrugged.

"Thought so. Have a seat, I'll be right back."

Cooper left Pyx staring at the comfortable brown velvet sofa. She fought the urge to make a leap and land all snuggly and reclined. What was it about mortal furniture that screamed comfort to her?

Now was no time to get comfortable.

Pyx had come to earth with a mind full of spells and invocations innate to the Sinistari. If pure physical force could not get the job done, then she'd facilitate demonic magic. She knew a spell that would enhance the Fallen's sensory perceptions—specifically to his muse.

The Fallen saw the world in vivid color, or so she understood. Much like herself, he'd been denied that color while in angelic form. But the Fallen's muse was unique in that she could literally blow out a Fallen's senses and his ability to see, taste and smell became rather muted as a result. Then, the only means for the angel to spy a muse was to notice the telltale sigil on the muse's arm. It was like a tattoo, but not. The sigils were unique and only one muse sigil matched to one Fallen sigil.

That didn't mean only one muse for one Fallen. There were actually more muses walking the earth than Fallen ones to match them to, thanks to the Sinistari having slain three or four dozen Fallen after the original fall. But once the Fallen found his own muse, and had sex with her, he could then move on to another.

Pyx hadn't gotten a look at Cooper's sigil. It could be anywhere on his body. And the only way to locate it was a thorough inspection.

She ran her tongue along her lower lip, considering such an inspection. It would involve removing clothing and lifting up hems. Running her fingers over warm, tan flesh. He'd agree, for sure. The man was a heathen. But so was she.

Or so she should be.

Why didn't the sin of lust appeal to her more? Was it simply that it intimidated her? It was the one sin she hadn't attempted yet. Wasn't quite sure how to go about it. It wasn't as though she needed instruction, but then again, she could use a few pointers.

Cooper had guessed right, she was a virgin. That didn't make her stupid, just…inexperienced regarding that one small aspect of mortal life. She'd pick it up as easily as she picked pockets. But what was the rush? She didn't need a romance, not while she was focused on slaying the Fallen.

He just had to quit distracting her.

The kiss Cooper had given her had been excellent. And easy. Pyx suspected what followed a simple kiss would be a bit more complicated. And desirable. Probably as delicious as bananas and chocolate crepes.

Nothing was going to intimidate her. Not the curiosity about sex. Not even a sexy Fallen one who liked to flirt and made sure the lusty compulsion never left her thoughts. He certainly had sex on the brain.

And that made it weird that Cooper had no interest whatsoever in his muse. Pyx knew the Fallen could have sex with any mortal woman, but could only garner his own pleasure from a muse. Which also meant his flirtations with *her* meant little. He couldn't get pleasure from her, so why bother?

Angels. They were a strange lot.

"So what's this spell all about?" Cooper returned and sat on the velvet sofa. He set a ceramic cellar of pink sea salt on the table. He leaned back and patted the cushion next to him. "Take a load off."

Relenting to the draw of comfort—and not his invitation—Pyx sat and picked up the salt cellar. "It'll open your senses to your muse. You okay with that?"

"I could be."

Tilting her head so she could not see the flex of muscles that moved his powerful thighs as he shifted his weight, Pyx poured out the salt on the table. He smelled...not bad. Warm? Couldn't be; the angel's blood was cold.

"Bubble gum."

His sudden remark made her almost drop the salt cellar. "What?"

"That's what you smell like."

"I know, but…" Could he have been aware she was just trying to place his scent? Impossible. An angel could only influence mortal minds. "That was an easy one." She snapped her gum. "But you?"

"Do I smell?" The voice whispered so close to her ear, Pyx did drop the cellar. Salt spilled in a pile on the coffee table. "Sorry. Do you know what you're doing?"

"I do." Slipping off the sofa to kneel on the floor before the table put a little distance between them, but he was still close enough that his knees were right there, next to her shoulder. "You do smell. Can't figure what it is."

"Cedar."

"What?"

"The headboard of the bed is made from cedar, as are the drawers. I think that's what it is." He sniffed his sleeve. "I kind of like it."

She kind of did, too.

Oh, bloody stupid demon. Focus!

Forcing her attention to the task, Pyx tightened her jaw and began to draw a warding symbol in the salt that she innately knew was correct. Crystal stones would prove helpful to focus the energy, but she could work without them.

"I thought salt was dangerous to demons?"

"It is if you shoot it at the normal ones."

"Normal demons?" He scoffed. "I think that's an oxymoron."

"Who are you calling a moron?"

"No one, sweetie."

"Darn straight. We Sinistari are tough. Hard to permeate our steel flesh."

He stroked her elbow with his thumb. "And yet, you feel oh, so soft."

Pyx ignored the twang in her belly that his touch ignited. Cedar, eh? "Just a costume. As is yours."

"But you like mine. I've seen you looking."

"It's…fine."

And warm. And smelled good. And strapped with muscles she wanted to touch and maybe… lick. And he still stroked her skin, which made her want to move closer so he'd stroke other places on her, and that would make her forget about what she wanted to do right now. It was all tied to her lacking indulgence in lust and if she really wanted to prove herself to the Sinistari then she should dive in, deep.

But not with a Fallen one.

"Can I get started with this?"

"We agreed to bargain if I'm to allow you to perform such a spell. I go first."

"I thought it was women first?"

"Not in this situation."

With a sigh Pyx pressed her back against the sofa. Tapping the coffee table with her fingers, she tilted her head all the way back to look upside down at Cooper. "Fine, thought you wanted to hunt halos?"

"Changed my mind."

"So? What do you want?"

"Another kiss."

Pyx sat upright. Why did that request not surprise her? As well, how could those two simple words flush her neck and send the heat down across her breasts? It had just been two words!

"Why do you want to make out with the one who wants to kill you?"

Cooper slid off the sofa to sit next to her. He leaned in close to her face. His scent teased at her need to stay focused. "Maybe it'll earn me a reprieve from your death wish."

He was pushing it. And those gray-and-azure eyes sparkled with thoughts Pyx didn't want to know about.

Yes, she did.

No.

Oh, crap, she did.

It truly fascinated her that this Fallen one wanted to go on a quest for his halo as opposed to wreaking havoc. Angels were experts at havoc, and smiting.

Yet here he sat, completely shameless and oh, so charming. He could have her in the palm of his hand with a "please." The enemy!

Well, as Cooper had stated earlier, the best place to put the enemy was as close as possible. And close was looking pretty good right now. And, man, did she like the smell of it.

Pyx closed her eyes. And waited.

A minty snicker huffed across her mouth.

Not opening her eyes, she asked, "What?"

"You're waiting for *me* to do all the work?"

Wasn't that the man's job? Besides, she needed time. There was a learning curve to this kind of interaction. And he'd had two weeks longer than she to perfect his moves.

"You wanted a kiss, angel, you come and get it."

The invitation was answered more swiftly than expected. He slid a hand behind her back and pulled her to his body at the same time his mouth found hers. Pulled onto his lap, Pyx couldn't decide if she wanted to struggle or snuggle closer. His insistence was overwhelming, yet the kiss was soft and gentle, not so commanding as to put her off.

Sliding a knee to either side of his thighs, she straddled him without breaking the intense contact.

The sensation of touch was extreme with her mouth pressed to this man's mouth. She could feel…everything. His lips were soft, the skin tender and different than on his arm or face.

The sensual feeling didn't stay at her mouth.

It scurried over her flesh and left a tingly wake. And those sparkles absolutely beamed. This was... nice.

And did she really need to concern herself with slayage 24/7? There wasn't another Sinistari within miles of this Fallen. No one would know.

Drawing a hand along Cooper's thigh, Pyx couldn't help but note how firm and muscled it was. Powerful.

Power impressed her. Power made her feel... safe. Protected. It was an odd feeling to have, but she didn't question it. Not now. Now was for the moment. A moment to learn and experience.

Cooper groaned into her mouth. The wanting sound softened her last defenses. His entire body sought hers, pressing chest to chest, hands gliding over her arms, and melding muscle along muscle. He sought touch, and she'd be darned if she didn't want to give it to him and in turn, receive touch.

Threading her fingers into his hair she tugged him closer, deepening the kiss. Despite the minty coolness of his breath the kiss was hot. It melted her like the gooey chocolate inside a folded crepe.

So this was why the Sinistari jumped right in with the indulging in lust stuff? Certainly was more satisfying than cramming a blade into an angel's heart. Mostly. She had nothing to compare it to. Yet.

"You taste like bubble gum," he muttered as he

nudged his nose near her ear and licked the lobe of it.

"I swallowed it when you kissed me."

A new sensation made Pyx flinch giddily. His thumb brushed over her nipple, strangely hard beneath the soft cotton T-shirt. The quick zing surprised her, yet she could go for another, so she melted against his palm, encouraging his exploration.

"Mmm, yes, tilt your head and let me lick your neck." Hot breath skittered down her skin as he kissed her neck, under her ear. "Never thought a demon would be so damned delicious."

The stroke of his tongue along her neck reminded her of what he was capable. "You're not giving me an angelkiss?"

An angel could lick a path on mortal skin that would itch interminably, and act as a beacon so the angel could track said mortal. Usually it was the muse who received the angelkiss.

"Only works on mortals," he murmured. "My tongue won't make you itch, Pyx, unless it's an itch for more. Mmm, down here?" He tickled the rise of her breast with his tongue. It felt so good she couldn't think about how wrong this was. "You are definitely all woman."

By now that declaration shouldn't bother her, but for some reason it did. Pyx pulled her fingers from Cooper's hair and pressed a palm at her breast where he was moving his tongue lower beneath the T-shirt neckline. "I can still take you, even if I am a girl."

"Didn't say you couldn't." He nipped her finger. When she pulled away, he softly bit her nipple through the T-shirt. "Kind of like how you want to kill me but at the same time you're having a bit of fun, aren't you?"

"Kissing is a new experience." She tried to sound bored, but really, this was fabulous. "Oh, what's that?"

He ground his hips against hers. The hardness she felt against her groin was long and thick. "I have a dagger, too," he said. "And it's not called Joe."

"Let's see."

Cooper suddenly pulled out of their embrace. He gave her the wonkiest look, half concerned, half bizarre with a raised brow added for effect. "You have no idea how all this works, do you?"

"What works? Kissing?" She tugged a lock of her thick red hair and wrapped it about a finger. "Don't you think I kiss well?"

"You do." He kissed her quickly, then kissed her finger through the hair wrapped about it. "But you're not up on what comes next, I figure. You *did* walk the world?"

"Yes."

"Did you happen to watch any couples having sex?"

"That would be rude!"

"A demon with morals? Where in your handbook does it say pillage and steal without a thought, yet close your eyes to the sexy stuff?"

"I thought it was personal. You know."

"Yeah? Well, the dagger in my pants is not something for show and tell. When I bring this guy out, it means business. And I don't think we're ready for sex."

"Sex? I thought we were just kissing?"

He jumped up from the floor and shrugged a hand through his hair. "I can't believe I said that. Woman, you are confusing my sense of wrong and right."

"Sounds like a problem." She turned to the table where the salt ward needed some readjusting. "Perhaps you should let me guide you down your destined path and you wouldn't have all this extra silly stuff to worry about?"

"Kissing isn't silly."

"I was talking about finding your muse."

He didn't seem as though he would kiss her again. Bummer. That had been fun. Somehow she had led him to believe they could have sex. She had definitely missed something between the kisses to her neck and him touching her nipple.

Oh! This was complicated.

"Let's get to it then." Cooper eased a hand over his jeans in the front then sat on the couch. Not touching her.

Yep, what they'd just done felt wrong. But she couldn't quite put a finger on why. Hmm, guilt? Another sin to add to her list.

Pyx sighed and leaned over the salt circle. It was as good as it was going to get without the crystals. She spread out her fingers and closed her eyes— then remembered. "I'll need your blood."

"Are you trying to attract vampires?"

"No."

She drew out Joe. The dagger was three-pronged down each side of the blade and the tip of it had been soaked in qeres, an angel poison. But it only worked when embedded in the angel's heart. It would serve little harm to the mortal flesh the Fallen wore as costume.

"For the spell to work it has to be focused on you," she explained. "Just a few drops. Give me a finger. Unless you're scared?"

"Not scared of anything, especially not a pretty little demon with a big bad blade she calls Joe."

He pointed out a finger, and Pyx grabbed his wrist. "I'm not afraid of anything, either."

Well, it had to be said. She couldn't let him think she was scared of something. Which she was not. Nope, not even kissing.

She poked the tip of his finger with Joe. Vivid

blue droplets dripped onto the table in the center of the salt circle, puddling and misting as if dry ice. Angel blood was cold, opposite her hot blood. She bet if a vampire bit into Cooper's neck the blood-sucker would get a major brain freeze before the inevitable explosion.

She noticed Cooper looked away. "Sight of blood make you woozy? So you are afraid of something."

"No, I… It's just…" He shook his head and ran his free hand over his scalp.

"Hurt?"

"No, it's blue, damn it! It's not red like mortal blood."

"Yeah, and mine is black. So what?"

"It's a reminder of how much I don't want what I am right now."

"I don't understand that. You are very powerful. You're an angel. You can flash all over, persuade mortals to bend to your will, never have to spend a dime, rip hearts out of vampire chests…"

"The less you understand about me, the easier it will be to shove the blade in deep when the time comes, eh?" He tugged his finger from her grip and stuck his hand in his pocket. "Get on with your spell then."

Demonic power vibrated through Cooper's living room. It shook the salt crystals on the table and rattled the plates and glasses in the kitchen.

Pyx stood over the table, shoulders proudly thrust back and one hand held over the salt ward, fingers splayed. She recited a spell in myriad tongues. It echoed bellicose and then harmonic. Cooper recognized a few of the tones as angelic in origin. He wagered the Sinistari had no idea that some of the languages her magic encompassed had originated Above.

As the spell took on weight, the air in the room lightened so Cooper felt he could float. Pyx's hair spread about her like a fiery crown, defying gravity.

He admired her beauty and elegance. Yes, she was possessed of both those aspects, though she herself felt awkward and as if she did not fit in anywhere. She fit into his idea of life, no matter that her intentions against him were deadly. For this moment, at least. Tomorrow may change his mind.

Truthfully, he feared her power. The blade she carried close to her heart could kill him. But he also embraced the challenge of turning her head, if not her heart. And if he could convince the demon that he wasn't such an awful angel he would not have to kill her in self-defense.

Pyx, alive, and in his embrace, suited him fine.

Suddenly Pyx swung toward him, bringing her hand up and facing it palm-out. The force of the ward, imprinted upon her palm, surged outward.

Cooper took the supernatural punch against his lower left torso—right where his sigil marked him from the angelic dominions.

Set off his feet, he toppled and caught his hands against the wall behind him. His sigil burned and he let out a yelp.

The room settled.

Pyx's hair spilled upon her shoulders and down her arms. She lowered her arm. The clatter of kitchen porcelain stopped.

Cooper gasped in a breath and slapped a palm to his abdomen. The sigil no longer burned.

He met Pyx's eyes, and as a grin curved her red lips, he found himself smiling in response. It was a drunken reaction to what she'd just done to him. Violated him in a way. Marked him. And he'd given her permission to do so.

Now he'd be more open to finding his muse.

He slid down against the wall. His legs were weak for no other reason than he wasn't sure what he'd allowed the demon to do to him. Did she have the upper hand now? No, he could resist if he happened to stumble across his muse. It was ridiculous to think he'd be *compelled* to have sex with her. A farce! He'd agreed to let the demon do the spell only so he would see the muse coming before he stumbled onto her—and that would allow him time to turn and run the other way.

"I'll leave you to stew," Pyx said. "Let that

spell sink in nice and deep, big boy. Dream sweet dreams of your muse. Nighty night."

The demon strode out of Cooper's apartment.

"The only woman I'm going to dream about," he muttered, and now managed a genuine smirk, "just touched me with a wicked spell."

Chapter 6

It was nearing nine in the evening and the patio outside the café was lit with lights strung about the posts and along the iron railing. The autumn air was sharp and cool. Cooper appreciated the four seasons and looked forward to experiencing winter. His mortal costume felt extremes of weather acutely. Snowboarding a packed run appealed to his sense of adventure.

He thanked the waitress who had refilled his coffee and then looked out at the Seine. It twinkled with the reflection from the passing tourist boats, which were strung with lights.

A couple walked hand in hand outside the iron railing that blocked off the café from the street.

The man pushed a stroller. Cooper nodded and tipped his cup to them.

It seemed a long shot to give a moment's thought to some day having a family and walking along the Seine to the Tuileries where he could push his children on the swings and toss bread bits to the ducks in the octagon pond.

What he'd not told Pyx about his time Above in the ranks was he had served his master without question. He had slain many because he was told to do so. No question whether the person deserved to die. He'd wielded a sword and bloodied it often. It was all he had known, and he'd served his master well.

So when had he suddenly decided it was wrong to kill and he'd prefer living a life with mortality attached to it? It hadn't even entered his mind until Kadesch had said something.

It had been a particular event in a Mesopotamian village long ago. The village was new and greed had festered throughout the population. His orders had been to smite the entire village, and he did so, washing the land with flames and striking off the heads of those who'd fled the destruction.

Only he'd missed a child. A small boy, perhaps three years old, whom he'd found bent over the blackened body of what had once been his mother. Juphiel had approached the boy, sword wielded to decapitate him, when the child had looked up into his eyes.

Into his eyes. Not pleading. Not asking why. Only seeing a part of Juphiel that even the angel had not realized existed. A compassionate shard of his heart had actually pulsed then, and he'd given thought to his actions.

All it had taken was one moment of connection to make him wonder and to take survey of what lay before him. Humans were not animals herded into his path of destruction. They possessed bright and vital souls, and those souls made them more than Juphiel could ever hope to be.

Kadesch had stalked up to his side. Two angels in all their divine glory stared down at one frightened child.

"I cannot do it," Juphiel had said. He lowered his sword, as well his head.

"I am pleased."

Kadesch's remark had shocked him. Juphiel swung about to find the angel extending a hand to the boy.

"But this is wrong," Juphiel had argued. "We've orders."

"Orders make it right?"

"Yes!"

Kadesch had stood straight, shoulder to shoulder with Juphiel, and looked across the vast destruction. The world was blackened with ash. "Is that what you really believe, Juphiel? Speak to me from your heart."

"My heart holds no compassion."

"Yes, it does."

"No, it— I don't...know."

"Good. Not knowing is a strong position. It leaves you open to choice. There is no right or wrong, Juphiel. No good or evil. Only choice."

"We have no choice."

Kadesch's voice had whispered on fine tones lighter than the ash flakes dusting the air, "Choice is yours if you dare to take it."

Juphiel had not heard such talk before, not within the angel ranks. But as Kadesch spoke, Juphiel began to nod in agreement. Knowing, for the first time, that it was possible. And so Juphiel had made a choice.

That day the angel had traced a circle in the ash around the child and his dead mother. And then he'd flashed them both to Babylon, ensuring a mother who had recently lost her son to the pox sighted the child. She'd taken him in and raised him as her own.

Kadesch had then suggested they join with the rebel ranks that spoke of falling. Humanity, Kadesch had said. It is a marvel.

Cooper spread his fingers about the warm coffee cup. He wondered what had become of the child. Had he grown into a fine, strapping young man who had served his community? Or had he become a pyromaniac because of how his mother and village had been destroyed?

Didn't matter.

What did matter was the boy's eyes were all Cooper saw after that whenever he wielded his sword. And though he continued to serve his master, he looked forward to the day he could join the human race and live, love and suffer along with them. And ultimately, make more choices.

Kadesch had been right about everything. He wondered if the angel walked the earth now, or was still imprisoned in the Ninth Void.

Pray, the angel had not been destroyed by Sinistari. Cooper found it hard to imagine Kadesch, the master of a compassionate heart, could answer the compulsion to find a muse.

A sip of creamy coffee burned down his throat, but he enjoyed the sensation. Feeling pain or discomfort was new to him. When in complete angelic form he hadn't experienced the like. Not physical or emotional. Save for the wonder in the boy's eyes.

It wasn't right. While he knew Above and Beneath existed for a reason, and that mortals would always cling to their distorted beliefs in the two realms, he had wanted to step away. To fall away to something better, more substantial and real. To face the consequences for wrongs and rights.

He would be a fine mortal, he knew it. Yet whether deserving or not, would he be lonely?

In this mortal costume, Cooper could attract any woman he desired. But could he keep one? Would any woman be attracted to a man whose only history was killing myriads and betraying Him by falling?

The chair across the table from him scraped across the sidewalk. A man plunked onto it and propped an ankle over his knee. Scruffy running shoes peeked from the tattered hem of faded jeans. He slapped the iron table. "How's tricks?"

Setting down his coffee mug and leaning back in his chair, Cooper sized up the man who wore sunglasses though the sun was but an orange strip on the horizon. Hair cut military-short and a square jaw gave him a rugged, don't-give-a-crap appearance.

He wasn't mortal, Cooper sensed, which left the obvious choice of vampire since they seemed to be following him of late.

When the man grinned, his top lip curled to expose the tip of a fang. He did it as a warning. A futile one. Cooper still had the throwing stars in his pocket, and he carried the blade tucked at the back of his jeans. But who needed weapons?

"Tricks are just fine," Cooper offered with an

air of indifference. "What brings you up from the coffin?"

"Ha, ha, ha. I don't do coffins, but that was a funny one."

"But you obviously don't do sunlight."

"Actually, I do." He tilted his head and the dark sunglasses glittered with the reflection from the café's neon sign. "But the guy I work for is one of those SPF 1000 kind of guys. Sunglasses are a bad habit I picked up from him."

"Who do you work for?" If the vampire wanted to chat, Cooper intended to get whatever information he could from him.

"Antonio del Gado."

Surprised a name had been offered, Cooper filed that one away. "And is Monsieur del Gado looking to connect with me somehow?"

"You are one smart angel, Juphiel."

He knew his name?

Maintain composure, Cooper coached. No need to start a scene in a public venue that could result in him holding a bloody heart.

"I do have knowledge of the entire world," Cooper offered coolly.

"Let's not get cocky now. Because you're stupid, too. Hanging out with a Sinistari? That's idiotic, man."

"Keep one's enemies close. Isn't that the saying?"

"Obviously that doesn't apply to all your enemies. I heard what you do with vampires."

"Did you now?"

"Yeah, you rip out their hearts with your bare hands. Stylish. But I'm telling you right now, I'm not that dumb. I'm protected."

"Wards?"

"Can you feel them?"

Cooper now noted the subtle hum emanating from the vampire. It was as if the breeze was electrified. Weaker than the spell Pyx had tossed at him, but nothing to sneeze at. "Not stupid, but still a bloodsucker."

"Gotta survive somehow. So about your muse?"

"What about her?"

"You fixing to hook up any time soon?"

"Why? You want front-row seats?"

That was crass. Cooper forced back a wince because he didn't want the vamp to guess anything about him. And why was it every paranormal creature within sight wanted him to get it on with his muse?

"Too bad. I'm all for crashing parties. So, my name's Bruce." He offered a hand to shake, but Cooper crossed his arms. "Right. Just wanted to introduce myself since I do know your name, and I'd like to think we'll become good friends. Until you and your muse decide to put on a show, I'll be on your ass like a tick, buddy."

"I'll save you the trouble, and me the itch. I'm not going anywhere near my muse."

"Oh, yeah? Sorry bit of feathers and halo you are."

He didn't have feathers, or for that matter, a halo.

Fisting his fingers under the table, Cooper fought the urge to push the vampire's nose into his cranium. Patrons sat everywhere. Tourists walked by on the sidewalk.

"I can deal with that," the vampire offered. "For now."

The waitress walked by and the vamp flicked the hem of her skirt, which garnered him a sneer and a huffy "What do you want?"

"Give me one of those fancy little cups of high octane, will you?"

Confusion twisted her pretty pink lips.

"An espresso, please," Cooper offered in French since the vampire preferred English. "Make it a triple."

"Trying to keep the vampire up all night? Works for me. Not much of a sleeper, anyway." Bruce leaned forward, catching his elbows on the table. "So here's the deal. You don't want to look for your muse? Fine. Then you'll have to make me happy another way."

"I don't have to do anything for you."

"Yeah? Well, if you want that pretty Sinistari

to remain pretty I think you will, at the very least, hear me out."

"There's not a thing you and your bloody ilk can do to harm a Sinistari demon."

"We may be a lesser physical match to the Sinistari, true, but I know a psychopomp who'll match her blow for blow, and won't stop until he's raped her heart for all the stolen souls within."

Cooper looked aside, coaching his expression to remain impassive. The Sinistari were known to steal souls from the angels they slayed. It pissed off the rightful receiver of those souls, the psychopomp.

He wondered if Pyx had any souls. He couldn't take a chance. "What do you want?"

"Names," Bruce said.

"Names?"

"Of your fellow Fallen. Need them to match to the angel sigils Monsieur del Gado has collected."

Cooper put two and two together quickly. "This vampire leader of yours… He's summoning the Fallen to earth?"

"Summoned you, big boy."

Cooper had no response to that. It went against any explanation he could imagine for his summoning.

Bruce persisted. "Give me a few names, and I'll hang in your wake for a while. What do you say?"

The waitress dropped off Bruce's espresso and he tipped it down in one swallow.

"I say—" Cooper stood "—you get the bill."

And he flashed away from the café and landed at the Pont Neuf. Cars passed over the bridge behind him. He waited for Bruce to search the area, and waved when the vampire sighted him. "Idiot vamp."

The vampires had summoned him to earth?

This was not what he'd expected. What would a bloodsucker want with a Fallen?

Flashing home, Cooper strode through the apartment and scattered the throwing stars on the kitchen table. "Vampires," he muttered.

He glanced to the laptop, which flashed a flying toaster screen saver. He'd set the email program to alert him if he received a reply from Eden Campbell. Until then, he could only wait for more information on the halos.

But why not organize a halo-hunting mission on his own?

"No idea how to start. How does she track them?"

It wasn't as though he could sense his halo. But then, who knew? If he got close to the thing *would* he sense it? Would it send out some kind of vibration? There was nothing online to answer those questions. And he couldn't ask another Fallen because he didn't know any.

Had the vampires summoned other Fallen ones? To what purpose did the Fallen finding his muse serve the vamps?

Scuffing a frustrated hand over his hair, he decided he couldn't sit around and do nothing. He had to be proactive. He shouldn't have left Bruce alone. He could flash back to the bridge right now and follow the vamp back to his lair.

He hoofed it down the stairs to the lobby, but before flashing, noticed someone stood outside the doors.

Cooper stepped outside. He hadn't expected her to look quite so alluring. In an awkward trying-so-hard-it-works kind of way.

"Care to hunt some vamps?" he tossed out.

Strolling his gaze down her body, he thought what an incredible figure she had. The black silk hugged her breasts and tucked in snugly to emphasize her waistline. It stopped high on her thighs, and he followed those long sexy gams down to—

"I'm so there," Pyx said, flipping a stake through her fingers like a high school majorette's baton. "What's wrong?"

"You're wearing a dress."

"Yeah. So? It is what girls wear. Shows off our legs and other curvy bits."

"Right, but how many girls in dresses hunt vampires?"

"You don't think I can hunt properly in this?" She sashayed her hips side to side, which put visions of sexual positions into Cooper's brain. Her on top of him, moving like that?

"I think you can do about anything you like in that." He smiled and crossed his arms over his chest. Peering down, he waited for her to heel out one of her feet, displaying the black combat boot laced high up her ankle. "What's with the boots?"

"I like them. You got a problem with them?"

He was about to comment that combat boots did not go at all with a slinky black silk number, but stopped himself. Mr. Blackwell, he was not. And for some reason, the look worked on Pyx. Sexy *and* I-can-stab-you-faster-than-you-can-wink.

Yeah, he liked it, he really liked it.

"All right then. Let's go stake some vamps."

Chapter 7

Pyx led Cooper onto the dance floor in club *Exsangue*. Dancing in this silk dress was a voluptuous experience. She was beginning to take to heart Cooper's quest for all things sensual. He was right. Every experience opened her senses, and ignoring it was stupid.

The airy fabric slid across her bare flesh as if it were a lover's hand. Or so she suspected. She wasn't sure what a lover's hand felt like. She'd only had the two kisses from Cooper, and he didn't count because any accidental seduction between the two of them was part of her master plan to lure him into trusting her.

Cooper danced to the beat of a song called

"Disturbia." The music became him. It was as if he didn't have to try at all. Music moved within him. He'd bounce a bit, then groove his hips, and then wink at her.

Oh, that fluttery wink. It made something in Pyx flutter. Definitely not her heart, though.

Why was she having a problem with the things her breed would normally swallow in large gulps and then go on to more, more and more? The Sinistari were known for their decadent indulgence in mortal sin.

She had indulged in theft, gluttony, vanity and greed, but not yet lust.

When she closed her eyes and surrendered to the sound it was as though her body was the instrument, and she liked the feeling. The frantic beat directed her body.

Cooper's hand slid to the back of her waist. He swayed closer to her, enticing her into the same delirious beat that toyed with their closeness and threatened forgotten goals.

He gave her that big white-toothed smile, like he was proud of her. Man, did his eyes glimmer in the club's weird flashing lights. Angel, warrior, dancer. He occupied a place in her mind that didn't know how to process the experience. Or maybe that place had already accepted what the demon could not.

Demon, warrior, slayer.

Focus on the task, Pyxion. You're playing up to the angel to keep him close, remember?

Despite the sexy clothing, she still kept her dagger strapped close under her arm. This demon would not trip over silly mortal emotions.

Bending her knees, Pyx lowered, shifting her hips side to side. Screw the overthinking. She was here to hunt vampires.

Gliding up to standing position, she allowed Cooper to wrap a hand around her from behind, and spread his fingers across her stomach. His touch was not warm, but not disturbingly cold.

They moved in time with one another. Pyx bumped him with her derriere and she discovered that hard weapon he possessed was ready and willing again.

I have a dagger, too…but it's not called Joe.

Is that what men were like? So focused on their…parts. Could it be, they were literally controlled by their penises? And she was so worried she hadn't been a man?

Yet a woman could easily control that appendage without even touching it. She merely had to smile prettily at him and bat her lashes.

Cool.

Pyx swept her gaze about the dance floor and high along the balcony. A man lingered at the railing above, elbows propped and eyes taking in the scene. Tall, thin and too pale. He was unmistakably vampire. It was a sense she got for the longtooths; she couldn't explain it more than to say she got a shiver in her veins.

Gliding up to Cooper, she pressed close to him. He secured her hips with each hand and slowed their rhythm to a rocking sway that made parts on her body tingle. And that wasn't a vampire tingle, either.

"There's one standing directly over you," she said at his ear.

The sweep of his breath across her face made her want to nuzzle in closer. And she did, quickly, just long enough to breathe in his musky male scent. It was subtle, yet she wanted more of it. To drown in it.

He turned her in his embrace, his fingers brushing over her breast. That set her insides to a jiggly quiver.

So maybe the male had as much power over the female with mere touches and looks. That left her on uneven playing ground, for Cooper obviously had much more experience in the sexual arts than she did.

They moved slowly, rocking and blending with the dancers. He turned her so he could get a look at the vampire.

"I know that vampire," he muttered over her shoulder. "He's warded against angels."

"Seems a lot of them are."

"Not all of them. We've taken out unwarded vamps. And who is to say if he's warded against demons?"

"How to determine which ones have wards and which do not?" Pyx said. "Probably the leaders. Let's get him out of here. See if he's got minions."

"I do like to slay minions."

He clasped her hand and led her from the dance floor. While she wanted to walk beside him, to catch up and even surpass him, Pyx decided it would look better if the vampire saw the angel leading her out. Maybe the vamp would even think she was the muse.

Cooper kicked open the exit door. They entered the night with hands clasped and Pyx hugged up next to him. Just to make things look good. Certainly not because the shim of his sleeve across her bare arm tingled wickedly and made her weigh the benefits of slaying vamps against the thrill of more kisses.

Or was that the thrill of slaying vamps and the benefits of kisses? Certainly kissing was more thrilling than slaying.

The club parking lot opened to a narrow alley-way, but she didn't want to take out any vampires so close to the building, in case an innocent walked out. And Cooper's method of annihilating vampires was rather messy.

"I know you're using me," he said as they crossed the lot, hands swinging.

So what else was new? "You're using me."

"So we understand it's not real affection, then." He drew her hand up to press at his mouth.

Affection? Did he mean between *them?* Was the angel developing feelings toward her? No, couldn't be.

Pyx tugged her hand out of his, away from the allure of his kiss. "Nope, just a game."

"Fine."

"Fine." Seriously? Why had it been necessary to confirm what had been so obvious?

Angels didn't fall in love any more than demons did. Unless she'd been assigned to slay a broken one. Had the man landed on his head after his Fall? It was possible because his utter lack of interest in finding his muse was just wrong. And since when did angels kiss demons?

You kissed him back.

"There's a couple on the rooftop," Cooper said over his shoulder to her. Then he leaped and landed on the roof of a brick-sided building.

Happy to abandon her mutinous thoughts about kissing, Pyx followed, landing beside him.

Cooper pressed a hand to her hip, to keep her behind him. She did not like to be stifled, and peeked around his shoulder. Three vampires flashed stiletto grins at her. Behind her, the vamp from the club had matched their leap. Now he pulled out a length of chain from his jacket and swung it over his head.

Pyx pulled out the wooden stake tucked in her boot and swung around, prepared to connect with flesh and blood. The vampire dodged and waggled an admonishing finger at her.

Cooper flicked a throwing star. It landed in one vampire in the skull above his ear. The vamp grabbed the razor-edged star and yelped as it cut open his palm.

"Nice one," Pyx said. She kicked high to heel a vamp in the jaw. "But watch this!"

Her head still angled downward from the kick, palms to asphalt, she pushed off and flipped high into the air, landing on another vamp's shoulder with her thighs. She squeezed but that wasn't going to take out an immortal bloodsucker. Lunging forward over its head, she plunged the stake into his chest, and somersaulted to land on both feet. Behind her the air filled with vamp ash. The smell of that stuff was like burnt, rotting meat.

"Not bad—"

"Cooper, watch out!"

He had been aiming for the vampire wielding the chain in front of him, and didn't see the vamp who leaped for his back and clung like a monkey. The vampire slammed a gun barrel against Cooper's back.

The angel shouted viciously. His arms and legs snapped out from his body, shaking, as if touched by a Taser.

The decoy vampire laughed and turned right into Pyx's space. She shoved a stake in his heart.

Cooper let out a biting string of mortal oaths. His body shuddered as if pinned in midair. He struggled, fighting the weird effects of whatever had been done to him.

The vampire who'd been on Cooper's back lunged for Pyx. She booted him in the chest. He dropped the gun and landed against the brick wall with a thud. Stake held ready to stab, she was about to take him out when Cooper's painful cry stopped her.

"I will not relent," another vampire said to Cooper, whom Pyx had not turned to look at yet. "I want a name, buddy. I'll return when you're not sporting a demon on your arm."

Cooper's growl was unnatural and glassy. Something wasn't right.

Turning about, Pyx's stake hand dropped to her side. Her mouth may have dropped open, too, but only momentarily.

Cooper wasn't in human form.

The angel had shifted. Whether purposefully or as a result of the strange attack, Pyx couldn't know. He shook his glass head as if trying to shake off a daze.

The vampire who had spoken ran down the alleyway. She let him go.

There were more important things to concern her right now. She slapped her hip, but the dagger wasn't there.

Now was her chance! So what if the muse wasn't around. She didn't need one. The angel had assumed the form in which he could be slain.

Pyx frantically scanned the rooftop, but couldn't locate the dagger.

The angel moaned, and let out a high-pitched shriek. It resembled no earthly sound. He could blast out mortal eardrums, and eventually their brains, if he continued—but he did not.

Pyx stared at the shifted creature and forgot about Joe.

Magnificent was a poor word to describe Cooper in his half-shifted form. The man's shirt had torn away and his chest had become hard, solid blue glass, which flexed remarkably like liquid ice. To touch him in this form would invite a chill no creature could withstand. It wouldn't kill her, but it would freeze her solid.

Within the blue glass, Pyx saw the red heart. All angels had glass hearts. Not glass as mortals would define it; this particular angel was formed of ineffable substance that resembled glass.

All angels were different; some were fashioned from metal, wood, mist, razors, paper. Their

structure was related to the craft each angel possessed and had taught the world upon their fall.

The creature standing before her looked like
Cooper, but his face was glass and where his hair
should be a vapory substance clouded about his
skull.

But the most spectacular sight was the wings
stretching out thirty, maybe even forty feet behind
him. A pseudo-peacock's array ruffled out from
between his shoulders. No feathers. Angels did
not do feathers until the final death. Instead, the
illusion of feathers designed of what looked like
stained glass shivered and moved with the air as
if weightless. Titanium, blue, silver, emerald and
violet glass glistened under the streetlights and cast
lasers of color across the brick walls.

"Pyx?" His voice shuddered in a bell-like tone.
He slapped a glass palm to his chest and the skin
rippled as if flesh to flesh.

"You are an incredible sight," she said, and then
caught a lump in her throat.

A lift of his brow, cocky—even in half form
the angel was still a Casanova—made Pyx realize
what she just said.

"I mean, your wings. They're…gorgeous. Why
did you shift?"

"Wasn't on purpose." He suddenly fell to his
knees and bowed, catching his palms on the asphalt. His wings swept the air beyond the roof of

the three-story building to his right. "Shot me...
with something. In the back. Like...electricity running through me. Couldn't help it."

"Yes. The vampire had a gun."

Pyx scanned the ground and sighted a small
silver gun. She grabbed it. It was more an injection gun with an empty glass cartridge barrel than
something that fired bullets.

And where had Joe gone?

"I think they injected you with—"

The piercing cry sounded again. Pyx winced
and covered her ears.

She turned to find the wings gone and Cooper
had resumed his mortal costume. His lower half
hadn't shifted so he wore jeans, though his boots
lay beside his bare feet. His chest heaved, flexing
the muscles.

He looked up at her, huffing and exhausted from
the shift. "Injected me? I felt it at my lower back.
Take a look."

She crawled over to him and noticed Joe lying
not two feet away from the angel's feet.

"What do you see?"

A missed opportunity.

The chance to prove herself had been stolen by
her misplaced wonder. For now. She would have
another chance, and next time, she would not be
distracted by the angel's beauty.

Pyx bent over him, but didn't see any marks on his flesh. "The light here is bad. Can you flash?"

"Of course I can. I'm not an invalid."

"I mean, so we can go home and take a better look. Come on." She swept up Joe and holstered the dagger, patting it once. Next time, for sure. "Whatever the vamps are up to, I want to figure this out."

Missed opportunity or some kind of weird angel worship? She'd been utterly aghast at the beauty of his form. Sinistari did not admire the Fallen.

You're not going to fail again, Pyx.

But had she already accepted the failure?

Cooper put a shaking arm across her shoulders and together they flashed.

Bruce had never seen a shifted angel. Not unless it had been a painting. In the moment when he'd clung to the Fallen's back, it had freaked him out. He wasn't sure the GPS had been injected correctly. It had been designed to go into the mortal flesh the angel wore when on earth.

Why had it shifted? Was it because of the injection? Weird.

He tapped the receiver. Static buzzed.

"This had better work."

Chapter 8

"You've been quiet since we left the rooftop."

Cooper turned on the light in the bedroom with a flicking gesture. Pyx lingered in the doublewide doorway between the two rooms. The pocket doors were shoved inside the walls.

He shrugged and rubbed the back of his neck. "Just didn't expect to shift in front of you."

The involuntary shift had felt weird, as if he'd stripped naked before Pyx. Normally stripping naked for a woman would have felt great. As well, it would have been a powerful, sexual thing.

Shifting to half form had exposed a side of himself he didn't wish anyone to see. On the rooftop he had felt shamed, and remnants of that shame still shivered across his mortal skin.

He'd revealed himself to Pyx.

And now he wondered what she had thought in that moment as she'd stared up at his angelic half form. Had it offended her? Had it appealed to her? She was a demon; she could have only felt the urge to shove a blade into his heart. Yet he wished now she had seen beyond that urge and into him. The real him.

And why did it bother him what she thought of him? Did he have feelings for her?

Maybe.

No. She wanted to slay him!

Yet he wanted to connect with Pyx in a way he felt was not all right. They were two alike in this world. They should cleave together instead of trying to kill one another. But it hurt his brain right now to try and sort out this emotional stuff.

"That gun they used delivered some kind of electrical charge to shock my system."

"Here it is." Pyx handed him the weapon she'd claimed from the rooftop.

He examined the small injection gun. The barrel was glass or some kind of Lucite and he suspected whatever had been put in him was still there. "It set me off and I couldn't control the shift."

"That's the first time I've seen an angel in half form," Pyx said.

"You didn't slay any of my kind before the flood?"

She shook her head. "I was summoned to slay a Fallen but a week before the flood. Never did track that bastard down before the waters came."

"Lots of Sinistari survived the flood," Cooper noted.

"Yeah? Doesn't that figure. Pyxion the Other is always getting the short end of the stick. I got sent Beneath as the flood waters covered the land. Other Sinistari were Beneath. You can't imagine the razzing I got from them."

"Because you didn't complete your task?"

"You got it."

Cooper had only walked the earth a short time before the flood had come to sweep away him and his Fallen brethren and imprison them in the Ninth Void as punishment for falling. But he'd always thought all the Sinistari had been allowed to walk the earth following.

"I thought I heard about some great Sinistari warrior," he said, "who stole hundreds of thousands of souls from the Fallen he had slain and tallied quite the number of kills."

"Ashuriel the Black." Pyx punched a fist in her palm. "He's no longer the great one though. He accepted his own mortal soul months ago after an angel kill. And get this, it was because he was in love with a mortal woman. Yuck. I hate saying that word."

"Ah." He knew what word troubled her. "Love will get you every time."

"Not me."

"Even the mightiest are not immune to love's seduction."

The scent of her drew him, but he stopped himself from approaching her. He sensed she wasn't putting two and two together. That men and women could fall in love, have feelings for one another, even if they were not of this realm. Even one who was slightly confused about her sexual nature.

"So if you were unable to slay a Fallen," Cooper asked, "does that mean you've no souls?"

"Nope." She pounded a fist over her heart, where the Sinistari interred stolen souls. "Not a one."

When the Sinistari slayed an angel they interred all the souls that angel had stolen by teaching the mortals the arts into its black heart.

Which meant, no psychopomp would be interested in Pyx. The vampire had won that round. Damn.

How to open her eyes to what was happening right here between the two of them? Or was it just him? No, he sensed some burgeoning emotion from her. A desire to connect that must be driving her insane, for her mission was not to connect but to kill.

Did he want to make it hard for her? Making

her job easy meant surrendering. That, he would never do.

"Let me take a look," Pyx said. "See what we're working with here."

Cooper's shirt had been torn away during the shift. Her fingers probed along his spine and he stood straighter. It wasn't a gentle touch, more clinical. Still, he liked the feeling of their connection. Even if she wasn't into it.

"Lower," he said. "Can you see a mark of entry?"

"No. Skin's flawless. You heal quickly, as I would expect."

"Not as fast as I once did. There must be a bruise."

"Maybe. It's discolored." She pressed a fingernail into his flesh. "Right about here?"

"Yes. Have Joe help you."

"What? You want me to...?"

"Yes, damn it, cut into the flesh. There's something in there. I can feel it rubbing against bone. Whatever a vampire wants inside me is not something I want to remain."

She tugged out the dagger from her combat boot. Cooper roamed his gaze up her long, slender legs made for running, or wrapping about his waist. Oh, sexy siren in black silk and shitkicking boots. "Your dress is ripped."

One copper brow arched over her kaleidoscope

eye. She tugged the tear and it revealed skin to the top of her thigh. "Yeah, maybe hunting vamps in silk wasn't such a good idea after all."

"I like it." He fingered the black fabric that hung before her thigh.

"Hands off, horny angel. Lie down."

"Ah? You want me prone and facing down?" He spread out his arms. "Helpless to whatever devious pleasures you decide to employ?"

"Whatever I do to you, it will be devious." She tapped his shoulder with the tip of Joe. "Not so sure about the pleasurable part though."

"I can mix pleasure and pain. You up for it?"

Her brow arched higher, a thin arabesque of deliciousness Cooper wanted to lick. But she was all business. "Turn over. You want pain, you got it."

Cooper let out a groan as the blade cut through his mortal skin. He would not discount the pain for the mortal experience, though. She cut in the area where he felt the intrusion.

"Go deep. To the bone," he said around a wince.

"Yeah, yeah. Masochist." He felt her fingertip prod his insides.

For some reason it didn't hurt after the initial cut, but instead made him wonder at the demon touching him so deeply. She was inside of him. Tenderly. Cautiously. A man she labeled enemy. Yet right now he trusted her.

The mortal air had surely toasted his better judgment.

"So your wings," she said, still probing about, "they were like stained glass, or something. But I suspect not so fragile."

"Ineffable." He cupped a fist under his chin and closed his eyes to the now tender touch.

"I understand each angel is unique."

"In relation to the skill we master. I was a crafts-man of glass. Despite popular belief, we did not fall simply to mate with mortal females. Some of us sought to teach mortals the arts. I taught them artistry in colored glass."

"Deemed a sin at the time."

"Yes, all artistic endeavors and crafts were. But not so much now, eh? I knew I was doing right at the time. Look at all the beauty in the mortal realm. Every stained-glass window you see is be-cause of me."

"I also understand when an angel taught mortals the creative arts, that mortal's soul was ransomed upon his death to the angel."

"Yes, unfortunately. Because the mortal had sinned in the eyes of his peers so his soul could not rise to Above with death, but it was not des-tined for Beneath either." Cooper propped his chin on a fist. "You ever wonder who decides what is sin and what is not? Some cultures believe eating certain kinds of meat a sin, others do not. So who is the ultimate judge of a sin? Not who you would expect."

"Him?"

"Not at all. A mortal's sin is judged by his peers, which is such a shame."

"Yeah, whatever. How many souls do you have within you?"

"Just the one." He winced as the blade cut through muscles.

"Impossible. I've heard Sinistari tell about stealing thousands upon thousands of souls from one angel kill. You guys spread your creative mojo across the lands. You can't convince me you taught one single person the craft and it became what it is now."

"Just the one," he repeated. "He was a Mesopotamian potter. Ouch!"

"I think I found it," Pyx said. She stood from the bed. Cooper saw her wipe blue blood down the side of her dress. "Can't get it out."

"Why the hell not?"

"It's a small metal piece fused to your bone."

"Carve it out with your big bad knife."

"Can't."

"Pyx. Come on!"

"I'm no surgeon!" She marched into the adjoining bathroom and Cooper heard the water gush in the sink.

He reached around to inspect the wound. It

wasn't completely healed but he could not feel deep enough to touch bone. He wiped the blood on his jeans and sat up. Muddy blue stained his fingers. So different.

Would he ever earn the right to fit in? To belong on earth?

Why did he believe obtaining his halo would give him the right to live here? He wasn't like any other. His experiences were too vast and tainted by murder at command. Was it wrong to want what he'd never been designed to have?

"What is right?" he whispered. "What is wrong? Who's to judge?"

Could it be only his peers who would judge him? But he was no longer a peer to those angels still Above.

Rubbing his fingers along his jeans was like trying to erase his truths. The stain of their existence would never be washed away.

It felt wrong—it *had* been wrong—he'd committed sins against mankind.

"You okay?" she called out from the bathroom.

No. He wasn't sure what he was anymore. A fool for thinking he could have what He had gifted to the mortals?

"I don't understand. Why vampires?" he said. "And why me?"

"This is a guess." Pyx appeared in the doorway,

shoulder to the frame. "Maybe it's some kind of tracking device."

"Why?"

"So they can keep an eye on you and when you've found your muse, can move in."

"I'm not going anywhere near my muse."

"They don't know that."

"Yes, they do. That vampire, Bruce—the one who tagged me and left with his dramatic threat to return when you weren't there—he talked to me earlier today. He wants names of my fellow Fallen brethren."

"Why?" She tugged at the torn skirt.

"Because the vampires are summoning we Fallen to earth hoping we'll find our muses, and... well, then I don't know."

"I had a tussle with a vamp myself."

"You did?"

"Yes, they're after me, too. Supposedly, I'm their greatest threat. And now it makes so much sense. If the vamps want you to find your muse, I could step in and slay you before you get a chance. So keep the Sinistari out of the mix and they get what they want."

"Except I'm not going after my muse. This is ridiculous. I will not be bagged and tagged like an animal. Give me that blade."

"Joe belongs in no hands but mine."

"Then I'll use a kitchen knife."

She flashed to the bedroom doorway, feebly blocking it with her narrow frame. Cooper could have easily pushed by her. But instead he slid a hand up her back and pulled her close, hip to hip.

Garnet hair fell over one of Pyx's eyes. She looked up at him with that one wide kaleidoscope eye and Cooper thought surely if his heart could beat, it just did. As the mortals liked to say, the eyes were a window to the soul. Yet though Pyx had no soul he saw in those myriad colors the promise of what could be.

"Did I tell you that you do the female thing well?" he asked.

"I'm trying."

"Stop. I like it better when it's a happy accident with you. Look at you. Your hair all tousled and wavy. Most women would spend hours before the mirror to get it this way. And your style. It's I-don't-give-a-damn meets sex kitten. And your mouth." He thumbed her lips. "You want me to kiss you, don't you?"

"You got *kiss me* out of my threat with Joe?"

He nodded and leaned in closer to her. She didn't back away. Challenging him or maybe stubborn. He figured stubborn, but he liked that about her, along with her crazy fashion sense.

And the element of danger.

"You smell like bubble gum again," he said, tracing his nose along her tense jaw. "And demon."

"What does demon smell like?"

"Sweet and spicy, and…warm."

Her mouth parted and her breath hushed upon his lips. Prolong the moment. Read her easy compliance. Her daring to stand before him and not step away. Her quiet breath tickled his lips.

"Pyx?"

"Mmm?"

"You think this is wrong, the two of us?"

"You mean standing so close like this?"

"Yes, and having kissed already." Drawing his lips along her cheek, but not quite touching, he sensed a shudder minutely move her shoulders. And she couldn't realize that her breast hugged his chest, her hard nipples teasing him. "It doesn't feel wrong."

"It's wrong."

"Then step away from me."

"I, um…don't want to."

"Then your only other option is to kiss me."

"I could punch you. Or stab you with Joe."

"Let's not draw any more blood tonight, shall we?"

He touched her lips with his, no pressure, just moving closer, taking in her apprehension, her growing confidence. The sigh of breath across his mouth felt surreal, dangerous, and prohibited.

Breathe her. *Taste of bubble gum and heat.*

Learn her. *Not so sure of what she really wanted or could do.*

It was a rare gift he didn't want to open too quickly. She wasn't his death; she could very well be his life.

"Very wrong," she whispered, yet her body melded against his chest, her breasts crushing the black silk to his skin.

"Don't want it to be wrong," he said.

He combed his fingers into her hair and savored the slither of a curl across the inside of his crooked thumb. He clutched her hair, not wanting to lose her.

One slip of Joe and he would lose. She wouldn't miss him. Or would she?

He couldn't stand it any longer. Cooper crushed his mouth to Pyx's.

Sighs echoed in his mouth. The sweet sound of surrender.

She clutched him tightly, her fingers digging into the flesh on his back. All the hurt she could give him was no match to the taste of her desire. It flamed in his veins, warming his icy blood. And when their tongues dashed across one another, he moaned hungrily.

His hand wandered down her waist, and he toyed with the rip in her skirt where the skin felt softer than the silk. He flipped his hand, and tucked his fingers behind the dress, softly stroking over her mons.

"Oh, I don't know." Pyx broke the kiss, ceasing their contact, the sublime connection of skin against skin. Slapping a hand to the door frame, she steadied herself.

"Sorry, that was wrong to move so quickly."

"Enough with the right and wrong of everything! There is no right or wrong. Only choice."

Cooper's mouth dropped open. The air hummed with the echo of her furious statement.

"That was weird," Pyx said. "I don't know where that came from."

He did. By the divine Above, could she be?

"You were speaking your truth," he said. "Kadesch?"

"What?" She didn't know. Couldn't remember. Wouldn't, surely.

But he did.

Stepping backward into the kitchen, Pyx shook her head. One hand went down to subconsciously pull at her skirt. "That's enough vampire hunting for one night. Gotta go. Bye."

"Wait!" He rushed down the hall after her. "I moved too fast. I won't do that again. Not unless—" The door slammed shut. Pyx was gone. "You ask."

What she'd said about there being no right or

wrong, only choice. It is what Kadesch had said to convince Juphiel to fall.

Of course, anyone could put those words together and form a similar statement.

"But she is like me," he muttered. "Her eyes. They are like mine. And she doesn't even know."

A little bit of his salvation had just run away from him. He felt it every time he touched her. Pyx was the key to him becoming completely human and earning his soul.

With a hunger for pizza on her tongue, Pyx flashed to a pizza shop and was back at her apartment five minutes later with a steamy pie laid out on the coffee table. Food put her mind from deeper issues.

Like the angel.

"What the hell was that about? Letting a Fallen one touch me like that?"

And liking it. That was the part she couldn't rationalize.

She'd wanted to remain in his embrace and encourage his touch as he explored her skin. He'd been a little cool, not so warm as she was, but she knew it was because his blood ran cold.

And she would have liked to remain in his bedroom to see what would have happened next. So why hadn't she?

Tossing a crust onto the greasy pizza box, she

sat back against the sofa and put up a boot on the edge of the coffee table.

She didn't *like* the angel Juphiel, who called himself Cooper, and who flirted with every woman he saw. Did she?

She wasn't hungry anymore.

Padding into the bathroom, she stripped naked along the way, leaving her clothes in a trail. She flipped on the light switch and looked in the mirror. A dribble of black blood ran from her ear. Cooper hadn't pointed that out. A vampire had clocked her good.

"Can I do this?" she asked the woman staring at her. "Can *you?* You're just a girl. You're an anomaly. And I don't understand why."

Leaning in closer, she studied her eyes. They were green, blue and violet with flecks of gold, white and black. Kaleidoscope.

"Just like his." She leaned her palms on the cool vanity, head hanging. "That's odd. Why are my eyes the same as the Fallen's?"

They were two of the most opposite creatures walking this world. One from Above, one from Beneath. They had nothing in common. The angel sought his halo for reasons she could only imagine were not good. And she sought to kill him.

Nothing in common.

Except when they touched it almost felt right.

Pyx recalled telling Cooper there was no right or

wrong, only choice. It was the weirdest statement. She didn't know where it had come from, only that she had spoken it as if she'd meant it.

So could she choose to like his touch? Perhaps she had already done so.

Chapter 9

"You successfully implanted the tracking device in the Fallen?"

Bruce hooked a thumb in his pants pocket and forced a confident grin. "You know it. I am the best." And don't ask any more questions.

"That's all well and good," Antonio offered, not as impressed as Bruce had hoped, "but wouldn't it be easier to track the muse? The angel will probably rip the damned thing out."

"If I knew where the muse was, I'd go after her. Best scenario finds me tracking the Fallen to his muse. Then I'll have them both where I want them."

"Which is where?" Antonio asked in his deep,

hissing tone. "We need them in a controlled environment."

"We need the muse. Pregnant."

"And we're going to simply allow the Fallen to trot off to his next muse after that?"

"If he's still wearing the tracker, then yes. It's a win/win scenario. Every muse he finds, we track him to her and reap the rewards."

The leader of tribe Anakim sat back in his chair, dissatisfied, but clearly he could not find a better argument. That pleased Bruce.

Now to get that damned tracking receiver working.

He sat across the table from a demon, who sipped a macchiato. Basking in the coppery glow of the setting sun made Cooper feel alive. After centuries of survival in the nonexistence of the Ninth Void it was an amazing feeling to experience life. He hadn't had it for millennia. And this mortal life was so much richer, full, and exquisite.

Mortals had an idea of heaven. It was all angels, clouds, pearly gates and love, love, love.

Where Cooper had been imprisoned hadn't emanated love by any mortal imagining. It was truly like the mortal's idea of hell. A void without sound, color or surface. If he'd uttered a word or cried out, he hadn't heard his voice. He'd floated, endlessly. He could not see anything. Sensation had not existed. Thought had eventually left him, and he had become a sort of embryo awaiting final judgment.

Yet the slightest thread of hope had bound his being and kept him from completely surrendering to the void. Mortality. Humanity. As Kadesch had implied, it could be his.

Could Pyx know? Could he be right about her? He had no proof. He knew the origins of the Sinistari. Yet Pyx did not, so to simply ask her would serve little purpose.

He turned his wrist where the sun beamed across the flesh. It felt like a gift. Kept vampires away, too.

"You've come here every day since you arrived?" Pyx sipped the cream-swirled macchiato the waitress had dropped off. She sat across from him before the white iron café table. "I think I know why."

He followed her gaze to the waitress's swinging hips. He hadn't seen the dark-haired beauty here before but she didn't appear to be in training. Must have been working different hours the past week.

Hmm, she was a vision. Obsidian hair and lush lashes gave her an Italian heartbreaker look. Curves, so many curves, his eyes didn't know where to start.

"She is pretty," he agreed. "But the coffee here is what draws me."

"Uh-huh." No belief in that tone. The demon leaned over the table. "It wasn't her breasts as she leaned way over the table to pour your refill, Casanova?"

"I do like that particular body part. You jealous?"

"Please."

Yes, she was. Because she tilted an elbow on the back of the chair, which lifted her small breasts nicely. Score one for the angel trying to soften up the killer demon.

"Why do you want to waste any more time here on earth than it takes to find your muse?" she suddenly asked. "And don't tell me it's because of some stupid quest for your halo. Look around you. All of creation is a mess. His sons and daughters are an equal mess. They kill, steal, maim, cheat and lie. And you want to be a part of it?"

"You do, too. Doing a great job of blending with the locals too, to judge from your penchant for kleptomania."

She had been playing with an iPod since they sat down. And he'd also seen her shuffle a cell phone and car keys in the pocket of her jeans jacket. The demon didn't own a car that he knew of. She must be starting a collection.

"Not for all the bubble gum in the world. I'm just here to do a job, buddy."

"And when that job is done, you'll return

Beneath? No arguments? No lingering memories of earth?"

She turned her cheek to him, scanning the street. "We're not talking about me. I asked why you want to stick around in this mess of humanity."

"I have my reasons."

If he told her the real reason for the halo search she'd never buy it. Who would? He was an angel, for heaven's sake. For as lacking as his power was now that he'd Fallen, he was still stronger, wiser and smarter than any mortal alive. And who would give that up?

Cooper leaned over his coffee cup to bridge the distance between them. From the corner of his eye he noted the waitress. Man, she could swing her hips. Did she smell sweet? Nah. He couldn't possibly scent her all the way across the dining area.

He averted his attention to the smirking demon. "Why do *you* want to be here? To prove yourself? That's weak. If you'd wanted to prove yourself to the Sinistari you'd have knifed me last night after I shifted."

Pyx glanced aside, worrying her lower lip with her teeth. He'd guessed right. There were deeper reasons she walked this earth.

"Truthfully?"

Now they would get somewhere.

Pyx put up her boot on the nearby chair. No silk dress today, but instead a leather miniskirt and a tightly fitted leather vest over a soft red sweater. "I'm certainly not perfect."

"No one is."

"Angels are perfect. Or in your case, you *were*."

"Angels have mastered perfection. But once my feet touched mortal ground I lost my divinity. I have never considered myself perfect, even when I was blessed by His grace. But that still doesn't answer my question."

She tilted the iPod up and down between two fingers. The sun crept across her cheek and glinted in one of her eyes. A riot of color danced there. The most beautiful part of a demon was not the costume but that one bit of its true self that remained—the eyes.

Yet again, if she knew her origins…

"I do need to prove myself. But…"

"You can tell me. I won't tell anyone else."

"I guess I wouldn't mind becoming a part of this realm. Earth, as it is. I've never felt…in place. I told you this already."

She set the iPod on the table and clasped the coffee cup with both hands. Unable to meet his eyes, she scanned everywhere around her. Teasing the end of a long red curl, she couldn't realize how dragging it across her lips ignited Cooper's libido. Made him imagine dragging his tongue across soft parts of her.

"Beneath is the demonic realm, but don't you

think a demon should feel like they belong there? And look at me. I'm a chick!"

"You fit in well here on earth. You've mastered the female costume. You are comfortable with the ways and means to procuring material things."

"Then I must belong here. As messed up as *here* is."

"It is a crazy world." More so than Cooper had expected. But that made it all the more interesting. And a greater challenge to try to assimilate. "But it will be such an adventure to become mortal, don't you think? So many things to do," he encouraged. "Entertainments and education. Food and commerce. To hold a job and feel good for accomplishments. And the people!"

"I do like the men. They are interesting to look at."

He winked. "As are the women. Short dresses and pretty shoes." Where had the waitress gone?

"Tight-fitting shirts and kilts—er…pants."

He caught the demon's slip. She was into him. Poor girl.

"I really like the food," she added quickly. "But so far your cooking has been the best."

"I'll cook for you any time you ask."

"I've cold pizza at home."

"That sounds not good at all."

"I'm doing the mortal experience, buddy. You

should be proud of me. So what else do you like about earth?"

"Everything. The variety of cultures and the art. The exquisite architecture. I want to go to India and see the Taj Mahal."

"My guess is no place on earth is quite so glorious as Above."

"It'll be even better then because imperfection makes for beauty. What about you? Where do you want to go? What do you want to do?"

She looked down toward the sidewalk paralleling the café's patio. The tip of her tongue dashed out to trace her upper lip. When she looked to Cooper a resolute indifference tilted her head. "I just want to belong."

He touched her hand, smoothing over her narrow fingers. They were warm from the hot cup. "Me, too."

Cooper felt the connection as their gazes met. She didn't try to look away. And in those moments they shared far more than simple words could ever equate.

"I do think discovering this imperfect civilization will be an adventure," Pyx said. "But are you implying you want to become mortal, too? I thought you were just doing a halo search?"

Dare he tell her?

"You don't want your halo because you can use it as a weapon," she said, her voice growing more confident as she guessed his secret. "You want it for the earthbound soul within."

Cooper crossed his arms and leaned back in his chair.

"When an angel Falls its soul gets trapped in the halo. You want to become mortal."

"As do you."

She nodded, silently allowing him to join her club of wanting something so simple yet so meaningful. When he didn't remove his hand, she did, slipping it under the table and sipping her coffee.

He confused her. Good.

"Who'd a thought," Pyx said. "An angel looking for his soul. Well, you'd better hurry."

"I run into my muse, you slay me, right?"

She nodded, but it wasn't quite so adamant as previously.

"I'm still not feeling anything," he said. "Your spell must not have worked."

"Give it time. I believe you were drawn to Paris for a reason."

"I told you I came here because I wasn't drawn here."

"Whatever. Whew!" She set down the coffee cup. "This stuff is strong."

"Yeah, you'll be able to kick my ass to Sunday after that double shot."

"So since we're not going to get in any muse action today, what do you say we hunt some vampires again? You must be itching to get your hands on them after last night."

He rubbed his lower back. "Don't remind me."

"I brought holy water."

"You have holy water? What, did you rob Nôtre Dame?"

She shrugged, a silent admission. Pyx shaded her eyes with a hand. "Sun's setting. We can sniff out the vamps in less than an hour. You going to pay your standard way?"

"Yep. I'll be right back."

Pyx leapt over the iron fence surrounding the sidewalk tables, completely oblivious to the fact a woman in a miniskirt would never perform such a feat. "I'm going to cross the street to that record shop. It looks just goth enough to maybe have a clue on the vamps. Meet me there."

Cooper nodded and turned to find the waitress. She smiled as he neared her. Her name tag pronounced her "Sophia." He pressed a palm to her forehead. "Thanks, Sophia. You must be new here?"

"Not at all. Just back from vacation in New Jersey, of all places, with family. Oh, that tip was generous. Merci."

He winced. Sometimes it made him feel sick to utilize the trick on mortals. He was stealing from her, which was the truth of it.

"New Jersey, eh?" Now why did that—?

"Yes, it's a pretty state. We spent a day in New York shopping as well."

New Jersey was where he'd initially landed when he'd been summoned to earth. And Sophia had been there? This did not feel right.

"Lisa says you've been here every day for a week." She itched her wrist and tugged up her sleeve. "You must love our coffee."

"It's delicious." Cooper started to fall into the bruised-rose color of her voice, until he noticed her forearm. He touched her hand and tilted her arm toward him. Subtle vibrations shimmied up his arm and he quickly released her. "That's an interesting mark."

"Oh, this? Been there since I was born. A birthmark." She rubbed her forearm. "It looks like two sexy number sevens to me."

He sucked in a breath and slapped a palm to his abdomen where a part of him had begun to warm. He wondered what it would feel like if his heart could beat. Probably be racing to the finish right now. "Got a rash?"

"No, the itching just started. I think I must have burned it when I was brewing the macchiato. So, I'll see you again tomorrow?"

"Sure."

He turned and stalked out of the café and weaved through the tables outside. Feeling as though a china shop bull were on his heels, Cooper couldn't make it away from the café quick enough.

Before crossing the street to join Pyx, he turned and eyed Sophia. She spoke to another waitress.

Suddenly he saw every fine detail about her. Her dark hair was highlighted with deep red strands that matched her lipstick. Her eyes, initially he'd thought brown, were flecked with gold. And those curves—he'd like to get his hands around that flesh.

"Hell." He exhaled gruffly and forced his focus away from Sophia. He slapped a palm over his gut where his sigil unique to the angel dominions curved like two funky sevens. "She's my muse."

Chapter 10

Bruce hunched down in the Smart Car's driver's seat, parked across the street three car-lengths away from the record store the Sinistari had gone into.

He wasn't concerned with the demon. Leave her for Stellan. Though she was a gorgeous looker, he wouldn't bite a demon for all the money in Switzerland. He had a healthy respect for the Sinistari. Most paranormals—if they were smart—did.

Stellan was an idiot to assume the task of taking out the Sinistari. Though this one was female, which should make her much less a challenge than if it were male. Heh.

What turned his crank now was the scene he

witnessed outside the café where he'd tracked the Fallen.

The GPS receiver sat on the passenger seat, un-blinking. The injection had gone wrong. The track-ing device had either fallen out or had been damaged when the angel had shifted. So he had to do this the old-fashioned way or risk Antonio's wrath.

The Fallen was talking to a waitress who had an amazing figure. Reminded Bruce of Sophia Loren in her heyday. That tight little waitress uniform en-hanced every curve. "Nice."

But when the Fallen touched her wrist she pointed out something Bruce thought looked like a tattoo.

Bruce sat upright and honed his sight on the pair. "Is that…?"

The woman smiled and put a flirtatious hand to her throat as the angel stroked his fingers along her wrist. Then the angel abruptly dropped her arm and stepped back. He looked away, then back at the woman. The angel's fists clenched and flexed out as if unsure how to react to what he'd seen.

It was a visceral reaction, and it made Bruce wonder. And when the angel left, he began to cross the street, but kept looking back at the café. Something about the waitress had disturbed him.

And Bruce was willing to bet what that some-thing was.

"Score."

* * *

Pyx strode out of the record shop blowing on her wet fingernails. The girl behind the counter had been painting her nails a grapey purple and when Pyx asked about it, she offered to do hers.

She met Cooper and replied to his silent inquiry. "Nothing. The store owner is not into vampires, and I didn't want to push by asking if she'd seen any. But I think we need to let them come to you. If they find you we know that's a tracking device stuck in your spine."

"I still want you to dig it out." He tossed a look over his shoulder to the café. When he turned back to Pyx his wistful expression disturbed her.

"Anything wrong? You want another shot of espresso?" she asked.

"Nope. So what, we stand around waiting for a vamp to find me?"

"Thought we were going clubbing?"

"I don't like that idea. Let's be proactive. Walk around and find them before they find us. You can sniff them out?"

"Not exactly. But I can sense when they are near."

"Well, then, we'll follow your senses." He hooked an arm in hers and walked onward. "Pretty nails."

"You think? Yeah, I like them, too."

He lifted her hand and kissed it, and she didn't

try to pull away. He didn't really admire the nail polish, Pyx sensed. So that meant what? That he'd needed an excuse to hold her hand? Smooth.

They strode past a Smart Car and took the sidewalk hugging the Seine away from the inner city.

This was unexpectedly nice. Holding the guy's hand. Like some kind of normal woman and man on a date. So this is what made mortals happy? Pyx could get to like it, too.

A blur of motion stopped them both. Cooper tugged Pyx up against the wall of a building. "Vampire?" he asked.

"Yep. They're the fastest moving things in this city, besides us. He's moving north."

"Let's flash ahead. Maybe we'll get lucky and find their lair," he said, squeezing her hand.

"Their lair? Vampires still have lairs? That sounds so nineteenth-century."

"Like you would know, so new to this world."

He had a point. And yet. "Like you would know, too."

He chuckled, then embraced her and they flashed together. They landed on the north side of the same building just in time to see the vampire take a right turn down a dark alley.

"This way."

Pyx took the iron staircase hugging the side of a building and Cooper followed. He liked the rear view. He preferred clothing that accentuated a woman's figure. And Pyx, while tall and slim, had a nice, shapely bottom. He gave a shove to her derriere, and she protested, but he didn't relent, he wanted to touch. All the time.

They topped the building and Pyx gestured for him to remain crouched. Creeping to the high brick edging the roof, they peered down and saw a man enter a building across the street.

"That's the vamp?" Cooper whispered.

"It's the one I told you about."

They both ducked when the vamp scanned the street before closing the door behind him. The building was different than the surrounding residential buildings. Fashioned of red stone, with crumbling parapets that still held on to the mangled lace of iron railings that must have once kept out intruders. Windows were boarded up and a chain and lock were strapped across the door on the corner.

"Looks like an old church," Cooper said. "Blasphemous."

"Yeah? Look who's talking."

"I resent that."

"Hey, I wasn't the one who fell."

"Neither—" He stopped himself. What Pyx did not know about herself he could not explain right now. She'd never understand. Not without a lot of convincing and proof. And how would he show proof? "So the vampires are holed up in a church?

That's a new one. No one would think of looking for them there."

"How many people do you think actually *look* for vampires?"

"The crazies."

Pyx tilted her head close and muttered, "I like crazy."

Cooper smirked. "And beating up vampires, apparently. So, we going in or we going to do reconnaissance first?"

Raindrops spattered their heads. *Pling. Plonk.* Cold and startling. Cooper tilted his head to catch the rain on his face. He did like the rain. It was something he'd never experienced and he could stand in it all day.

"I say storm the vanguard," Pyx said firmly.

"Don't you think day would be a better time to invade a vampire lair?" he wondered.

"Probably. But not as much fun."

"You really enjoy kicking ass."

"About as much as you do. I like that about you."

"Did the demon admit to liking the angel?"

"Heh. No."

Pyx slammed her arms across her chest and strode to the small brick cupola where an inner stairway opened to the roof, and leaned against it. The rain quickly dampened her hair and trickled over the leather vest.

Cooper blinked at the raindrops. "It's a weird wonder that I find myself chumming around with my destroyer. But I can't complain. If you do go through with your task of murdering me, at least I'll have had some fun before I go."

"Aren't you willing to fight for what you want?"

"I am. But I don't want to hurt you to get it."

"Oh, come on, Cooper. Show me some fight."

He shook his head. "Nope. No hurting girls."

"So if I was a male you'd have no problem?"

"Not at all. If you were male I wouldn't be thinking how much I'd like to kiss you right now."

She blew out a frustrated breath. "We both want different things."

"That we do."

"Only one of us can have what we want."

"If I find my missing halo, you'll never have the opportunity to slay me."

"Because with your halo you'll become mortal. But you could fight me with it first."

"Probably. I'm sure it could take off your head with ease."

She leaned forward, catching her palms on her knees and flipping her hair back over her shoulder. "I want a fair fight."

He was all about a fight between equals, too, but wasn't cool with fighting Pyx. If the Sinistari had been male, Cooper would have ripped out his heart by now.

He patted the concrete roof next to him. "Come sit by me, Pyx."

"What for?"

"I'm going to kiss you."

She folded her arms across her chest.

"You like my kisses," he challenged.

"Mostly."

"Mostly? Way to make a guy feel insignificant."

"Okay, I liked your kisses more than mostly, and probably, maybe a lot. But it's not cool to say it."

"Why not?"

"You know." She glanced upward, blinking at the rain. "Someone could be listening."

He looked about, having no idea whom the someone could be. Cooper wasn't able to cast his gaze Above since he'd Fallen.

"You come over here," she prompted.

Cooper made a show of thumbing his chin as he thought about her offer. "If I go over there to you, I will push you against the wall and suckle at your nipples—which the rain is making very hard—until you beg me to stop. And even if you beg, I may not stop."

She considered his statement, an equal opponent to his play to appear aloof. Then she leaned against the cupola wall, lifting one knee and pressing her boot to the wall. Arms down at her sides, she tilted up her fingers and crooked them ever so slightly.

A challenge.

Cooper stood before her in a flash. In fact, he did flash, moving at the supersonic speed his kind were capable of. He resisted the urge to clasp her wrists and pin her immobile before him. He didn't need to. She remained submissive, hands down, and open to him.

Drawing one hand along her slick thigh, he savored the wet flesh. Warm. Wanting. All woman, despite her obvious longing for it to be otherwise.

He quickened his pace upward, skittering his fingers over wet leather and gliding over her narrow hip. The red shirt was heavily soaked. First touch to the skin on her stomach was cool. Her body shivered. He felt the goose bumps rise. Heat flooded her flesh. He groaned at the warmth. It was as if he'd never known such heat—and he had not.

He cupped her breast. No bra. Small, like a prize in his hand. Bending, he bit gently through the fabric, then pushed it up to expose her breast. Pyx's flesh was an idol he wanted to worship.

He nudged his nose across her hard nipple and was gifted with her wanting moans. Her fingers hooked at his waistband. Instantly hard, he cursed the tight jeans as his cock thickened and ached for release.

Hooking her leg along his hip with his other

hand, Cooper pressed his torso against hers, holding her where he wanted her, and teasing her moans with his insistent need.

The raindrops splashing his face and neck, he slicked his tongue about her nipple. Taste and touch blended with the sweet bite of the rain. Pyx ground her hips against his.

In all his millennia Above, he'd never imagined the human connection could be so exquisite. Angels could not have this connection, nor could the Sinistari when in full demonic form.

It was the craziest thing that they two stood in this illicit embrace. He'd been programmed to believe this act of connection between a man and a woman wrong, but he was now making the choice to let it be right. Kadesch would be proud—and someday she would share that knowledge.

"I know I'm supposed to be the bad guy," he whispered against her ear. "And you're the good guy."

"Girl," she corrected. "Or I prefer chick."

"Mmm, sexy demon chick, you do it for me."

Her fingers dove under his shirt and her purple nails zinged his nipple. "You like that?" She flicked his nipple a few times.

"Pyx, can you feel how hard you're making me?"

"I can. Pressed against my hip like some kind of battle weapon. Maybe I'm not so good after all."

"You are a very bad good girl. I like that." He kissed the lobe of her ear and trickled more kisses along her jaw. Drawing her around in front of him, Cooper leaned against the wall and kissed the back of her neck through her wet hair.

"Oh…" She sighed. "That. Is. Don't stop. Just. Don't."

Here she smelled wild and dangerous. Nothing about her was hard or vicious. She was all woman. And for now, Cooper was all man.

"You know what you said earlier about there being no good or evil?" he asked. "No right or wrong. Only choice."

"What does that have to do with what you're doing to me at this moment?"

"Everything." He stopped kissing her and clasped his hands about her body, hugging them beneath her breasts. "I agree with you, Pyx. The world is not black and white. We can be whoever and whatever we wish to be."

She pushed him away, her fingernails slashing the skin of his fists. Her expression did not say "more, please" but rather "now you've done it."

"You're wrong," she said. "What I said was just something stupid. I don't even know where it came from. This—this embrace is wrong."

Sensing the demon had returned to Pyx's eyes, he raised his hands in placation. He should have kept his thoughts to himself, and his tongue wrapped around her nipple. Idiot.

"Leave me," she demanded. "I've had enough of you tonight."

"As you wish."

Settling to sit on the wet rooftop, Pyx spread her legs before her and tilted her head, opening her mouth to catch the rain. Her entire body shivered and her muscles flexed. Her mouth was warm and tingly where Cooper had claimed her. Her breasts ached for his hands and tongue again. And her loins were hot with desire. It was as if he could mold her to any shape he desired.

Except the one shape she couldn't bear—compliance.

Yet she continued to struggle with proving herself to the Sinistari and simply being a woman who could be desired by a man.

So this was desire? The feeling encompassed so much; it was overwhelming and making her nervous and giddy. She wanted Cooper at her mouth—and she was glad he was gone.

The taste of him tainted her sense of mission, confusing it with need. She didn't need anything but to slay the damned angel. But what she wanted was more than anything she could grasp since she had arrived on earth.

Sucking in her lower lip, she closed her eyes and

squeezed her hands between her thighs. The erotic tingling at her mons lingered. It wasn't going to go away soon. She needed him pressed against her body. She wanted to feel what a man could do to a woman.

No one would have to know. Her Sinistari brethren would have no idea what she did before slaying the angel.

And what a sweet triumph over the Fallen should she lure him into her arms, to sully himself with a demon.

Cooper stalked the rainy streets. Rain soaked his clothes and he was growing angry at the insolent weather. Ridiculous, eh? Only minutes earlier he'd been devouring a gorgeous woman in the rain as if they stood in a shower surrounded by the world.

With a shake of his shoulders he assumed a new pair of jeans and sweater, both dry.

Why couldn't Pyx remember her origins? She'd spoken the words yet claimed to not understand why. Frustrating. She was Kadesch, he knew it. But how to be sure? Kissing her was not a means to learn that answer. Yet the sensual distraction always reared up when he and Pyx were together.

He enjoyed kissing women. That's as far as he'd gotten—kissing. The sensual exploration was so intense. It had been millennia since he'd had full-on sex with a woman. Did that make him a virgin as well?

He couldn't remember what it had been like. Which was why he languished in the slow seduction now. It was almost enough to satisfy and giving pleasure was an immense reward. But he knew he could never achieve complete satisfaction by having sex with a mortal woman. Only if she were his muse.

Yet was that one goal, the orgasm, so sweet when it was with a woman he'd rather not touch? A woman he must stay away from?

And what about demons? He had no idea how that would go.

Pyx was so ready. Hungry for the mortal pleasure of sex.

Sex between a Fallen and a Sinistari could only end badly. What was he thinking?

Yet if he thought about it even harder, he could come to some remarkable conclusions about their origins, and how maybe they *should* be together. They were more alike than different.

"Kadesch," he muttered.

He passed the café. A few lights were still on inside, yet the interior was bare of patrons. The closing crew must be cleaning up for the night.

Cooper paused across the street from the café and sighted two waitresses. One was Sophia, elbows propped on the counter, talking to another waitress. Thick black hair spilled over her shoulders and she laughed. He felt those gorgeous tones in his chest as if she stood before him right now. He clasped a hand over his heart and winced. She'd unbuttoned another button on her shirt, revealing her voluptuous curves.

How sweet it would be to draw his tongue along those curves. To taste her skin and read her flesh as it slipped under the whorls on his fingertips. If he had whorls. Cooper rubbed his fingers together. Smooth. His skin had not the telltale signs of mortality. Not until he got a soul.

Sophia was one hundred percent mortal, all soft skin and luscious laughter. To touch her and watch as her breathing grew faster, her back arched and her legs would part in welcome.

Cooper blew out a sigh.

The moment he surrendered to the muse's allure Pyx would have her wish. And he wouldn't have to dream about a soul or about someday having stupid, frikkin' whorls, because he'd be dead.

All this time he'd been drawn to the café because his muse worked there. She hadn't needed to be in the exact place, and still he'd been compelled to it. What strange irony the one place he felt hadn't been calling to him, had been luring him after all.

He didn't need the muse. He could have sex with women and take pleasure from their pleasure.

He would not be curious about Sophia. He must not be.

He'd walk around the café, taking an extra block out of his way. If he was lucky, he'd find his halo and then wouldn't have this problem.

Like that was ever going to happen. Who was the mysterious MD mentioned between Eden Campbell and her online friend, and could MD help Cooper?

Forcing himself to walk onward, Cooper punched a wooden street pole. The half-foot diameter pole cracked, but didn't break. He restrained himself from delivering the coup de grâce.

"I can do this," he muttered. "I need to get serious about finding my halo. No more chasing vampires with the Sinistari. And no more kissing her. She is the enemy. Don't forget that, Cooper, or you're a pile of angel ash."

He entered the foyer of his building and shook off the rain from his wool sweater. He shook his head, spattering rain droplets over the heavy carpeting. Glancing to the mailboxes, and thinking some day he too would receive mail, like a normal mortal man, gave him a smile.

His mood lifted, Cooper decided to take the stairs instead of flashing up to his apartment.

Leaving a wet trail to his front door, he paused, noticing the door was ajar. Muscles tightening, he scanned the hallway. No sign of anyone near.

Reaching behind his hip for the throwing star, he pushed the door open noiselessly and stalked down the long narrow hall toward the kitchen.

Though the world appeared to him in vivid color and sensory feeling, he could not pick up the scent of anyone close to him. He couldn't get a read on whether there was an intruder inside or if he'd been robbed and the thief was long gone.

He passed the living room, slinking against the wall. Everything was in order. Moonlight cast shadows across the sofa where he and Pyx had once sat, kissing.

Kissing a demon. What kind of idiot was he?

The warrior angel he had once been would have already slain the nuisance.

Pressing a shoulder to the wall, Cooper listened for sound from the kitchen, and beyond, perhaps his bedroom.

He stepped around the wall and into the kitchen, which was lit by the small lamp over the stove. A man with short dark hair and a scar bracketing his left eye sat before the table, one leg crossed over his knee. He nodded to Cooper.

"Michael Donovan," he introduced himself. "We need to talk."

Chapter 11

Cooper's simmering rage boiled over at the man's insolence. He tossed the throwing star, landing it on the table between the man's arms.

Donovan lifted a brow, but didn't look down at the weapon. "After the hell I've been through the past few weeks, that impresses me little. Got anything better?"

"Oh, I do, but you'd piss your pants and I happen to like that chair."

The man opened his jacket to reveal the handle of a gun. "Let's see who pisses first."

Cooper lunged, grabbing the guy by the shirt and lifting him from the chair. The man's blue eyes remained cool. Then Cooper noticed the hard gun barrel poking his ribs.

Anger took over. Screw humanity. Juphiel was not completely absent from this mortal costume.

"I can see we're going to have to do this the hard way," Cooper said. He shoved the man and he landed the chair with an "ouf!"

The change came over him swiftly. Cooper growled as mortal flesh gave way to his natural angelic state. He could only shift halfway, from hips up, since he'd Fallen. That's all he needed. In twenty seconds he stood before the man whose smirk had dropped, as well as the gun barrel.

"Holy shit!" Donovan stumbled out of the chair and Cooper backed him toward the wall.

Cooper knew what he looked like. Not for human consumption. His eyes glowed blue, as did the sigil on his abdomen. His upper body was of liquid glass designed to emulate human ribs and gut. His glass heart glimmered between crisscrossing glass rib bones. And his jaw clacked when he opened it wide to growl.

"Impressed now?" Cooper asked in a voice edged with a bell-like scrape that, to mortals, sounded like glass cutting stone.

Donovan nodded furiously. "You're a-an angel?"

That he knew what kind of creature he was surprised Cooper, and in that moment the irrational anger subsided. He released the man and stepped away, folding his wings in to his body. They collapsed in a manner that tucked up neatly, and took less space than their full expansion did. Neat trick. Came with the territory.

"All this time I've been hunting halos and I've never seen one of you—wow. In your real form." The man had dropped the gun on the floor. Now he shrugged his hands through his hair, and gestured as he exclaimed, "Christ, it's amazing!"

"Christ *is* amazing. Me?" Cooper stepped closer. "Not so much. Now what did you just say you were hunting?"

"Ha-halos."

"Halos?" He smashed his fist into the wall near Donovan's head. The Sheetrock dusted. "Who the hell are you?"

"I—I already said—"

Cooper gripped him by the front of his polo shirt. The man jumped at the cold sting of glass flesh to his feeble mortal flesh.

"I'm a halo hunter!" he pleaded. "I've dozens of halos I've collected over the years."

"Angel halos?"

"What other kinds are there?"

"Michael Donovan?" MD. The MD he'd been trying to get more information about from Eden Campbell. Well, well.

"Could you let me go now? My girlfriend gave me this shirt. Dude, you are cold."

Dropping the man and stepping back, Cooper released his half form and wriggled his upper body as it took on human costume. It was scare tactics. A stupid move. He shouldn't angel up for any mortal who pissed him off. But his privacy had been violated and he had been in a fine temper.

Gotta watch his temper.

His shirt had been sacrificed for the shift. Cooper slapped a palm against his biceps and shrugged off the final shiver of the change.

"That was incredible."

Cooper winced. He was not a performing circus act. "Michael Donovan?"

The man nodded effusively.

"So you're the MD I've been reading about online?"

"Maybe. I'm careful about my posts online. Usually code them so no one can track them."

"There was mention of an MD in Eden Campbell's posts to Cassandra Stevens."

"You know Eden?"

Cooper shrugged. "Not exactly."

"You're honest. Eden is the one who told me you'd contacted her asking about me. She had no idea who you were, but the way you worded your post made her believe you knew angels were real. And now I understand why." He reached behind his hip and Cooper clenched a fist. "Just getting my wallet."

Michael produced a brown leather wallet and opened it before Cooper. He took out a folded paper and handed it over. "Take a look. I can't believe it."

With one eye on the man who had violated his sanctum, Cooper unfolded the paper. He swallowed down an oath at sight of the image. It looked like one of those fantasy paintings artists designed on the computer. But the most shocking thing? Blue glass body, and emerald-and-azure wings. And the sigil was exact.

"It's me."

"Yes! What you looked like just now, shifted and all. Eden Campbell painted that."

"I don't understand. How?"

"She's a muse who dreams about angels. Never thought she'd be so spot on though. Wow. Just... wow. I've never experienced angelophany."

"What the heck is that?"

"It's you. Appearing before me."

"I didn't appear. You broke in. Big difference."

"Sorry. The door wasn't locked." Donovan raked fingers through his hair. "What does an angel want with me? You're Fallen, right?"

"Yes. According to Miss Campbell—"

"It's missus now. She got married last month. To a, erm..." He scratched his jaw, dismissing the thought. "Right. Back to why you wanted to find me."

"You have halos from angels," Cooper said to the man who wiped the sweat from his brow. He still couldn't get over the painting. It was him, all right. Dreams? And another muse? "How do you find them?"

"It's difficult, but they're all over the world if someone knows what they're looking for. Buried in the earth. Stuck in an Alaskan iceberg. Shoved in a box sitting on the front lawn of a garage sale."

"A garage sale?" Cooper gaped. That the one thing most sacred to him could be found by such a means. He gripped Donovan by the shirt. "Do you have mine?"

"I—I don't know. It's not as if I can match your sigil to it. Very striking by the way." He glanced downward where Cooper's sigil was impressed upon his abdomen. When not glowing it assumed the color of muddy tea. "I wouldn't know it was your halo unless you held the thing and it glowed."

"And how do you know that?"

"I've seen it happen."

The man had *seen* an angel holding his halo? Wait. "I thought I was the first angel you've seen? Angelophany, and all."

"Oh, you are. It's complicated. Trust me."

"Not even going to go there with the trust."

Cooper laid the paper on the table and studied it further. She'd even got the red glass heart right. He shoved upright and turned on Donovan.

"Where are they?" Cooper asked. "I need to see them. All of them."

"Not with me. I sure as hell am not going to carry them around in this city full of vampires."

"You know about the vampires, too?"

"Hard not to. If you know anything about what's up, you should know they're after the halos. That's why I'm here. Well, that, and I promised Eden I'd check you out."

"How did you know I lived here? Have you been tracking me?" Cooper reached for his lower back. He hated that the vampires had a connection to him. "Are you allied with the vampires?"

"I am as far from allied with the vampires as a man can possibly be. At least when it comes to terms of engagement with the enemy. There are many ways to an alliance—"

"Is that so?" Cooper gripped the man's chin and jerked his head aside to expose his neck. There, behind the high collar of his black shirt, two faint marks sat right over the jugular vein. "Seems to me you're about as allied as a mortal can be. You've been bitten."

"By my girlfriend. She's a vamp."

"And you're *not* allied with them?" He shoved

the man hard and his chair toppled. "What sort of lies are you telling me? Let me take a look—"

Cooper went to place his palm against the man's forehead, but Donovan scrambled away. "Oh, I know how that one works, buddy. I don't want you playing around inside my head. Just let me explain."

He knew too much. Cooper couldn't decide if that was an advantage or just plain wrong.

"I'm listening. Make it fast. Make it the truth."

"It's a long story, but my girlfriend recently escaped from the control of the vampire tribe Anakim. They reside here in Paris under the command of Antonio del Gado."

That much Cooper knew was true. "Continue."

"Vinny—my girlfriend—is on my side now, which is not the vampires' side."

"I don't believe you."

"You don't have to, Grigori."

Cooper dismissed the term with a wave of hand. He did not like the old term. It implied he'd Fallen for one purpose only—to fornicate with his muse. But if the mortal did not know that he wasn't going to provide the complete rules and regulations of his kind.

"I've been collecting for a dozen years," Donovan said. "Never ran into any weird shit. Just happy to pick up another halo here and there, you know? Then six months ago I meet Vinny. She knew where a halo was hidden in Versailles, and took me to it, but she also wanted me to get her away from del Gado's control."

"And did you?"

"Yes, I did. And she bit me because she needed mortal blood to survive on her own. It was a sacrifice I was willing to make because, well, I love her. That was the beginning of my education in all things supernatural and paranormal. Oh, and a few months ago I talked to a Sinistari."

Cooper rubbed his jaw. The man's acrid scent indicated he was either fearful or lying. "Why? How? The demon revealed itself to you?"

"He wanted to kill me because he thought I was going to harm his girlfriend—Eden Campbell. Which I had no intention of doing. But you know demons."

"Yes, I do." He paced the kitchen floor, wondering at the turn of events. If there was another Sinistari stalking the lands his luck just got worse. "So Miss Campbell is married to the demon now?"

"The Sinistari won a mortal soul and he's human now. Their wedding was nice," the man said with a nervous smile.

Cooper swiped a hand over his face. Everyone but him was aware of the vampires' involvement in whatever *this* was. But seriously? *Vampires* were the key to him getting his halo?

"Why do you want a halo?" Donovan asked. "To use it as a weapon or to claim your mortal soul?"

Cooper flinched at Donovan's knowledge. By all of Above! "That's not something I'm willing to share with the man who just broke into my home. I want to see the halos you have. Where are they?"

"In a safety-deposit box in an undisclosed country on this planet. Which is where they'll stay until I've done what I've come to do."

"And what, exactly, is that?"

"Ensure the vamps don't get their hands on any more halos. They're using them to lure in the Fallen, or haven't you noticed?"

"I've fought with a couple vamps lately. None had halos in their pockets. I assume most Fallen could care less for a mortal soul, and I don't believe the lure of using a halo as a weapon should be strong enough. But they did have a little injector gun that put something inside me."

"They injected something into you?"

"Someone I know thinks it's a tracking device."

"Clever. It makes sense. If they can't lure you with a halo—and your thoughts on the use of a halo as a lure are feasible—then they would like to keep track of you. So you obviously haven't found your muse yet?"

Cooper sighed heavily.

"So you don't know what's up? They want you and your muse," Donovan insisted. "The vamps want to keep tabs on you. Take the muse into custody as soon as you've fuc—er, you know… attempted her. Then they'll take the baby and, well, after that I don't want to know."

"I think I do."

And bloody Beneath, it made perfect, but horrendous sense. For the first time he put two and two together and came up with something far worse than any mortal could imagine.

It made Cooper's cold blood turn to ice.

"The nephilim are the original blood drinkers," Cooper said, summoning the knowledge from when he'd once walked the earth in biblical times. "They may have well been the ones who created the vampire race. But I assume since nephilim have not walked the earth for millennia, those vampires they created are growing weak. A nephilim would prove a boon to a vampire."

Donovan whistled. "Whew!"

"It's got to be the reason," Cooper said.

"I'd lay bets it is. I'd hate to see one of those things walking down the street."

"Nasty sons of muses," Cooper hissed. "They're giants who feed on blood and meat. Anything walking will do, whether it be four-legged or two-legged. So you're sitting here in my home, waiting for me to come home, and if I can believe you, had no idea what I am. What did you think I could do for you by coming here?"

"Nothing. Like I said, I was just checking you out for Eden. But now, things have changed. We need to work together," Donovan said. "If the vamps happen to lead you astray—"

"That's not going to happen."

"I'm just saying. I know you don't have control of all your senses when in the presence of a muse. You say it's not going to happen, but a compulsion is a powerful thing."

"Save your theories, buddy. I know myself."

"I've sent my girlfriend to check out their lair."

"Your girlfriend? What is she? A slayer with a death wish?"

Both men looked to Pyx, who had entered without notice and asked the question. She swept a thick chunk of wet hair over her shoulder and leaned over the table toward Donovan.

Donovan glanced to Cooper, who remained poker-faced. So the whole world felt they could waltz on into his home without knocking? He'd never felt less in control than right now, and it was not a good feeling.

Pyx looked Donovan right in the eye. "Er…" he stated uncertainly. "My girlfriend is a vampire."

Pyx sneered.

"Stranger things have happened." The halo hunter made a show of glancing from Cooper to Pyx. "Like a demon and an angel getting together."

"He's not mine," Pyx said quickly.

"Nor is she mine," Cooper added gruffly. "But how did you know she's demon?"

"The eyes," Donovan said. "That wild riot of color. Never seen it on a human before. Very specifically Sinistari. Although…" He thought about it, looking Pyx over. "The last guy I met with eyes like that was really…"

"You spend too much time gazing into people's eyes," Cooper interrupted, because the man knew too much and he had no intention of letting Pyx learn all of that right now, "you'll soon enough fall under a vampire's persuasion."

"Already happened," Donovan said with a smile. He itched his neck where the bite marks had left a raised red welt. "My girl does it once in a while. She gets a kick out of it."

"I don't trust this guy." Pyx gripped Donovan's arm and wrenched it around behind his back. "The vampires sent you, didn't they?"

"No! And why would they if they've a tracking device on him?"

"That's a guess," Pyx provided. She took out Joe and shoved the tip under Donovan's chin. "You lying or telling the truth?"

"The truth! I want to destroy the vampires as much as you do."

"I said nothing about destroying vampires," Cooper hissed.

"But it would be a fun time," Pyx commented. She released Donovan and sat on the kitchen chair, slumping and putting up a boot on another chair. Noticing the painting, she leaned in to study it. "Who made this?"

"There's a muse who dreams angels," Cooper said. "She's the reason he's here. She's not putting those pictures out for the whole world to see?" he asked Donovan.

"Eden was showing them at a gallery in New York until someone bought all of them. And that someone was Antonio del Gado. He's gathering information on the angels any way he can. You'd better be careful."

"There's not a vampire alive who can tempt me with anything," Cooper said.

"Not even your halo?"

Cooper met Pyx's querying gaze. He averted his eyes away from the question she had no right to ask.

"Awkward," Donovan finally said. "So I should go now. Don't want to interrupt anything like a date between the two of you."

"It's not—" Cooper and Pyx both spoke at the same time and both stopped when the halo hunter cast them a smirk.

"Yeah, right." Donovan eased around Pyx. "I'll check in with you after my girl gives me a report."

He thumbed the throwing star stuck in the table, then nodded to Pyx, and offered a hand to shake to Cooper.

Cooper stared at it, then shook, and held firmly. "We're not finished yet. In fact, we've only begun. Where you staying?"

"The Regina. You can find me there, or call my cell." He handed him a business card. "You cooperate with me, and I promise you can look through my collection of halos. Deal?"

"Cooperate?"

"Help me take down the vamps."

"I'll consider it."

Donovan prowled down the hallway, and Cooper left him to close the door on his own. He eyed Pyx who didn't seem too curious over the man.

"Halo hunter?" she asked.

"Yes. I won't even ask how you know."

"Did you walk the world at all after you were summoned, Fallen one?"

He shook his head and went into the bedroom, calling, "I'll get you a towel. You're soaked bone-deep."

When he returned from the bathroom she stood in the bedroom, admiring the stained-glass pocket doors. Rain glimmered on her pale flesh like moon drops. He bet it tasted like sweet summer.

She tapped the window where violet glass segued into a curve of green that represented a leaf. "The windows in this apartment are crazy gorgeous."

"So we're not going to discuss the halo hunter?"

"We will."

He approached her and spread out the towel, pressing it to her shoulders. "You like? I enhanced them a bit."

"How?"

He took her hand and led her to the outer bay window that curved and looked across the right bank. He'd not touched these windows yet, because he wasn't sure if the building's owner would notice the changes from the street and protest.

But who could protest beauty?

Skating the fingertips of his left hand over the glass, Cooper drew wide arcs and dancing lines. In the wake of his touch bloomed gorgeous color. It seeped into the glass and where he wanted the colors to change, lead stripping cracked into the glass and formed.

"How do you—" Pyx asked, but stopped. With a sigh, she nodded. "Beautiful."

"It's my skill," he said.

"That's right, you said you taught mortals this craft."

"Just the one." He rapped his chest. "Only one soul inside this angel's heart."

"Right." She touched the window emblazoned with violet lilies and emerald stalks of grass in the

Art Nouveau style Cooper appreciated. A warrior who could dance and create beauty *and* rip out hearts without blinking an eye. "You make me want you, Cooper."

"I didn't do anything to you, sweetie."

"I'm not so sweet."

"You like to think you're tough."

He stroked the hair from her cheek and tucked it behind her ear. One kiss meant no turning back. Because he'd stepped over the need to linger at her mouth. Now he wanted all of her.

Cooper crossed his arms over his chest, but didn't step away from her.

"You are tough," he said. "But you were made that way. Forged of metal and costumed in silken human flesh. But in there? Your mind? You're a newling learning the world, trying new things, making mistakes and winning emotion and compassion and even trust."

"So are you."

"Exactly. Here on earth we're just people, Pyx, trying to make our way."

"We're more than that. Why is it so easy for you to overlook differences, to think of yourself as one of them?"

"Because I want to be one of them." He leaned against the windowsill, and put up a leg on the bench. He sighed. "I told you, I don't want my halo for the weapon. I want to claim my mortal soul. I want to become like them."

"You think the halo hunter has your halo?"

"It's a possibility." He scanned the street outside. "I should have followed him."

"He'll be back. And you know where to find him. You just wanted to be alone with me."

"I did. Ah, Pyx, mortals fascinate me. Not a one the same as the next." Cooper tilted his head back against the window frame. "I know it won't matter to you, but you need to know why I fell."

"It won't matter." Pyx nodded. "But go ahead."

"I admire the human race," he said. "I have always wanted to be one of them. I put myself no higher or lower than the common man, yet in angelic vestments I am deemed higher."

"Not anymore. You've fallen from His grace."

"True." He flicked a look out the window, but didn't cast his eyes so high as Above. He wasn't privileged to look that high now. "Wanting a human soul is a selfish act."

"No more selfish than falling to have sex with human women."

"That wasn't why I fell."

"It's your story. It works for you."

"It's not a story. It is what I desire. But lately I've been thinking how selfish it really was. Who am I to deserve the soul He gifted only to them? What right do I have to take one for myself?"

She approached and leaned against him. It was interesting to watch Pyx as she became less hard and more interested in actual emotions and the feelings of others. "You're not trying to take anything that wasn't already there. The soul has always been in your halo, hasn't it?"

"Yes. I would ransom immortality for a human soul," he said wistfully. "Only problem is, there's a demon on my ass with blood in her eyes."

"I bet it's a sexy ass." She kissed the corner of his mouth. The taste was bittersweet, lingering not long enough to savor. "I won't kill you tonight, Cooper. Promise."

He had to give her credit for at least trying to be compassionate. And what the hell? He was considering her offer. Because he did desire her. And if his days on earth were numbered, then he had no intention of living them unsatisfied.

On the other hand...

"You know how angels work? Sexually?"

"You have to wear this human costume, because in angel form you are sexless. Same with demons."

"Yes, but you know the muse is the only woman who can give me the ultimate pleasure?"

"You can take none from me?"

"I get delicious pleasure in making you happy, and it is enough to satisfy. But no orgasm, I'm afraid, with any but my muse. Unless, of course, I found my halo and ultimately, my soul."

She worried her lip, considering what he'd said. "So you don't want to do this?"

Cooper chuckled. "Oh, I want to do it. I just wanted you to be clear on a few things first. You are so fine."

A curl of his fingers brought her into his embrace without Pyx taking a step. He wanted to feel her against his skin, but it still wasn't right.

She didn't want this. She hadn't sunk into his arms like she had earlier. She was nervous. This closeness was merely a ruse. A means to ingratiating herself to him—to soften him for the kill.

"Leave, Pyx," he whispered.

"But—"

"You want this for the wrong reasons. Unless and until you change your mind, this won't happen."

"Oh. So until I come over to your team, you mean, and let you call the shots. I see. Typical male."

"You have no idea what the typical male is like."

"Nor do you realize what you're allowing to walk away from you." She turned and strode out of his apartment.

And a painful ache opened in Cooper's chest. She was right. He was making the mistake, not her.

But he didn't know how to do this from her point of view. He was the man. He needed to be in control.

The door slammed, and Cooper winced.

Had he just lost what he'd never had in the first place?

Chapter 12

"The angel seems indifferent to finding his muse." Bruce stalked the floor before his boss, the leader of tribe Anakim. Stellan stood in the shadows below the window that sifted in silver moonlight through the panes. "He's more interested in beating on us."

"You said he's working alongside a Sinistari demon?"

"Yeah. Isn't that remarkable?"

"As well," Stellan said, "I've seen the halo hunter, Michael Donovan, in town. We cannot allow them to join forces."

"But, we're losing men to the angel. A freakin' angel." Bruce fisted a hand into his palm with a crisp smack. "We can't risk approaching him again. Even with the wards, he's too powerful. When he shifts, there's no telling what power he has at hand."

"What about the tracker?"

"It's not working. Something went wrong. I think when the angel shifted the tracker got embedded too deep. I don't know, but it could have been crushed."

Antonio shook his head. He'd yet to look up at his men from his position before the granite-topped desk.

Here aboveground in the Hôtel Solange, he reigned over the Anakim tribe during the night. Yet he could only walk the day, as could those of his tribe, as long as he wore protective gear to keep the UV rays from his sensitive skin. It took less than ten seconds to burn his flesh and eat into his bloodstream. Thirty seconds later, he'd be one fried vampire.

That would change, Bruce knew, once a nephilim was born and the tribe could use that creature to strengthen their blood. Ancient bloodlines would be renewed with the infusion. They'd be able to walk in the day. Anakim would fear no enemy.

"Bring Michael Donovan to me," Antonio directed Stellan.

"Of course, sir." Stellan bowed his head and moved into the shadows.

"As well, kill the demon."

The tall vampire remained in the shadows, but Bruce detected a catch to Stellan's voice. "You want *me* to kill the Sinistari? You know those bastards are impossible to kill."

"You said the demon was female."

"Yes, but—" Stellan swallowed.

Bruce smirked. So glad he hadn't gotten demon duty.

If Stellan argued, he'd appear weak for whining about his inability to kill a mere woman. "It will be done."

Antonio rose and approached the far wall where the blood grimoire he used to summon the Fallen sat upon a lectern. It had a fancy name: *Rituals and Invocations of that Which Join Above and Beneath.* Bruce had not been in the room when Juphiel had been summoned and the crazy noise and flashing lights under the door had kept him out.

"Bruce, why is it so difficult to keep track of one fallen angel?" Antonio tapped the grimoire. "He is in Paris for a reason. The Fallen are compelled to their muses. She must be here. Somewhere."

"Don't worry. I've got a handle on it. I think I located the muse."

"You had better get a handle on the muse, if you know what is good for you."

"Yes, sir, monsieur. I'll leave then?"

The lead vampire gave him a look that could

only be construed as "get the hell out." Bruce turned and left, glad to be away from the old vampire's intense…existence.

He owed Antonio one for rescuing him from a vicious wolf attack. And the idea of being allowed to drink nephilim blood intrigued him. He already could walk during the day, but what other powers would he gain? He didn't mind sticking around to find out.

Cooper intended to leave town to avoid his muse. But first things first. He looked up the Hotel Regina online and marked the address. Instead of flashing there he decided a walk in the fresh air would serve him better.

This was his farewell walk through a city he'd come to love.

The high moon glamorized the puddles on the sidewalk from the rain earlier in the evening. A crowd of youth ran past him shouting for one another to hurry to catch the Metro. One of the girls sporting pink hair and too much eye makeup slowed and cast Cooper a smile.

If she only knew the man who'd quickly looked away wasn't even a man but something closer to a monster. Unless of course, she was religious and believed in angels. Then she might deem him divine. Mortals had a tendency to glamorize those things they did not understand. To find the heroic in even the darkest and most vile of creatures.

Funny how that worked. Would he do the same should he find his halo and claim his mortal soul?

Crossing the street to take a shortcut through a field of railroad tracks, Cooper noticed some action ahead.

Gorgeous garnet hair flashed as it caught the moonlight. That was definitely Pyx. She delivered a high roundhouse to her aggressor, sending him crashing against the brick wall of the Metro tunnel.

"Has to be a vampire," Cooper muttered.

Yet he held back. Pyx wouldn't like it if he rushed in when she was capable of handling one idiot vampire all by herself.

He winced as she took a skull blow and staggered, spitting black blood through the air. She did not relent, rounding on her hissing opponent and returning a bruising blow to the vamp's jaw.

The demon was like a work of movable art; gorgeous, defiant, exquisite and kick-ass.

"We're so different," Cooper said. "Black and blue blood. Will we ever earn the red blood we desire?"

Because despite Pyx's reluctance now, they had once both desired it. She had to be the angel he'd once called friend.

And if so, he wanted Pyx to bleed red. She deserved it. She didn't belong in the demon realm. Sure, a female demon could kick ass and slay as well as a male. But the mortal realm had so much more to offer Pyx.

Like home and family. Dresses and pretty things to adorn her body. Food and walks in the park. Love. Cooper wanted her to have it all.

Which meant he'd have to sacrifice his chance at red blood. "Or else find another Fallen for Pyx to slay."

He shook his head. It was unthinkable to consider putting another Fallen in his place so he could have his selfish pleasures. Much as he could get behind the halo hunter's reasoning to slay all the Fallen and prevent the nephilim.

The vampire snarled and hit Pyx so hard, she stumbled across the rail tracks. Dazed, she stood there, gathering her senses. The bright headlights of the oncoming Metro train alerted Cooper.

Cooper's glass heart clenched. He tracked the headlights; switched to Pyx's dazed stance. "She doesn't see it. It's going to—"

He flashed to the rail track, right beside the vampire. Shoving the vamp forced him stumbling away from Pyx.

Cooper leaped before the train, which twenty feet away and speeding fifty kilometers an hour. He wrapped his arms around Pyx's shoulders.

He felt the impact—twenty tons of metal to glass bone and human flesh—at the same moment he began to flash....

Sophia St. Michel worked at the coffee shop until it closed tonight at 11:00 p.m., according to the schedule hung above the register. It was only nine.

Bruce crept up the iron staircase hugging the cool, outside cinder-block wall to Sophia's apartment. Below sat a small, contained courtyard, encircled by four-story rental buildings. Shadows concealed his movements, though he moved so swiftly and stealthily no one would notice.

Her back door was bolted and chained. He rammed a shoulder against the door. The metal chain assembly on the inside cracked the wood with little resistance. He slipped inside without opening it too far.

The door obviously wasn't used, because he walked right into a hanger of clothing. Must serve as her closet. Rubbing a bit of silk against his cheek he inhaled the lingering perfume.

"Roses. I love the taste of a woman who smells like flowers. Too bad she ain't around. We could have had some fun."

Much as he'd like to sink his teeth into the muse's neck, Bruce intended to remain in his leader's good graces. Stellan was walking a fine line. That vamp's days were numbered.

Bruce wasn't one hundred percent positive this woman was the muse, so detective work was in order. Creeping through the darkness of her bedroom he eyed the vanity lined with glass bottles and girly stuff. Hanging over the mirror, a flowered scarf dangled red fringe. Women liked all that frippery. He liked taking that kind of stuff *off* women and tossing it over his shoulder.

Smirking, he prowled into the kitchen and spied a secretary desk against the far wall. That would have bills and papers, and maybe notes of interest.

Slinking between the kitchen table and the counter—most Paris kitchens were narrow aisles— Bruce lifted the rolling door on the secretary and poked about.

She sure as hell bought a lot of shoes. Owed two thousand euros on footwear alone from what he could determine. The urge to feel a spike heel pressed into his hip sent a shiver up his spine.

"I could hang around until later, greet her when she returns."

He pushed the button on the answering machine, but the robotic voice reported no messages.

In the living room the sheer white curtains were drawn. An array of fringed pillows smothered a green velvet couch. Bruce plopped onto the couch and settled into the nest of feminine overload. His hand flicked a stack of books tucked beneath the glass coffee table and he tugged one out.

He read the title, *"Angels and Demons: Of Heaven and Hell."* Inside were paintings by various artists of feathery winged angels and horned demons. "Stupid."

He replaced the book, which shoved a red velvet-covered journal to the floor. Picking it up he opened it to a random page—and sat up straight.

"No kidding?"

A black ink design scribbled across the page. Bruce recognized the design, or rather the style of it. He paged through and noted a different design had been marked on each page, and beneath were notes about date, season, what she'd done that day.

"Bingo! These are angel sigils. The muse knows about them? She must have drawn these. Antonio is going to love this."

He tucked the journal into his waistband and clapped his hands together. "This will definitely put me in the boss's good graces."

Chapter 13

Cooper flashed to the surface of the Metro tunnel. His knees hit the loose gravel. The woman in his arms he clutched against his chest as the train rumbled by below.

No sign of the vampire staggering outside the tracks. He had to be an ashy hood ornament by now.

Wincing, Cooper moved his right shoulder. The train had hit him the moment he flashed. It felt like his skin had been peeled from the bone. And that mortal flesh hurt like a mother.

Pyx moaned and clutched his forearms. "What hurts so much?"

Inspecting her arms and face, he couldn't find

any damage. Until he lowered his gaze to her stomach. Black blood oozed from a wound that hadn't come from the train.

"The vampire must have stabbed you."

"I've never felt anything like this before. Ohh..." She pressed her fingers over the wound and tarlike blood oozed between them. "Cooper?"

"Your flesh is mortal. It's called pain, Pyx. Humans feel it all the time."

"Yes. Hurt before when a vamp shot me, but... Can't shift now. Not...in front of you. Oh, that hurts."

She didn't want to shift before him? Because she thought that would spoil his attraction to her? He'd felt the same when he'd accidentally shifted. Seeing her in demon form would not offend him, but he wouldn't force her to do it.

He inspected the wound. It was a deep cut, but once beyond the mortal flesh and muscle the demon's inner organs and structure were metal. She would heal, but not as quickly as she would were she in Sinistari form. "Just sit still," he said, hiding another wince from his own pain. The shoulder had dislocated, surely. The muscles strapping it burned like molten iron. "Let it heal before we move. Or I've a better idea."

He wrapped his arms around her shoulders and flashed—landing in her living room. Jumping up, he raced into the bathroom and tossed a towel in the sink. While he waited for warm water to cover the towel, he jammed his shoulder against the door frame. Biting back a yowl, he gritted his teeth and swallowed the bile that had risen.

You want this kind of pain, buddy? Because it'll be a common thing after you claim your soul.

He turned and inspected his back in the mirror. Bold bruises formed an ugly tattoo. The skin was abraded and it looked like someone had started to peel it off.

"Cooper!"

Pain, he could handle. Pyx in pain? That was not cool.

Cooper wrung out the towel then returned to find Pyx sitting against the sofa, clutching her gut.

"I'll be gentle. Let me take a look."

She allowed him to press the towel to her stomach and wipe away the thick black blood. Her blood did not offend him. It only reminded him how desperately he wanted to get a soul—pain be damned.

"Maybe this mortality thing isn't what it's cracked up to be," she said tightly. "It doesn't hurt as much now, but I sure don't want to feel that kind of pain ever again."

"I like the pain. It's another choice the mortals have."

"That wasn't exactly a choice back at the tracks."

"Of course it was. You chose to engage with the enemy. You knew the risks would not be a day in the park."

"You got me there. I'd never walk away from an angry vampire. What about you? You've blood on your shoulder." She stroked his skin through the torn shirt and showed him her blue fingertip.

As his skin knit together and the muscles snapped into shape he felt it all. And yes, he did like the pain. He'd never once felt it while serving Puriel, though there were times half of him had been consumed in flames in the midst of a massive smite. As an angel he'd simply walked from the destruction and shook off the ash.

Without a thought for the damage and murder he'd caused.

Never again.

"I'm fine. It's healed. And your pretty skin is still pretty, sweetie. Bastard vampire."

He threw the towel and it landed on the bathroom floor. The motion ripped a searing cut through his shoulder. He bit back an oath.

"Choice or not, I'll kill all the vampires," he said through gritted teeth. "Screw the halo. No one hurts my girl."

Pyx's mouth dropped open. Her wide, multicolored eyes touched his. What had he said to put such wonderment on her face?

Oh.

"I mean it," he offered, "about the halo. It can wait. I want to kick some vampire ass for what they did to you."

"Yeah, that's cool. Vampire butt. Kick it to oblivion. Now about that other part."

"What part?"

"About no one hurting your girl. Do you...?" She gestured between him and her, speaking silently the dangerous connection neither would admit to.

The girl in question was the oddest girl he'd encountered, and the most appealing. Nothing about her was like the average woman. And everything about her twanged at his better senses. Senses that knew she was his enemy, yet wanted a go at it anyway.

And it wasn't as if he was feeling a compulsion. It was more a genuine fascination and interest in someone he admired. Yes, he admired Pyx. He felt as if he had known her for millennia.

And maybe he had.

Cooper shrugged. "Well, you know."

"I know I heard a Fallen one claim a Sinistari as his. What's up with that? Do you think the two of us...? That we have something going on?"

Her tone berated more than agreed. Damn it.

"No." But to be truthful? "Yes." He wasn't about to let her off with a free pass. "You don't think there's something between us?"

She slammed her arms across her chest. Sitting, her legs bent and fiery hair tousled about her shoulders, vamp blood smeared across her neck, she looked more the fallen angel than anyone else in the room. "Absolutely not."

"Are you sure?"

"What part of absolutely and not didn't you understand, Fallen one?"

Cooper sensed she wasn't being true to herself. But who was he to claim to know her mind? And what in all of Beneath had gotten into him besides a frisky Sinistari?

Humanity had begun to permeate his glass heart. A precursor to getting his soul. And he liked it. Hell, he loved this compassion that allowed him to relate to another being's pain or confusion, or even to sense when they were not being truthful with themselves.

Lunging forward on his knees, Cooper slipped a hand behind Pyx's head and drew her forward to kiss. She didn't struggle; in fact, she wrapped her long legs about his hips and pulled him closer so he straddled her.

This time he did not make his touch tender with gentle exploration, but instead dove in deeply. He had to taste her, to feel her, to claim her in a way that he hoped would knock the doubt from her brain.

"What in all of Beneath is this then?" he asked. Their breaths meshed in urgent desire. "The two of us. Kissing every time we get within a foot of one another. Touching. Acting as if we're the greatest of friends instead of mortal enemies."

"Lust. Greed."

"You can't excuse a kiss as sin. Does this feel sinful?" He brushed his lips over hers. The warmth of her made him moan.

"You forget sin is what makes me tick. I need it."

"Pyx, I don't want this—" he kissed her full on the mouth "—to be classified as a sin. It's a good thing. You can have goodness, too. It's your choice. A choice you made once already. Just take it."

She pushed him away and he landed, arms splaying across the glass coffee table. His shoulder had stopped hurting, but now, he felt a twinge of pain in his chest. It wasn't as if he'd been stabbed or hurt with a physical object, no, this pain pulsed in the muscle and hurt his thoughts more than his body.

That familiar ache.

"Last night you push me away. Tonight you pull me back." Pyx strode out of the living room, unbuttoning her shirt as she did. "You're confusing me."

"I'm not trying to."

Just trying to get a little action without having to argue over the right and wrong of it every time. What was so wrong about that? He was following his…well, his heart. And yes, admittedly, his heart was cold, out of touch, and unfamiliar with the whole process. He should not have pushed her away last night.

"I want to connect with you, Pyx. Don't you… remember things?"

"Remember?"

He got up to go after her but the bedroom door slammed in his face. Cooper beat his fist against it.

"Yeah, maybe mortality isn't what it's cracked up to be," he muttered to the solid wood door. "Do mortal males have to deal with such indecision from their females?" He scuffed fingers through his hair and ended up tugging until his scalp hurt.

"I can have any woman I want," he said, yet not convincing himself. "Just have to step inside the club and they fall all over me."

He turned and leaned against the door. His shoulder had healed as had the skin on his back. So why wasn't he walking away? Heading to the clubs? He had an itch and he knew how to get it scratched.

By all of Beneath, there was a perfectly good muse in the city and she literally had his name imprinted on her flesh.

Was it because Pyx had become a challenge? If he could land a Sinistari demon in his bed then look out, angelic ranks, because he was king of the Fallen.

Yeah, whatever. He had no inclinations toward achieving such a stupid accomplishment. He could care less what his fellow Fallen thought of him. They didn't think of him. Each was single-minded, focused on the goal of finding their muse. *If* they had been summoned.

"The vampires are summoning us to catch a nephilim."

A creature that rivaled any of the boogies and monsters the mortals had nightmares about. It fed on blood and flesh, and did not discern from man, woman or child. One drop of its blood could give great power to the vampire bloodline that had descended from nephilim.

Cooper had much better things to do than sit around waiting for the girl to get her act together. He had some vampires to slay.

He flashed out of Pyx's apartment.

After changing shirts, Pyx opened her bedroom door in time to see the Fallen flash away.

She leaned in the doorway, and bowed her head. "Thought he was interested in me. Huh."

Studying her fingers, she toyed with the dried

blue blood. Cool to the touch, it had come from a man more hot-blooded than even she.

A man she admired for he thought of her more than himself. His easy acceptance of humanity was rubbing off on her.

It was ridiculous to think she could have a relationship with Cooper.

But she still thought about it.

Why prove herself to her fellow Sinistari when, if she did slay a Fallen, she could take a human soul and remain on earth. Never return to Beneath. Never again concern herself with what some demon thought of her.

The hitch was the slaying an angel part.

If the vampires were summoning Fallen to earth, could she get them to summon another for her to slay?

"Interesting idea." It implied she work with the vampires. Not a chance. But the notion was worthy of some consideration if it saved her from slaying Cooper.

Chapter 14

The hunt had been fruitless. Either the vampires hid themselves well, or they were tracking him while staying cleverly hidden and snickering behind cupped hands.

He couldn't pick up their vibrations, as Pyx was capable of doing. Nor could he sniff them out. He'd returned to the rooftop and watched the church for most of the day. Just outside the doors a painting crew had begun setting up ladders and scaffolding, obviously to work on the building next door where thick strips of gray paint were peeling off.

Cooper had not felt so ineffective in a long time.

When he'd served the angelic ranks he had done

his job well. Too well. But at least he'd accomplished something.

Weird how he could consider murder and smiting an accomplishment. Truly, he was so far from humane, he might never deserve a soul.

Striding toward the one spot in this entire city that gave him comfort, Cooper walked through the white iron gate and seated himself before at a small table outside the café.

Sophia brought him a coffee and a hot cinnamon roll dripping with honey butter. She wore a ruffle-sleeved white shirt today that revealed her slender arms. But though the sigil on his abdomen was humming, it wasn't the sigil on Sophia's forearm that caught Cooper's eyes.

No, much as he tried to keep his eyes from her face and remain unconnected, Sophia's deep red lipstick beckoned his attention.

She smiled at him, then rubbed a palm along her arm, the one she'd tied a pretty black bow around right about where he'd seen the sigil. "You like our coffee, monsieur?"

"Coffee? Oh, yes." And leave it at that. It was a good thing he'd not told her his name. The less personal, the better.

Why'd he come here? He knew it was wrong.

Because you were compelled.

No. Really? Damn, he should leave. Right now. He was thinking about moving. He wasn't going to stare at those red lips. He would not. Red lips made him think of kissing. Kissing made him think of touching. Touching made him think—

He grabbed the cream pitcher and poured some in his coffee. Pyx. Pyx, Pyx, Pyx. *Yes, put the demon into your thoughts to keep from more dangerous wiles.*

"You work here every day, Sophia?"

"*Oui,* except Saturdays. That's my day to study at the Louvre."

"Ah? What are you studying?"

"Renaissance art."

"You a painter?"

"No, just a fan. But I do some sketching."

"I love the paintings, myself. I've been to the museum a few times since arriving in Paris. Could stare at the *Mona Lisa* for hours."

"*La Joconde* was so sad."

"You think?" He knew differently. An angel could read a painting as if he were tapping in to the artist's mind. "I suspect the painter was more angry with his subject that day over her secret happiness."

"Really?" She sat on the chair across from him. Her dark eyes glittered.

Cooper's eyes went to the black ribbon. Her fingers absently moved over it, scratching lightly. She seemed unaware of the move.

"The Mona Lisa was secretly happy about

something?" she asked. "There is her enigmatic smile, but that she was happy is such a common device. What is your theory? Did they have an affair, she and da Vinci?"

Wrong move, Cooper. Avoid the muse, remember? Don't engage with her. It can only end badly. Where had gone thoughts of the demon?

"Well, or so I suppose. It's a guess." The truth, but he didn't want to explain that he could read the artist's thoughts from the art they'd created.

She ran her tongue along her upper lip. How's a man supposed to look away from that? All his blue angel blood rushed to Cooper's crotch. He was thankful for the linen tablecloth hanging over his lap.

Sophia's perfume caressed his skin, skimming his lips, cheeks and eyelids. Something floral with a taint of alcohol. He didn't mind it at all. Could lap it up and suck it in…

Control yourself. You will not attempt to have sex with this woman. You. Will. Not.

"Was that your girlfriend you were with the other day?"

Her out-of-the-blue question startled him from the sensual ocean currently drowning him. He gripped the imaginary life preserver, relieved for the rescue.

"I don't have girlfriends," he muttered. A

charming smile curved before he could curb his flirtatious nature.

He thought it wiser to take a sip of coffee than to look up again, because he'd noticed that tiny second button was undone on her shirt. And wow, did she seem to stand out from the entire world. It was as if she were in hi-definition and the rest of the café, the sky and the street, faded into a blurry background.

The black ribbon at her forearm, tied in a perfect bow, stole his attention. What lay beneath marked her sure death. "New fashion?"

"I wear it sometimes." She blushed. Actually blushed.

Oh, those rosy cheeks warmed his heart and hands, and— Blood flow alert! *Soon you won't be able to think, man.*

The muse stroked the black moiré ribbon with a delicate finger Cooper could very well imagine stroking his—oh, mercy. Time to leave.

"It's my birthmark and it's so odd, so sometimes it's easier to cover it than answer questions."

"I see." *Stop gritting your teeth. Act normal. Just stand up and walk away.* "I can't imagine anything appearing odd on you, Sophia."

Where was his focus? He glanced aside but the world remained blurred. He wanted to look only at the muse. He had to…inhale her.

Cooper closed his eyes and inhaled the lush soft scent of Sophia.

"What is that cologne?" she asked.

He opened an eye and saw Sophia doing much the same as he, inhaling...something. Him? "Er."

"It's very sexy." Throaty, her tone. So...alluring. "I've never smelled anything quite like it."

Did he turn her on, too? He wasn't quite sure how it worked for the muse.

"You buy that cologne in one of the boutiques on the Champs Elysees?"

"No, it's um...just me." Cedar. Pyx liked it. He winced. "Do you live close by?"

"Now why would you wonder something like that? And I don't even know your name."

He didn't have to be on the earth a lifetime to recognize the flirtatious lilt in her voice. It rang like church bells in his belly. He liked church bells.

"Er, sorry, that came out the wrong way. Name's Cooper Truhart. I just wondered if it was easy for you to get to work. If you lived close by."

And please buy that stupid excuse.

"I get off in half an hour, Cooper Truhart." The tip of her tongue dashed out to trace her ruby lip. Diamonds glinted in her dark eyes. "Perhaps you'd like to walk me home? I've a wonderful picture book from the Louvre. You can show me why you think the Mona Lisa was so happy the day she sat for da Vinci."

He clutched the coffee mug handle, and felt the porcelain crack. The handle came off in his grip, but he didn't react, didn't want her to notice.

"A half an hour, eh?"

Say no, say no, say *no*.

He smiled. "It's a date."

Pyx intercepted Michael Donovan on the front steps before Cooper's building. She charged up the steps and insinuated herself before the lobby door, her chest colliding with the halo hunter's chest.

"Whoa." He stepped back, raising his arms, but in a mocking manner. "Ladies first, I guess. You here to see the Fallen?"

"He's not home. And I am a lady."

"Didn't say you weren't."

"You implied differently."

Donovan gave her a frustrated twist of lip.

"What are you doing here? I thought Cooper said he would go to you?"

"My girlfriend found the vampire lair."

"So what's new? We found it, too. It's in an old church." Pyx huffed. "Where is she? Your girlfriend?"

"She's a vampire," Donovan offered matter-of-factly. He glanced toward the setting sun.

"Right. So you're going to stick your nose into

the vampires' business, and end up getting killed?" Pyx leaned in the doorway, crossing her arms. "Yeah, that'll work. At least it'll keep you out of my hair."

"I have yet to meet a Sinistari who's mastered the art of subtlety."

"Yeah, but you've only met the two, so give us time, buddy."

He had not come to deal with her, she guessed. Too bad for him. She was first on the list when it came to contact with Cooper. Everyone else could take a number and stand in line.

"So when's the Fallen return home?"

"Does it matter?" She eyed the man's posture, straight and not at all weak. The scar beside his eye made her briefly wonder how he'd gotten it. Probably walked into a door. "He's not going to get you what you want. You want dead vamps? I'm the one with the warrior training."

"Is that so?" Donovan shoved his hands in his pants pockets. "Don't get me wrong, but I think angels have warrior mode mastered."

"Cooper's not like most angels. He's not like most Fallen. He's...too soft."

Although he had been in the war angel's ranks. And she still pictured him holding that dripping vampire's heart after tearing it out from its chest. So maybe Cooper had been a reckonable force—

at one time. But since falling he'd sacrificed that warrior status.

Though the angel had rescued her last night.

No, not soft, but humane. Protecting what he'd felt belonged to him. And how weird was that?

"Maybe around you he's soft," Donovan said. "Any man would go all soft and senseless around you."

Pyx straightened and twisted a strand of hair around her finger. She snapped her gum and looked down through her lashes at the man, who was looking more appealing now he'd dropped the sarcasm. "Why's that?"

Donovan's smile melted Pyx's last defensive muscle. "Because you're gorgeous. But I suspect while you've mastered the warrior stuff, as well, you haven't quite mastered self-awareness. Stay fierce, Pyx. Someone's gotta slay the Fallen."

"Right. I'm here to slay the Fallen." Not kiss him. Even if his kisses were better than banana and chocolate crepes. "But if vamps get in my way—" She punched a fist into her palm.

"You give it to them, sister. Go, Sinistari!"

"You know it."

"I brought a couple halos." Donovan patted the messenger bag at his hip. "Thought they would serve as an olive branch to Cooper. Prove to him I'll do what I've promised. I suspect the vampires have a bunch of these, as well. Not sure how they intend to use them."

"A lure for the Fallen," Pyx guessed.

"But most Fallen could care little for the soul contained within their halo," Donovan said.

"That's true." Unless the angel's name was Cooper Truhart. That was information Donavan didn't need to have. "The halo serves as a supernatural weapon when in the Fallen's hands."

"Yes, I've seen that. You could take off a head with one of these things if it's yours."

"Let me see them."

"Nope." Donovan hugged the bag against his hip. "These are mine. You get your own. So I take it you're the guard dog here? No entrance to see the angel unless I can get past his pet demon?"

Pyx lunged a fist up into Donovan's gut. He made a gasping "buh" sound and slammed against the door.

Snapping her gum once, Pyx said, "You got it."

Cooper clasped Sophia's hand, because she held it out and waggled her fingers as if she expected him to take it. They strolled the dark street toward her apartment building. Moonlight twinkled on the windows and the silver trim on parked cars. He liked the older neighborhoods; less modernity. The air of ancient times was appealing to him.

This wasn't a date. Nor was it simply a man walking a woman safely home. He wasn't sure what he was doing.

Yes, he was. Taking the woman home to have sex with her.

It was his destiny. And hers.

Everything about her, smell, sight, taste and sound, was magnified to a delicious come-on Cooper sucked in through his pores as if air.

She smelled sweeter than anything he'd known—honey and fresh cream—more desirable even than Pyx. And her voice absolutely dripped with come-and-get-me when she purred her words.

The color of her eyes was deep and molten, like glistening dark chocolate. The shine in her voice shimmied against his glass heart. The softness of her skin defied categorization.

And she could give him pleasure. Something Cooper wanted more than anything.

More than claiming his soul?

No. Not going to do it. You don't need sex. You'd like it, but you don't need *it. Besides, you can have sex. With anyone! What makes this woman so special?*

He knew the answer to that one.

He could resist the compulsion. No problem. He was...curious. Yeah, that was it. He wanted to keep tabs on Sophia, know everything he could know so he could prevent the inevitable horror. He was being smart about this.

Right. That's his story and he was sticking to it.

The Smart Car crept along the street, a good distance behind the walking couple. The Fallen was leaving with the same woman who had scribbled the angelic sigils in the journal Bruce had turned over to Antonio.

"Most definitely the muse. And the Fallen has finally tapped in to his muse mojo."

Bruce settled into the seat and turned the radio down low.

"Wonder if there'll be fireworks?"

Chapter 15

Sophia stopped at the front door to a gorgeous building, which was tiled in blue, green and yellow glass across the curved outer walls. Art Deco mastodons curved their thick paws along both stair railings. She lived in the shadow of the Eiffel Tower on the opposite side of the Seine from the café.

Strange, how he'd ended up so close to his muse, without suspecting.

On the other hand, Cooper was beginning to think nothing was coincidence. He'd thought to travel to Paris because it held no interest for him. It was a big city where he could get lost easily and never bump into the same person twice. And it had been a lark, like a romantic destination for lovers. That's why he'd gone, because it hadn't *fit* him.

Stupid idea, that. He'd been following an instinct all along. He'd been too preoccupied with other mortal females to notice his muse right under his nose.

"Do you want to come up for a bit?" Sophia's perfect bow lips parted slightly to reveal a fine tease of white teeth.

"I—" Shouldn't.

He did not want to father a vicious, blood-hungry nephilim child that would wreak chaos across the mortal land. Not to mention kill its own mother after the birth.

Man, get a hold of yourself. You're stronger than that, yes?

"For a bit," he answered, gripping his fists as he succumbed to instinct rather than good sense.

Lush black lashes dusted the air. The woman had a way of saying "take me" without even moving her lips.

Cooper followed her through the lobby and was relieved when she didn't take the elevator. The enclosed space may be the thing to push him over the precipice. On the other hand, following her sexy, shifting hips up the stairs would tempt even a saint.

What in Beneath was he doing? He should be anywhere but here. Siberia, actually. Why hadn't he chosen the subzero climes? Because once Sophia kissed him he'd lose all resistance and push her against the wall—and shift to half form.

Because she *would* kiss him.

He wanted her to.

She must.

He wanted to taste her. To breathe her into his pores. To walk through her essence and wrap it about his skin.

"I'm here." She shoved a key in the door and opened it inward. Leaning against the door frame, she pursed her red lips in a sexy half smile. Her dark brown eyes gleamed with promises Cooper didn't want to process. "You want to come in?"

"I, ah…" Cooper winced and mined his brain for an excuse to race away from her. Yet while he did so, his hand strayed up her arm and teased the ends of the black bow. "Sophia, I'm not looking for a girlfriend."

She tugged the front of his shirt, pulling him into her living room. "Good. I'm not much for re-lationships. But I do have lovers. Lovers who smell alluring like you."

Damn. She wanted him as much as he should not want her.

Could he explain things to her? Hey, you're my muse, and I am the evil angel who fell from Above thousands of years ago to find and mate with you.

And then you'll get pregnant with my monster nephilim child. It won't go well for you after that.

The truth should make her think him a nutcase, and perhaps she'd try to protect herself by shoving him out the door and calling the police.

Trust was in the eyes of the beholder. It was up to him to strip her of that trust.

"You want to sit down?"

Cooper opened his fingers, ready to make a gesture that would move the muse closer to him.

No. Don't use your powers. You'll scare her.

That's what you want to do. Scare the wits out of her.

Cooper walked across the living room to the window. If she were not going to ask him to leave, he sure as Beneath would not.

"The view from here is amazing," he offered, noting the mansard rooftops across the street glinted with moonlight.

Redirect. Easier than turning and eyeing up all her curves, yes? *Idiot.* He wasn't going to walk out. He was here.

He wanted some muse. In his hands, at his mouth, wrapped around his body.

Her fingers spread over his hip, but inches below the sigil that had to glow right now. If he lifted his shirt she'd see it.

It was as if a butterfly had landed on his biceps. Soft lips placed quick kisses to his cool skin. His muscles tightened. His cock hardened. His glass heart may have even pulsed but he knew that was impossible.

"Sophia, I don't know."

"Ah, you are shy? Shy and so sexy."

To hell with it.

He pulled her to him. The ribbon slipped to her wrist. She pressed her hands to the window behind her, opening herself to him and tilting up her breasts as if to offer them, one for each hand.

"You don't know if you desire me? Is that it?" she asked. "I thought, from the way you looked at me at the café…"

Female breakdown coming on. It was enough to clear Cooper's head. He released her arms and stepped back.

"It's not that, Sophia. I need to…take things slow." He winced. Stupid. She'd think he was an asshole.

Better that way.

No, it's not. Take her!

"Yes, this is a little rushed, I admit." She shrugged her fingers through her hair and sighed. That moment of readjustment worked as if she were coming up for air. "Whew! I don't know what I am doing. This is too quick. I'm so sorry."

"No, I am."

"I barely know you. I just, well, I got a good vibe from you in the café. You're such a nice man, and so handsome. Look at your eyes. I mean, they're like the sky or something. And the way you smell. So…yummy. I don't think you'd do anything to hurt me."

Poor girl. Her instincts were off the map. And everyone knew when one fell off the map there be monsters.

Cooper glanced aside, fixing his gaze to the bookshelf and thinking thoughts of ice water raining over his hardened cock.

"Let's just talk. I said I had a book to show you." She wandered off and he couldn't force himself to turn and walk out of the room.

Leave her.

It was the honorable thing to do.

But she is what you desire.

He knew it was an innate and greater consciousness talking, a consciousness that belonged to the two hundred angels who Fell. A consciousness he did not agree with now, nor had ever agreed with.

Standing here right now, Cooper had gone beyond the simple desire to seek a muse. Hell, he'd never touched that desire. When he'd Fallen it had been for one purpose only. And that purpose was personal to him.

Maybe.

Had he been fooling himself?

"I can't seem to find it," she called from the next room.

Cooper joined her before a fancy mahogany secretary, which spilled over with papers and assorted office ephemera. Her pinned-up hair had loosened a bit during their embrace and the effect absolutely screamed sex as she flashed her big chocolate eyes at him.

"I keep it here. It looks so messy. I'm usually much neater. Oh, here's a page from it. I stick pages in here and there because I've already filled the journal and sometimes inspiration hits me so I scribble on anything I have available."

Cooper fisted his hands behind his hips and smiled genially. He could do this. He wasn't so out of control of his own body he would shift against his will and take the poor thing like an animal.

She handed him a sketch and he made show of looking intently at it. And suddenly, he was interested. What was on the paper moved his cold blood to his gut. Many little drawings. Of nothing in particular. Codes, devices, designs.

Yet he immediately knew what they were.

His shoulder hit the wall, unaware of Sophia's allure for the first time since he'd fallen under the spell of her sassy red mouth at the café. Sensual smells and sensations fell away. All that mattered was the bold curving lines on the page he held.

Tracing the lines of one symbol, he shook his head. "Did you draw these, Sophia?"

"Yes, I scribble. Have ever since I was a child.

Symbols, like the one on my arm. You had asked
about it, so I wanted to show these to you. I know
what they mean, too."

"You do?" He scooted a few inches away from
her. The front door was in sight. He wasn't going
anywhere. "Tell me."

"They're angel marks." She took the page he
held then handed him two more pages. "That one
is mine."

She pointed to the symbol on the page, a match
to the one he wore on his lower left abdomen. It
matched the sigil on her forearm. It looked like
an elegant long-limbed number seven that butted
heads with its twin. Two number sevens head to
head.

Each angel wore a sigil unique to the angelic
dominions. And for each Fallen there was a muse
who matched that sigil. But humans had not this
knowledge.

"Why do you call them angel marks?"

"Because they are. I just know. Sounds odd,
doesn't it?"

Like Eden Campbell had known exactly how
to paint him? Did mortal muses possess such
knowledge?

He stroked her forearm over the sigil. Her skin
was warm and smooth. Her blood pulsed against
his fingers. He could read her thoughts regarding

the marks, but he was too distracted to think that would do any good right now.

"I've been marked by one." She shrugged and gave a little giggle, and caught a strand of her hair and teased it across her lower lip. "Call it a silly childhood thing. But I still find myself drawing them when I'm chatting on the phone or bored. I wish I could find the journal with all of them in it."

"You have more?"

"A whole journal full. I counted one day. Almost two hundred designs. Ah! I almost forgot about the *Mona Lisa*." She skipped over to the coffee table.

He grabbed the other paper from the messy secretary desk. "Don't you understand what you know, Sophia?"

Startled at his outburst, Sophia let the big coffee table book on the Louvre slide from her grasp and land on the sofa.

Cooper crushed the papers in a fist and she silently protested, reaching out to grab her artwork, but he slapped away her hand.

"You're too perfect," he growled. That his voice had lowered and rasped didn't alert him.

He'd gone beyond control. His Fallen super-conscious had taken a step up and now it would not be ignored.

"I was a fool to think I could follow you up here and not take what is mine," he hissed.

"I don't understand. Your eyes…they've changed color. You should leave now. We probably are pushing things a little too—"

"Not fast enough for me."

He slammed Sophia against the wall and licked his tongue up the elegant column of her neck. She struggled but did not cry out.

"An angelkiss for you," he whispered in her ear. She truly did taste as delicious as she smelled. "I'll always know where you are now. Doesn't matter, we're going to get busy now."

"I don't… Please, you're too rough. Cooper!"

He ripped open the front of her blouse. A black lace bra cradled her generous breasts. So ripe for him. A lash of his tongue stirred a frightened moan from her.

"You must go!"

"Not—" he pressed a forearm across her chest to hold her against the wall, and ran his free hand down to slip under her skirt "—until I've had this."

Why had he walked the waitress home? Pyx thought he was into *her*. Was the angel two-timing her? Why did she care?

She didn't.

She did.

The bitch had to answer to her if she thought to steal her boyfriend.

Well, he was a male, and a weird sort of friend. The label boyfriend worked for her.

Pyx rushed up the stairs in the apartment building. She didn't know where the waitress lived, but she sensed the Fallen was close. By the third floor she heard the female scream.

Pyx kicked down the door. Inside, the angel, half-shifted, and his stained-glass wings tearing through the Sheetrock, held the muse pinned to the wall.

Chapter 16

The shift melted away her human costume. Beneath that, muscle liquefied and stretched. Bone grew to adamant black metal forged from Beneath. The Sinistari demon grew two feet taller than her mortal form, arms bulging with muscle and powerful thighs thickening. Skin was replaced with an armor of black metal. Horns curved down the center of the skull and back of the neck.

Hooves dug into the wood floorboards as it charged, the angel-killing Joe held ready to stab.

The muse, pinned to the wall by the angel, screamed madly.

The Fallen spied the Sinistari and howled, high-pitched and not of this earth, but did not release his prey.

Pyxion leaped over the sofa, a hoof biting through the green velvet and taking out a chunk. A backhanded smack flung the glass table aside. The demon growled, revealing square teeth designed for doing damage.

The Fallen ignored the nuisance, ripping open the fly on the mortal jeans it wore, for it was only half-shifted from hips up—it was the only way the normally sexless angel could mate with a human.

The muse's manic scream suddenly faltered. Her cries ceased. She fainted, wilting against the Fallen's blue glass chest.

The angel couldn't support the muse and tear down his jeans at the same time. He was also aware its shifted flesh would quickly freeze the mortal's skin. He dropped the muse and stepped back. Glass wings scraped the walls and tore gouges through the living-room wall.

Suddenly the Fallen jerked his head up. Glowing blue eyes sought the Sinistari.

Jaw tight, the Fallen struggled. "Pyx." The angel's voice was deep and metallic. "Do it!"

The angel spread out his arms, opening his chest and giving the demon a clear target for the red heart that glimmered behind the solid yet flexible, glass chest.

Lifting her arms overhead and gripping Joe with both fists, Pyxion charged toward the Fallen.

Toward an angel who had turned his back on his master by falling.

Toward the Sinistari's only enemy.

Toward the one being in this world who had opened her steel heart to the marvel of humanity.

The blade screamed through the air, yet Pyx's muscles tightened. As the blade tip touched glass her movement stopped.

The angel lunged, pushing the blade tip into the liquid blue skin. The tip was soaked in qeres, the poison that promised the first sweet breath of the afterlife when it penetrated the angel's heart.

The demon twisted a muscled black fist, withdrawing the blade and—Pyx threw the blade aside, landing it point-first in the wall near the door.

The muse, now conscious, slid away from the pair, her palms guiding her along the wall. Eyes wide and mascara running down her cheeks, she squeaked nervously.

"Get out of here," the angel bellowed at her. "Save yourself!"

The muse scrambled out on all fours, stood, and ran down the stairs.

Pyx stepped away from the angel.

"Do it!" the Fallen growled. "Kill me!"

"No." She turned from him, bowing her head.

Slapping a metallic hand against her chest clanged loudly. So hard on the outside, yet inside, something had changed. She had become…soft.

Pyx shifted to human shape. Her arms tugged and the heavy metal skeletal structure gave way to weak mortal flesh. Garnet hair spilled down her bare back. She turned and rushed down the hallway, not wanting to show her weakness to the powerful half-formed angel who seethed at her.

Slamming the muse's bedroom door behind her, Pyx plunged to the thick white rug spread at the end of the bed. Gripping the long, soft fibers and bending over her knees, she let out a keening wail.

Cooper shifted to mortal form. It was like shaking off ice adhered to his mortal skin, accompanied by a cutting sting as the ineffable glass cracked off his arms and vaporized. His shoulders hung heavily. The sigil on his abdomen ceased to glow. He bowed his head and closed his eyes.

The muse had fled.

Never had he witnessed such utter terror in a human being. Sophia's eyes had mirrored a creature—*him*. It sickened him he had been responsible for her fear. He was a soulless monster who could not control his own base lust.

Yet in the moment he'd worn wings granted by Him, his perception of the world had altered. Juphiel had taken control. All he'd wanted was to fulfill the original mission the Fallen had agreed to. The desire had been instinctual. No part of the man he had become since landing on earth this second time had been able to wrestle the unfeeling and mechanistic angel he was from the task.

More surprising? Even when he'd pleaded, the Sinistari had not slain him. Because the demon was Pyx and she had gotten to know him, Cooper, the man. And she hadn't been able to bring herself to kill him. What a pitiful demon.

"What a pitiful Fallen one you are."

Shaking his head, he let his eyes roam the walls where his wings had cut gashes and left behind disaster. Sophia would return and never be able to rationalize what had occurred. He could never face her again.

He must never face her again.

He'd get himself as far from Paris as possible. Until he found his halo, he was a danger to one vulnerable and kind mortal woman. She hadn't asked for this. She didn't deserve to be treated like a brood mare for the Fallen's vicious and twisted desires.

He would flash right now—

Sniffles from somewhere down the hallway distracted Cooper from his intent. Who was here? Had the muse…? No, she'd run out.

Pyx.

He padded down the hardwood floor. When he'd shifted, his shirt had shredded and fallen away. His jeans had begun to tear at the waist, but they were still intact. No shoes though. Why did the shoes get kicked off when shifting? His feet didn't change shape.

It was an anomaly that puzzled Cooper to no end.

If Pyx were still around she would be naked, for her shift to demon had ripped away all her clothing. The Sinistari was a hulking, muscular beast forged from metal. An even match to an angel. Perhaps a greater match to a Fallen, for the angel was grounded, unable to use his wings to fly away from a threat.

They were more alike than she could ever imagine.

Pushing the ajar bedroom door inside, Cooper spied the naked woman bent over and huddled upon a white rug. Her head was tucked against her knees and soft sniffles trickled tears down her leg.

"Pyx?"

"Go away!"

The vehemence in her tone cautioned his need to rush in and hug her.

Cooper clung to the door frame, his grip gouging the soft pine wood. He wasn't about to leave her. Mortal tears were supposed to burn the Sinistari. Cooper didn't know how that felt, but right now, each tear that plopped onto Pyx's leg felt like a demon's blade stabbing him in the heart.

Her blade had cut his flesh, and when he'd wanted to jam it deep into his heart and give her the win—and her mortal soul—she had pulled it out.

"Why didn't you do it?" he asked. "You had a clear shot at me. You could have claimed your mortal soul. It is all you want. So you can belong."

He wanted that for her, more than he wanted humanity.

She pressed onto her palms. Long hair concealed the side of her face closest to Cooper, so he couldn't see her expression. It also veiled her bare breasts.

"I couldn't do it. I cannot conceive of killing you. Some Sinistari I turned out to be! No wonder they snickered at me behind my back when I was Beneath. I'm just a stupid girl. A stupid. Feeling. Girl!"

Allowing himself a smile at her ridiculous argument, Cooper scanned the room and spied a red blanket folded over a wicker chaise. He summoned it to his grasp with a gesture and laid it across Pyx's shoulders, then knelt beside her on the thick rug. Tucking her hair behind her ear, he stroked his thumb along the tear trail painting her reddened cheek.

She rubbed her cheek with a fist. "Don't look at me. I'm a failure."

"You? Please. I'm the failure. I couldn't do what

my destiny demands of me. I should have shoved you aside and attempted my muse. But…"

He'd wanted it over within that moment. To have the situation resolved—either by his death or by taking the muse. But that he'd survived only meant he must face this dilemma.

He'd never wanted what his Fallen brethren wanted.

"Fine couple of murderous bastards we turned out to be, eh?"

She chuckled through her tears and a few final drops splattered her lashes.

"I didn't want to harm her, Pyx."

"I know that."

"It tears me up inside that I scared her. I was so close. You should have plunged Joe into my heart."

"I couldn't stab you because…" She tossed her head to the side. Bright multicolored eyes fixed to his and touched him. "I like you, Cooper. I'm pretty sure about that, even though I'm still learning things every day and I'm not completely up on all the emotions."

"Like is good."

"Yeah, well, it's not the strongest way to describe how I feel. I can't do the other…you know…"

"The other?"

She winced and scratched her head, avoiding his searching gaze.

Did she mean love? Could Pyx's like be love? The idea of it warmed Cooper's chest and he thought he felt a flutter deep inside. But that was ridiculous. Angel hearts did not beat.

Nor did demon hearts beat. Love was the one crime that would see a Sinistari punished with endless torture. It wouldn't be wise for Pyx to even *think* she felt it.

"Oh, sure. I understand," he reassured. "I like *like*. It's a good word. Not overbearing. But not weak, either. I like you, too."

"Really? I've never been in like before," she said, perking up. "But I think this might be what it's all about. This whole human experience."

"It's said that's why He put them here on earth. To learn to lo—er, like one another. To simply embrace like and all its goodness."

She lunged up on her knees, bracketed his face, and kissed him. "Yes. Goodness. Like. All that it embraces. Like you and me. Hold me, Cooper. Show me how much you like me."

"Pyx, we could do this."

"What?"

"Us. Do you want to?"

"Us?"

"I know you're scared. I am, too."

"I think so, but I can't—"

He kissed her to silence her protest.

"Let's not talk about this here," Cooper said.

"Sophia will be back. Or certainly she's called the police."

"Right. Poor woman. She's going to be freaked."

"Don't remind me. I may have damaged her for life. Damn it, I hate that I could not control myself. I never chose to Fall for the muse. You know that, right?"

She nodded. "You fell in lo—er, *like* with humanity. Stupid angel." She thunked him on the forehead with a snap of her finger.

Cooper took her fingers and kissed them. "Maybe so. So why am I like my other Fallen brethren? Why couldn't I stop myself from attacking the muse? Part of me knew it was wrong."

"Just like my need to slay you. I know it is what is expected of me."

"You need to prove yourself."

"Do I? There's a part of me that screams how wrong it is."

"But you have always loved humanity, Pyx."

"No, I haven't."

Cooper sighed. Yes, she had. Dare he tell her? How would that upset the balance that must exist— Sinistari stalking Fallen?

He looked aside. He didn't want Pyx to see his eyes, because she might see the truth he wanted to keep to himself.

He scooped her up and set her on the bed. Hastening to Sophia's closet he sorted through the clothes on hangers, his finger playing over velvet, silk and soft sweaters, and pulled out a black knit dress. He tossed it to Pyx. "Will that do?"

"Yep." She pulled it over her head and down her thighs. It was obviously too small, for it fit snugly. Everywhere. "Let's get out of here before we're arrested. Hell, you could be arrested for the way you're looking at me right now."

"I'd gladly serve the time. We've only begun, Pyx. I'm not letting you out of my arms until we've made love."

"Can we not use that word?"

"Oh? Right. We can make, er...like?"

"That sounds stupid."

He shrugged.

"Let's go have sex."

"I'm on board with that."

The muse hit the street in tears. She staggered along the side of the glass-tiled building, one hand sliding along the wall. Bruce, who had been standing across the street, eyes on the window of the muse's apartment, dropped the cell phone he'd been dialing to Antonio in the front seat and crossed the street, keeping far enough behind the muse.

Her frantic state kept her from noticing him. Had the angel screwed her? Nah, couldn't have. She was wearing the same clothes she'd worn when she'd invited the angel up, and it had only been about fifteen minutes.

That damned Sinistari must have stopped the Fallen. Bruce had seen her run inside the building, but hadn't wanted to race after her, knowing he'd have to face both a Fallen and a demon, and that wouldn't end well for him.

Why hadn't Antonio formed a full-assault tactical team? They needed one if they were to deal with both angels and demons. There had to be an easier way to get this job done. All tribe Anakim ultimately needed was the muse, pregnant.

So had the demon killed the angel?

"Hope not."

But it was likely. Why *wouldn't* the demon slay her prey?

This was Antonio's fault for not putting more men on the job, but it would also look bad for Bruce, who should have had the whole thing under control. So there was only one other option to save face with the boss man.

Picking up his pace, Bruce snuck closer to the sniffling muse. She stopped behind the apartment building, clinging to the wall. She had to be freaked if she'd witnessed either beast shift shapes.

He approached cautiously, knowing as well, she probably didn't need a stranger sneaking up on her right now.

Picking up pace to a normal walk, Bruce made

as if he was walking down the street. He passed her by, hands in his pockets, ready to cross the street, when he paused and look back at her.

He put on his most compassionate expression, and added his charming smile just for good measure. "Mademoiselle? Are...you all right? Can I get someone for you?"

She turned away from him, crying, her cheek pressed to the tiles.

"Oh, hey there. You need the police?" He stepped closer but didn't touch her. She shook her head in a manner he couldn't tell was yes or no. "Some asshole say something mean to you? I don't want to frighten you, but I can't let you stand here all sad like that. Is it okay if I stand with you a bit?"

She nodded it was okay. He was in.

"Fight with the boyfriend?"

She swiped the back of her hand under one eye, effectively wiping the smear of mascara away, but a black trail slid down the other cheek.

Bruce made to wipe it away, but paused, waiting for her approval. She nodded, and he gently touched her cheek. Man, she smelled great. Fear lingered in her blood, giving it a salty yet savory aroma. He loved fear-laced blood.

But a smart vampire would keep his fangs up. Even if the Fallen had been wasted by the demon, this muse was still prime. She could lure any number of Fallen to her; all Antonio had to do was conjure another one.

"Merci," she said in a tiny voice. "I just… It was so terrible. I couldn't believe it."

"Tell me. I'll call for help if you need me to."

"Yes. The police. They might still be in my apartment."

"I have a cell phone in my car. It's across the street. Come on."

Like a good little girl, she allowed him to lead her across the street. She even sat in the passenger seat when he offered, tucking her legs in before her and smoothing her torn skirt.

Bruce closed the door behind her, and marveled how easy that had been.

"One muse, coming right up."

Chapter 17

Pyx held Cooper's hand as they flashed to the door outside her third-floor apartment. Someone's apartment. It was hers for now.

Seeing him again in all his angelic glory had once again impressed the heck out of her. Whatever *heck* was.

A demon should not be impressed by an angel. But she was.

So there it was, all out there and ugly and, well—sue her. Good luck getting the money. This demon was walking her own walk, and if that meant walking hand in hand with a Fallen one, then so be it.

But he was wrong about loving humanity. That *L*-word didn't exist for her. She could endure humanity. She could subsist within humanity. But she'd never lo—

"Can I come inside?" Cooper whispered against her ear.

His hands roamed the curve of her hips. The heat of his breath stirred up her sigh. Pyx tossed aside all extraneous thoughts about how things were not as they should be, and she didn't really care what heck meant.

She walked inside and aimed straight for the bedroom. She was going to have sex with an angel tonight. She was going to have sex for the first time.

There would be no love involved, only want, desire, need and passion. It was about time this demon mastered the sin of lust.

There was one small problem.

Pyx turned abruptly, stopping Cooper with her body.

"I haven't done this before," she said. The confession felt blatant, but at the same time she trusted he would not laugh or think less of her.

Strong arms wrapped about her and he kissed her once. Perfect collision of want. Two opposites snapping together with a magnetic click. Another kiss melted them like summer reeds under the hot sun. The urgency of their mouths connecting was too sweet. But she enjoyed it. Wanted more.

Instinct demanded a surrender to something that felt so wrong.

You can make a choice.

It was all about choice. Her choice.

"You're sure you want your first time to be with me? After…" He bowed his head, pressing his forehead to hers. She could feel his tension radiate in the air between them.

After.

After what she'd seen tonight: Cooper going after his muse and nearly attempting her. After all she knew about him: he could not control his compulsion to mate when around the muse. And also knowing they could never be anything but enemies: the universe had decreed it so.

Sure? Never.

But hopeful and desirous? "Yes, I want to do this, Cooper. With you. You're the only one who understands me."

"Then I need to let you in on something. Since I've arrived on earth?"

She nodded, expectant.

"I haven't been able to get past kissing women. The sensory experience wraps me up and carries me away. I haven't gone further than second base."

"So you mean…?"

"Well." He shrugged his shoulders, straightening. "I'm not a virgin. I've had my share of women back in the day."

"Biblical times?"

He winked. "About then."

"So what you're trying to say is, it's been a long time for you."

"It has. And I couldn't imagine a better first-time partner than you, Pyx. You are a unique and incredible female. And as you said, we understand one another."

"But not the same understanding we had before, right? About us using each other."

"Never."

Whew.

"I promise this is not a ruse to get you on my side, Pyx. Whatever you ultimately decide to do—if things should come to, well, you know—is your choice, and I won't influence that choice one way or another."

"What if it is just a need because you couldn't get it on with the muse? Am I your rebound girl?"

Cooper laughed. "Be quiet, Pyx, or you'll talk yourself out of my arms."

He let down the strap of the dress she had borrowed from the muse. Cooper trailed his fingers along the neckline, lowering the fabric inch by inch to expose her breasts. Anticipation of where he'd place his touch made her bite her lower lip.

The skim of his thumbs across her flesh tickled

up goose bumps, and Pyx smiled and then laughed because the reaction was so…mortal.

"That tickle?" he asked, his eyes holding hers. "I can be more gentle."

"No, I like it." She moved his hand lower. His palm cupped her breast. "It feels great. But promise you won't get lost in this sensory experience and not move on to the rest?"

"Promise."

With a deft move from Cooper's hands, the dress slipped over Pyx's hips and landed at her feet with a *cush*. The angel purred in a deep lion's tone that said he was pleased with what she revealed to him.

Vanity infused Pyx's being and she stretched back her shoulders. The move lifted her breasts, and Cooper was right there with his tongue to greet them. This was better than any kind of food. This was lust at its finest.

Greed took over for vanity, and Pyx caressed Cooper's head, running her fingers through his hair, keeping him at her breasts where his ministrations sent erotic vibrations humming up and down her limbs and focused at her groin.

"This is going to be good," she whispered. "I can feel it."

He chuckled and she tripped her fingers over his hard, muscular shoulders. They felt like the steel that designed her bones. So strong and powerful.

The woman she had become sighed and squeezed his muscles when he playfully nipped at her.

"Sit down," he murmured in a breathy voice. "I want to give you all the good you desire."

He bent before her and she sat on the bed. He kissed her bare knee. She made a little noise of satisfaction. A flick of his tongue tickled the soft flesh behind her knee. It was so sensitive there, Pyx felt her belly twist in the best way.

Cooper glided his thumb up higher, along the satiny skin inside her thigh. The journey was slow, traced with his tongue and patient kisses.

"Yes, there." She guided his hand higher and put her foot up on his shoulder. Anticipation gasped from her throat. "Please."

He tickled his fingertips within her nest of curls, planting kisses in his wake. She slid her leg over his shoulder, inviting him to do as he pleased. One hand she threaded through his hair, loosely, no direction, just making contact.

He thumbed the apex of her folds, using her wetness to slicken his moves. Just the perfect rhythm and pressure, right—there.

Pyx whimpered. She clung to his hair and clutched his neck. The scent of his desire undid her in ways she could not comprehend, but accepted with open arms. Cedar and musk, perfectly man.

He kissed her inner thigh without stopping. Steady pace, focused only on her pleasure. Drawing his tongue up and pushing her skirt high, he replaced his finger with his firm tongue. Two strokes across her sensitive peak and she released, crying out softly, her body melting into the bedsheets.

"That was amazing," she announced.

"You're telling me."

"I can't believe I'm going to say this, but…I have to."

"What?" He looked up from between her legs, his chin nuzzling lightly upon her thigh.

"I'm so glad I'm a girl. Because if I wasn't then you wouldn't have been able to do that to me right now."

"Hallelujah. She's a girl! But we're just getting started, sweetie."

"Mmm…" She turned on the bed, pressing her cheek against the pillow. With her foot, she coaxed Cooper onto the bed beside her. Using his masterful tongue, he traced along her thigh and around behind her back, directing her to lie on her stomach.

He dashed heart-fluttering kisses down her spine. "Let me take a close look at your tat," he said. "Hmm… A skeletal angel. On fire. I should be offended."

"But you don't look like that angel," she said.

"I can be thankful for that."

"What about your body art?" She playfully pushed him into the pillows and kissed her way across his abs to find his sigil. It was an interesting design that mirrored itself with long, sweeping curves. The color was reddish brown. "Does it glow when you're around her?"

"It does." He tilted up Pyx's chin. "More kisses," he encouraged. "No talking about other women."

"I can dig it." She unbuttoned his pants. "Now to the dangly bits."

"They're not dangling now, sweetie."

"I need to take a look at what I didn't get when I arrived."

"Thought you were happy to be a woman?"

"Ecstatic." She revealed his hard shaft and gripped it firmly. "This is a nice handful."

"Oh, sweetie…"

"Do you like that? When I squeeze like this?"

He hissed through his teeth and could only nod his head, so Pyx continued to stroke him slowly, bringing her cupped hand up over the thick head and then down to the base.

"Mortals are supposed to get married before they do stuff like this," Pyx whispered, fascinated at the small bobs and movements his penis made at her direction. "Marriage seems so foreign to me."

"Demons don't marry…" He gasped and the muscles of his abdomen tightened.

"Angels?" she finished for him. "You want me to stop?"

"Oh, no. Faster," he managed to say.

It seemed his ability to talk slipped away as she

quickened her movements, so Pyx decided to concentrate and watch his reactions. It was amazing how she could control him with one hand. One hand! Go, demon!

"Go, me," she whispered, and bent to kiss him at the base of his erection.

"Oh, yeeeessss." He came, flooding over her fist in a marvelous display. Cooper slapped his hands to the bed and cried out an exhilarating shout.

Pyx slid up alongside him and watched as he rode the climax just as she had done moments earlier. His face was flushed and he gritted his teeth. And then he relaxed, sighed and sank into the pillow.

"That was impossible," he muttered, huffing breathlessly.

"No it wasn't. I just did it. Not so hard. Well, I mean, it was hard." She glanced south. "But not so much anymore."

"I mean…" He chuckled, still breathless, and slipped a hand into hers to bring it to his mouth for a kiss. "What you just did to me? That isn't supposed to happen unless I'm with my muse."

"Oh." Right. The angel only received pleasure from his muse. "What in Beneath?"

"I have no idea why that happened, but I'm not going to question it. Come here." He pulled her in to hug against his warm and heaving chest. "We'll think in the morning. Now is not for thinking, or discussion. We're going to speak with sighs and fingers for the rest of the night, okay?"

"Works for me."

Chapter 18

The old man led him to what Stellan decided was a form of domicile beneath the city of Paris in the 16th arrondissement. He'd jumped down a manhole and followed his guide about two hundred yards through a snaking sewer tunnel. Limestone and crumbling cement formed the seeping walls. Dirt and the occasional slab of stone, beaten down from centuries of footsteps, formed a path. It stank down here like a rotting animal corpse covered in maggots. Stellan knew the smell distinctly.

"Here it is." The clank of a fingernail against metal lured Stellan from his deliciously morbid thoughts. "Just like I told you."

The vampire leaned in and inspected the object

embedded in the rough-shod tunnel ceiling a foot above his head. The headlight helmet the old man wore beamed sharply upon the curve of what looked like dirty tin.

"Indeed, it is as you told me," Stellan said. "But it's not glowing."

"Every so often it glows blue. No specific time or length. Just flashes. You want it or not?"

Stellan reached into his jacket pocket and pulled out a few euro notes. "Will you take twenty-five euros for it?"

"Well, now, that's not a lot of money."

"Make it fifty then." Stellen handed over half the money.

The old man swiped the bills from his hand— all of them. "Hundred's fine. But you'll never get it loosened from the stone. It's stuck in there tight. Even tried to chip it out with my lucky horse-shoe."

"I can see that."

Stellan examined the chipped limestone hugging the two places where the halo fit halfway into the wall. Had to have been down here since the original Fall to fit in so tightly. But he'd found others in tighter situations.

He gripped the halo and worked it back and forth.

"You'll bend it!" the old man yelped.

"Shut up. These things don't break. Go spend your money before you die, old man."

In proof, the limestone began to crumble and bits of it exploded onto Stellan's leather coat. He pulled out the halo and held it high, as if that might make it glow. Didn't work. Didn't matter. The old man couldn't have possibly lied about something so unique as the halo glowing.

Stellan hooked the thing about a wrist and stomped away from the stench toward the surface. He detected the old man had turned a corner behind him, and decided it had been a few hours since he'd last fed. And really, snatching the whole hundred after Stellan had offered fifty was rude.

He turned and smiled to reveal fangs at the startled geriatric.

"Michael Donovan was here earlier."

Pyx sat nestled in the pillows, her garnet hair spilling across Cooper's shoulder like a bright winter scarf. They hadn't slept. They'd passed through the night making love and sharing quiet talk about things like mortality and companionship, and the possibility of sharing those two things together.

Cooper sat up in bed and stretched his back from side to side. His muscles were lax and every bit of him felt terrifically spent. The woman may have been a virgin yesterday, but she'd made up for lost time. Whew!

"Donovan. The halo hunter? What'd he want?" he asked over his shoulder. "Did his girlfriend go after the vamps? He said he was going to sic her on them, or something like that."

"He had some halos to show you. To prove he would stand good on his word to help you. I suspect he wants to keep tabs on you."

"Who doesn't?" He scrambled off the bed and grabbed his jeans. The waistband was torn, rendering them unwearable. "Where is he?"

Cooper stood and with a thought, assimilated the kilt, a crisp white shirt and combat boots laced neatly.

"At the Regina in the second quarter." Pyx leaned forward and toyed a finger along the hem of his kilt. "I do like this look on you. You've sexy legs."

"So the demon finally indulged in lust." He leaned in and kissed the top of her breast. "Hold that thought. I'll be back soon."

"You going to leave me, just like that?"

"He's got halos, Pyx."

"I just thought…" She spread an arm across the sheets where he'd lain.

Don't do that. That'll make me want to crawl back in bed with you to inhale your bubble-gum perfume.

Pyx sighed. "Don't mortals snuggle or something like that after they've had sex?"

Part of Cooper wanted nothing more than to snuggle up to Pyx and repeat everything they'd done last night. And then repeat it again.

But if Donovan had his halo and was willing to give it to him? Pyx could never understand. And she probably didn't want it to happen. If Cooper got his soul that meant she was tough out of luck to kill him and claim her soul.

Cooper wanted his lush, gorgeous demon who came wildly and let out her joy at the top of her lungs to have whatever it was she desired. Another part of him didn't want to sacrifice his happiness when he knew she had the opportunity to find another Fallen, while he did not have the opportunity to live again if she killed him.

"I have to go see them," he said. He knelt on the bed and kissed the curve of her spine there, where it was so sweet, just below the fiery wing of the tattooed angel. "Mortals do snuggle. But we're not mortal yet."

"I know. Snuggling would be too much like a commitment."

"Er, right. Wouldn't want to do anything so dangerous as commit." Especially after they'd discussed that very thing last night. Must have been the endorphins.

"You got that one right. Let me get dressed. I'll go along with you."

"To keep an eye on me?"

"You know it." She retrieved the muse's black dress from the floor and tugged it over her head. The hem stopped just low enough to cover the treats she'd offered him last night, and Cooper wanted to tug the skirt lower so no man would even think about what he was thinking. "And because I'm not sure I can function for any amount of time now with you away from me."

"Hey now, sweetie, don't fall in love with me. You know that's a no-no for the Sinistari."

She scoffed, but it came off as lackluster. Did the demon question herself? "I don't know what that word means."

"What word? Love? Say it. Come on, I dare you," he teased.

"No."

"Because you don't want to?"

"Because I don't want to bring Raphael's wrath upon me for succumbing to the one Sinistari sin."

Raphael was the archangel who commanded the Sinistari ranks. Yep, an angel led the demons. Didn't she question that? Was now a good time to tell her his suspicions about her origins? It could either bring them together or force them to opposite poles.

"I'm having a good time, is all," she said. "Aren't you?"

Right. Just a good time. Nothing intense or even resembling commitment.

"Having sex with the woman who intends to slay me? That's about as good as it gets."

And he meant it. This was one seriously screwed-up relationship. But he'd take it. Because she spoke to him on a level no mortal could ever understand.

And most important, it kept his mind from other women—specifically, his muse.

Damn, he'd come close to harming her yesterday. He could not have guessed how strong the compulsion would actually be. He'd not been able to stop himself from attempting Sophia.

His plans for leaving the city stood, but if a halo was in the vicinity, he wasn't going to flash away from it until he held it in his hand.

Pyx could find another Fallen.

"Let's head over to the hotel. I'll buy you something to eat on the way."

"Crepes with bananas and chocolate," she said.

He kissed her on the head, then bent to lick her neck. She squealed, but didn't move away. Instead, she sat on her knees and pulled his head down to pay both her breasts due attention.

They left for the hotel three hours later.

Striding down the hallway in the ultra-lux hotel put up Pyx's hackles. Fancy paper lined the walls. Gold frames caressed centuries-old paintings. Crystal chandeliers tinkled overhead. This fancy lifestyle wasn't her. Much as she'd take the human soul, she figured if human, she'd live on a farm somewhere chasing goats and eating fresh eggs for breakfast.

But winning a soul meant only one thing, and she was conflicted now regarding that ending after having made love to Cooper. Make that having sex. The *L*-word had not been involved. No way.

"Did he tell you what room number?" Cooper said over his shoulder. "Wait. He's close." The Fallen put out his hands, palms flat, as if reading the air. "Two doors down."

"How'd you do that? I thought I was the only one capable of reading paranormal vibrations, and the halo hunter is mortal."

"I think I'm sensing the halos." He grinned widely, a little boy nearing the end of his quest for the buried treasure. "Come on."

He held out his hand for her to take. Kind of old-fashioned, like boys and girls often did decades ago. Pyx slapped her hand into his.

But she wasn't sure how she felt about Cooper finding his halo.

The idea of him claiming his soul sat well with her. He deserved it. The angel fit humanity well.

But then that ruled out *her* getting a soul. Unless she could find another Fallen and slay it. It wasn't as though the Fallen were walking the world in numbers. As far as she knew a Sinistari was only summoned when a Fallen walked the earth. And she knew for a fact her brethren were not out in population in the world. Again, vibrations.

Cooper knocked, then drew up Pyx's hand and kissed the back of it. He winked at her. She guessed he was excited for what Michael Donovan may have, but wished it were because he was with her and was thinking about what they'd shared last night.

So this was emotion, she thought, focusing on the weird stir in her belly. It was complicated, but not so bad. She preferred it by far to memory of Beneath. And it could only increase after she'd claimed her soul—from this interesting, kind and sexy man.

A petite woman with bright green eyes to match her shirt and an even brighter smile answered the door. "You must be the angel and the demon," she said. "Come in, Michael's in the shower."

Cooper paced the elaborate room. Two twin beds had been pushed together, the sheets and comforter spilling onto the floor in evidence of good use. Marble-topped vanity, a writing desk and a television table were placed amongst the damask fabrics on the wall, windows and even the floor.

Pyx hung by the door, eyeing up the vampiress while Cooper tugged aside a curtain to look outside. The Tuileries gardens were in view and the bright evening settled a heavy golden glow across the emerald foliage.

"So you're Michael's girlfriend?" Pyx finally asked.

"Vinny." She offered her hand, and Pyx shook it. She sensed the shimmer, innate to vampires. The weird electrical tingle startled her and she pulled free.

Not going to trust this chick. Not after what she'd seen the vampires do to Cooper with their injection gun.

Vinny bowed her head. "You are a powerful demon to have recognized me. I am at your disposal. Whatever I can do for you, I will."

The deference was nice. The Sinistari were the most respected amongst the demon realm, simply because they were so powerful and fearless. They were angel killers. Nothing could kill an angel, save the Sinistari.

"Where are they?" Cooper asked, clapping his hands together in expectation.

Vinny pointed to the messenger bag on the striped Louis XIV chair and Cooper opened the flap top. He didn't reach in, but clasped his hands expectantly.

Michael strode out of the bathroom wearing jeans and no shirt. His short, dark hair and shoulders glistened with water droplets. "Cooper.

Pyx. I see you found what you're looking for. Did introductions get made?" he asked Vinny.

The vampiress nodded and stepped behind him. Interesting, Pyx thought, the vampire being submissive to the mortal. But what had been normal since she'd arrived on earth? No one was playing to character.

Most especially, the Sinistari demon and her prey.

"Will you take them out so I can look at them?" Cooper asked Michael.

The halo hunter did so, laying five halos on the marble writing desk. Cooper, arms crossed high on his chest, winced as each was laid out. The halos were each about a foot in diameter, the outer circle two inches wide and fashioned from what resembled unpolished tin. They clattered as they were laid on the marble.

Pyx had no idea if the Fallen could sense his own halo, or if he were so eager he didn't know where to begin.

She dug her fingers into her palms and sucked in the corner of her lip. If she had a heartbeat, it would be thundering right now.

Cooper glanced to her. In his eyes lived worry. Or maybe it was a question. A request. *Is this all right with you?*

The look set her back, and Pyx looked aside, out the window. Of course it wasn't all right. But it was his choice to make. And that he'd silently conveyed that question to her meant so much.

She would never tell him what to do. She respected him as much as she expected others from the paranormal nations to respect her.

Without touching them, the angel looked over the five disks before him. Nothing fancy, that was for sure. How they could be wielded as a weapon was beyond Pyx.

"Go ahead," Michael offered, "pick them up, look them over."

"Not necessary," Cooper said. "None are mine."

"But how do you know?" Pyx argued. She approached the table, ready to grab a halo and stick it on top of his head.

"I just know!"

Affronted by his angry response, Pyx felt a cold shiver move from her breast to her belly. The demon did not care to be admonished. "You didn't even touch them."

"I don't have to. I…can't. They're not mine. Put them away," he said to the halo hunter. "Thank you for showing me them."

"I'm sorry," Michael said as Vinny dutifully tucked the halos in the bag. "I have more, but not with me. The vampires have quite a few. Vinny was able to find out."

"How did you get inside their lair?" Cooper asked the vampire. "Did you just stroll in?"

"I've a contact on the inside," Vinny said.

"I don't like the sound of that. Whoever it is, he could be playing you."

"We've taken precautions," Michael said dismissively. "Now, what is the plan? I know the two of you have your own issues to deal with, and that concerns me."

"I wasn't aware we were working together yet," Cooper challenged Michael. "My quest for a halo has nothing to do with you wanting to stake a bunch of vampires."

"And yet the vampires are the key to everything." Michael eyed Pyx. "I'm surprised they haven't gone after the Sinistari. She's the biggest obstacle to their gaining a nephilim."

"They've tried," Cooper said. "And failed."

"They obviously know what they're up against." Pyx made sure Vinny caught her glare before walking over to the table and pressing a palm over the messenger bag. She didn't sense anything, but then, why should she?

And then…she did.

Pyx withdrew her hand from the bag. It hadn't burned, but she had felt something visceral. Deeper than the light shimmer she'd felt from the vampire, almost *internal*.

Seeing her reaction, Michael scrambled to open the leather bag and shuffle out the halos. They clattered onto the marble surface. "Did you feel something? I saw something."

"It was nothing," Pyx said. How could it be anything?

Both Vinny and Michael gasped when one of the halos glowed blue.

"But that can't be," Michael said. "She's...an angel?"

"What's he talking about?" Pyx looked to Cooper.

The Fallen shook his head and stalked toward the door.

He couldn't face her. He could not.

Cooper marched out of the hotel, aware Pyx followed. She didn't call to him, or try to catch up. She could not be aware of his struggle to fend off anger. And he didn't want her to see him in this mood. It had nothing to do with her—and everything.

The halo hunter should have kept his mouth shut.

Damn it, would it be smeared in his face now? The fact he may never find his soul, and she—a bloody *demon*—may be so close.

He kicked a stone and it zinged the hubcap of a Mercedes. With little thought, he'd probably caused a thousand dollars of damage. Cooper marched onward toward the river. The bustling city did not appeal to him. The rush of traffic gave him little concern as he walked across the street, causing cars to slam on the brakes and honk their horns.

Pyx yelled after him. He ignored her.

Have to get out of this city. Out of this country. Far away from the muse.

Far from the unknown. Would he ever have what he wanted? Did he deserve it?

The river was ahead. He could jump into that horrid muck of centuries past and drown. It would be that easy. Angels could not swim; hell, they could drown in a friggin' bathtub.

Cooper recalled the great flood. It had swept him from his feet and swirled him away from the earth, imprisoning him in darkness for so long. Interminable torture, the lack of all sensation and thought, had been his prison as he'd waited for final judgment.

He would not go back. He'd die before he did so.

The way to achieve that goal was to do the muse, or find his halo.

Only one sat well with his desperate heart.

But the other formed his very nature.

"No excuse," he growled to himself. "You're thinking like you did when you were in the ranks, smiting without second thought. You're not that angel now. I can make a choice."

Gaining the Pont Neuf, he slammed a fist upon the stone railing and huffed out tight, angry breaths as he stared down into the broth-colored water. Boats and barges lined both sides of the river. A tourist barge passed under the bridge and he sneered at a little boy who cheerfully waved up at him.

Then he was overwhelmed by the scent of her. Bubble gum and sex. The world muted and the sigh of her climax revisited his thoughts. Tender. Rushed. Devastating. If they had only the one night together, he intended to cherish that memory as if it were a stolen jewel.

Pyx approached him carefully, stopping five feet from him and propping her elbows on the railing parallel to him. "What's wrong?"

"You don't really care," he said. "It's an affectation you think I require to keep me on your side. We've already agreed we're only in this for ourselves so stop the act. I don't need it."

"All right then. No pussyfooting around. Although, what does that really mean? Pussyfooting?"

He shot her an arched brow, but controlled his desire to smile. Man, she could ease his anger like that.

"I want to know what got stuck in your craw," Pyx said. "It had something to do with the halos. Didn't you see? One of them glowed. It could have been yours."

"It was yours, damn it!"

Pyx stared unseeing at him. Her head shook slightly, not processing.

Cooper pounded the railing so hard, the stone cracked. "You know nothing, do you? You, the powerful Sinistari demon who came to smite me from the earth. You! You are like me. You *are* me. We are the same, Pyx. You are a Godforsaken angel."

Chapter 19

Stellan dropped the halo on the desk before Antonio. It wobbled and landed with a tinny clap. Antonio knew by now the things were indestructible, but he was still startled at the lack of care Stellan took when handling them. The thin disk of unknown-origin metal briefly glowed blue.

Antonio looked to Stellan, who smirked. "Told ya. I'm sure it's the Fallen's halo. I found it within half a mile of where he lives. Underground."

"I've never seen them glow before." Antonio touched the cold disk. "Are you positive that is why it's glowing? Because it senses the original owner?"

"It's only a guess, but I'd stake my life on it."

Antonio grimaced. Stake and life should never be used in the same sentence.

He trusted Stellan though. The man had been his right hand for over a century. Together they'd begun the quest to produce and capture a viable nephilim. The blood of their ancestors was all they needed to become stronger. More powerful. To walk in the light.

But if it had just flashed blue that could only mean the Fallen was nearby. "Have guards been posted at the perimeter entrances?"

"Yes, the Hôtel Solange is secure. We'll nab the angel the moment he sets foot on the grounds."

"Bruce found the muse," Antonio said. "She's resting in the dungeon."

"No shit? Now we've a full house. The halo. The muse. We'll have the Fallen before the sun rises."

"We can hope." Antonio crossed his arms smugly. "But I've another on my list I want contained. Venezia is back in town. Bring her to me."

Michael swept Vinny from her feet and into his arms. They sat on the hotel bed, both quiet since the Fallen and the Sinistari had left.

He nuzzled his face against her shimmery hair. Always she smelled like ginger. She had a spunky bite like ginger, too, and that wasn't even about her real fangs.

He smiled to think how they'd been together

only a few months but already he couldn't imagine living without her. Ever. Not because she sucked his blood every few weeks, which gave him an insane orgasm and made them feel closer than close. He genuinely loved this woman.

She had only bitten him three times, saying she didn't need to take more blood, and showing her worried face. That face said "I'm not sure how much before you die." Neither wanted Michael to become vampire.

It was a weird relationship, for sure.

But an angel and demon together? Even weirder.

Despite all that, Michael prodded at the thoughts troubling his brain. He'd been focused on stopping something he felt could be great evil—tribe Anakim gaining power and walking in the light. Yet what remained in the corner of his eye, and meant so much more, he'd ignored.

Seeing the angel's protective regard for the demon earlier had made Michael tilt his head and view what stood in the corner of his eye—Vinny.

Why hadn't he come to this conclusion before?

"I've been selfish," he whispered aside her cheek.

"You're the most generous man I know." Positioned before him and sitting between his legs, Vinny nestled closer, sliding down so her back rubbed across his crotch. Tilting her head back, she touched his chin with her fingers. "What's going on in that brain of yours, lover?"

"I've been so focused on going after Antonio and his tribe. Determined to bring them to an end so they can't enact their evil reign upon the world by arranging for nephilim births. But all this time I never gave a thought to you. Vinny, I'm so sorry."

"If we keep Antonio from getting what he wants…"

Michael winced because what she couldn't say, he should have taken to heart months ago.

"Then you don't get what you want either. They're your tribe. If they don't get the blood that'll allow them to become daywalkers, you will never be able to walk in sunlight."

She sighed and clasped her arms about his leg. "It's not so bad."

"It's not so good either. I want you to have the sun, Venezia."

He knew she didn't like it when he used her real name, but Vinny had never really appealed to him. Venezia was a bold and brilliant goddess, and a sneaky seductress who had lured him into her world. He didn't regret a moment of that capture.

Silence was her answer. He'd never asked her before if she thought it right they go after tribe Anakim. He'd set off on his righteous quest with his vampire lover in tow. Asshole.

"If Anakim drinks from a nephilim the entire tribe could gain the boon, yes?"

"I think so. I'm not exactly sure how it works."

"Then they need to do it once. Only once," Michael said. "And then we'll kill 'em all."

She wrapped her arms around his chest and hugged him. Another silent answer that he knew agreed with the new plan.

Pyx shoved Cooper's chest so hard he bent backward over the railing and his feet left the ground. The wily angel sneered and jumped to his feet, mocking her with that sexy grin.

"You lie," she said through a tight jaw.

Anger forced another punch into his gut. He bent double, but she suspected it was an act for her benefit. The angel was matched in strength to her, and he had the advantage of a male anatomy, which gave him larger biceps and stronger thigh muscles. More powerful, all around.

"I don't know why you are lying, but you are."

"It's not something you have knowledge of, Pyx," he said. "I think when the Sinistari walk the world upon summons, the information is somehow blocked to them. Sort of like if an angel gets his soul he then forgets he was ever an angel. But it's true. You were once as I. An angel from Above."

She shook her head furiously and twisted to pace away a few steps. The unbearably insistent noise of traffic beat in her ears. The whole world caved toward her and she felt…small. She didn't like the feeling, the not knowing. The lacking power.

Could she have possibly walked the world and not learned it all?

"Don't you remember?" he asked. "You are, or I believe you are, Kadesch."

"Kadesch?" The name meant nothing, and yet, speaking it did not feel wrong. The tones of the name sounded familiar.

"It was your angelic name. We were, I believe, good companions while Above. You chose to fall with the rest of us," Cooper said. "In fact, you were the one who encouraged me to fall."

"Ridiculous."

"Fact, Pyx. Two hundred angels fell, yet during that descent their ranks were decimated. You were taken before your feet touched the earth and then forged into Sinistari. Which makes you divine, and gives you the power to slay angels."

"Divine?" She scoffed. "You are on something, Fallen one."

"Yes, I'm on the truth. And it's about time you opened your eyes to it. I didn't recognize you as Kadesch. Not until you said the thing about having choice."

Spinning about and charging him, Pyx beat the lying bastard on the shoulder with a hard fist. Once, twice, and again. If they were both shifted her metal structure would clang against his glass form. But each punch boasted less anger, and more confusion.

Why would he make up such fantastic lies? To what purpose would it serve him? Is this how low the Fallen would stoop to get a Sinistari on his side? To win his freedom and live? It wasn't working. It was only making her angry that she'd trusted him in the first place.

Besides, she had never been on his side. The sex had been…fabulous. And so the emotions she had begun to feel for him were warm and squishy and possessive. But that was beside the point!

Cooper gripped her wrists and wrangled her close, forcing her to look into his eyes. "It's the truth, Pyx. You are Kadesch. I know it. Ask your archangel master, if you don't believe me."

Pyx had never questioned the hierarchy. But if the Sinistari had been forged from the Fallen, then it made weird sense because their leader, Raphael, was one of the angelic dominions.

But divine? No way.

"How do you know this?" she challenged. "If you say that you didn't recognize me…"

Though she was already beginning to accept, the infusion of such a bizarre truth rippled through her being, making her skittish and stepping from foot to foot.

"I just do," he offered. "It was apparent to me the

moment my feet touched the earth so many millennia ago. You are one of twenty original Sinistari
created from those two hundred Fallen."

"Mythology. As is the entire mortal Bible!"

"Only an angel can kill an angel, Pyx. You know
that."

"I…" Did know that.

Wasn't sure.

It *seemed* true. But she'd never thought about it
before. It was instinctive knowledge like all the rest
of her knowledge.

"But that's why I've Joe," she said, her words
losing some fire. "My blade is forged from an
angel's rib and dipped in the poison qeres."

"A poison made only for angels," Cooper confirmed. "I know of that nasty stuff."

"Yes, and that is how I'm able to slay an
angel!"

"That blade was forged from one of *your* ribs,
Pyx. Taken from you as you Fell. Which makes
Joe divine, as well." Cooper kicked the base of the
bridge railing. "You don't want to believe me. But
you know it's truth."

"This isn't possible."

She caught her palms against the cool stone
bridge railing. The brown waters swirling below
matched the wicked swirl in her gut.

After sharing her body with Cooper last night,
she had to be open to anything being possible.

"Don't you remember me?" he asked, slapping a palm to his chest. "Juphiel? Think, Pyx. Just dig deep."

She put up a palm to block his words, and shook her head furiously. "Lies."

"Not lies. Truth. It is why the halo glowed in your presence."

Cooper left the bridge, shoving roughly through a crowd of tourists posing before the Henri IV statue. Pyx raced after him.

"I don't intend to screw any muses today," he called back. "Why don't you bug off for a while and leave me alone, eh?"

Pyx let him go. He was in a fine temper.

Yet why should he be? It was *she* who had discovered she was once an— "Angel?"

She hugged her arms across her chest. "I have to process this. This is too incredible. And *my* halo?"

She glanced in the direction of the hotel, though could not see it from this distance for the buildings edging the Tuileries blocked view. She should march back and take the halo from Donovan and just see...

See what? If it granted her an instant soul? She'd always thought the only way a Sinistari could get a soul was by killing a Fallen. Could it be as easy as taking possession of her halo?

"An angel? I don't deserve a soul for all the sin I've committed since walking the earth."

Not a lot, if she was truthful with herself. She'd tried to do the big bad demon thing, but it hadn't come naturally. Weird. She was so wrong, in every way.

"What if I am wrong? What if..."

She was wrong because she had been an angel?

She couldn't speak it, but to think it gave her a shiver. What if she should have Fallen to earth and another angel should have been chosen as Sinistari? Would she be looking for her muse right now? Would the muse be a he? Would she be a he?

"Kadesch." Why couldn't she remember that?

Because there is nothing to remember.

Pyx stomped across the street toward her building, but when she reached the top step, she kicked the stone wall and turned to march down to the cobbled street.

"No way. Not me. I'm demon, through and through. I don't possess divinity. Never have and never will. Cooper doesn't know what he's talking about. He's trying to make me sympathize with him."

They'd been honest with one another: each was using the other to gain what they most desired. If Cooper wanted a soul he'd do anything to stay alive and convince her to not kill him.

Like have sex with her? Seduce her? Claim they were once friends?

You are an angel, Pyx. That is why the halo glowed.

"My soul? Could I…?"

Walking onward, Pyx toyed with the notion of calling out Raphael, her superior. She'd never met the archangel, and wasn't sure she was worthy anyway. No, she daren't make good on the desire.

Dismissing the longing, she eyed the café where Cooper's muse worked. Would she have had a muse?

You are not and were not an angel.

Striding onward she entered the café and ordered a latté double mocha with sprinkles. Whatever that was. Sounded fun, and she needed a little levity right now.

"Is Sophia in today?" Pyx asked the waitress, who turned and gave her a teary-eyed shake of head. "What's wrong?"

"She was attacked last night. Called in this morning to say she was staying with her mother for a few days. She sounded so frazzled, I thought she could have been in trouble right then. Poor girl."

"Oh. Uh. I'm sorry. She sounded frazzled?"

"Yes, she was breathing fast and speaking quickly. I hope she's not in trouble."

"Yeah." Pyx took the latté and pressed a finger

to the waitress's hand. "Paid. I hope your friend is okay, too."

And she did feel empathy for the muse. Poor woman had been through an awful experience, witnessing an angel and a Sinistari go at it in her living room.

Maybe she should swing by her building and check things out. No sense in letting a perfectly good muse slip through her fingers, right?

Chapter 20

Sophia came to from a faint. The air smelled dank and dusty. The left side of her black skirt was badly torn. Her white blouse was smudged with dirt and her arm—

Chains clanked when she lifted her arm.

Panic racing from her heart and up her throat, she stifled a cry. She sat on a stone dais. Her left wrist was shackled and chained to the stone wall behind her.

What in hell? Where was she? How did she get here?

She remembered…that man who'd been so thoughtful and had offered to call the police. She'd gotten in his car. *Stupid!* He'd retrieved his cell phone from the driver's seat, then tossed it in the backseat. His sneer had cut her like a blade. She'd screamed, and then she'd seen fangs.

Fangs? Yes, the man had long white fangs.

She slapped her free hand against her neck. He hadn't bitten her. Like he would have? Was he...?

"What's going on?"

Scrambling to her feet she pulled at the chain with both hands. The thick bolt drilled into the wall held it securely. She'd never free herself. And the tight shackle kept her from folding her fingers inward to slip out from it.

Scanning her surroundings, her gaze landed upon nothing but stone walls and floor. It was a cavernous room, yet high above beams of light flashed down from holes carved within the stone ceiling. Those holes beamed down a circle onto the floor at one side of the room.

On that far side the wall stood a picture of some sort. It was as tall as a man and featured vivid colors that formed a strange beast—

Sophia gasped on her breath. The painting looked similar to the creature that had been in her apartment.

That insane man had changed into a creature! She'd been foolish enough to invite into her home— Cooper, that was his name. He'd seemed perfectly sane and kind. Handsome. Charming.

He'd changed into a monster with wings! And

then another monster formed from black metal and sporting horns had rushed into her apartment and battled the blue one.

She could not wrap her head around it all. Why was she here? Where was here? Had one of those monsters returned and imprisoned her in a lair?

Nothing made sense. It was difficult to think with the pounding blood her heart surfed through her system. She had to be strong. And get the hell out of here before the monster returned.

Sitting and pressing her bare feet to the wall at either side of the bolt, she pulled until the skin tore at her wrist. Blood dripped onto her bare foot and she sniffed back tears from the pain.

"Ah! The fresh smell of blood in the morning."

The male voice clamped an invisible hand about her neck, tightening her scalp. Sophia did not want to turn and look. If it was Cooper she had no idea how to win against the weird creature he could become.

Why hadn't she stayed in Jersey with her girlfriend and helped her start the cupcake shop she'd been so excited about?

She struggled, tears spilling down her nose and cheeks as the shackles cut deeply. A cold touch to her shoulder frightened a warbling scream from her throat.

"Enough of that."

The man leaned in and with but a tug, yanked

the bolt from the wall. The chain dropped onto Sophia's thigh. Would he set her free?

Then he turned her about and knelt before her. It wasn't the same man. Not Cooper. He was dark of eye and hair and his voice was disturbingly calm.

"My name is Antonio del Gado. You are a guest in my home."

His home? This was…a…a dungeon!

"Let me go." She couldn't find calm. Her entire body shook as if ice flowed through her veins. "I won't tell anyone. I promise."

"There's nothing to tell, Sophia." He reached for her hair, but when she flinched, he did not continue that touch. Instead, he grabbed her shackled hand and tutted over the blood. "Smells delicious."

Fangs curved over his lower lip. *Vampire.* They were vampires!

Sophia tried to scream again, but the cry stuck in her throat. And she wanted to kick, but her legs felt leaden. Frozen in fear, she could but watch as the man bowed over her wrist and sniffed, savoring her scent.

Mon Dieu, help me.

The man abruptly stopped sniffing and smoothed his fingers over the mark on her forearm. "Mustn't get distracted." His fangs disappeared as if they were a movie trick.

Light-headed and woozy, Sophia struggled to stay alert. She was not going to become some horror-movie extra who gets killed halfway through the film because of stupidity.

The soft touch over her forearm tickled. "You know what this means, Sophia?"

She shook her head lethargically. The muzzy precursor to a faint pulled at her conscious. *Stay awake!* And look for escape exits. She scuddered a glance about the room. A huge medieval-looking wood door with iron studs sat about thirty feet to her left.

"But you must have some knowledge." He smoothed his thumb over the mark on her skin. "My man brought me the notebook taken from your home."

He left her lolling against the wall, weak and so frightened. Her brain envisioned her running out of here, but her muscles did not comply.

He returned and displayed the small red velvet-covered sketchbook that belonged to her. She'd thought the apartment strangely messy last night. Someone had been in her apartment *before* Cooper had walked her home.

"This belongs to you," the man said.

Was he a man? He had fangs. That would make him a creature. Not a man. Not human. But that was impossible. And yet, she'd watched Cooper grow wings last night. What had he been? She'd never believed in monsters.

Now was a good time to begin.

"Did you draw all these sigils, Sophia?"

She'd never heard them called that before—sigils. The word sounded odd. Sid-zel. She shook her head.

"So you must know what they mean? Which angel they coincide with?"

"Angel?" She nodded drowsily. So exhausted. She wanted to sleep, to close her eyes and wake in her own bed. "Don't know what they mean."

He knelt before her and gripped her hand again. It ached and she could smell the blood.

"You've worn an angel sigil all your life, Sophia. You draw angel sigils in your pretty red notebook. And you want me to believe you don't know what they mean? Come, Sophia, we will get along much better if you are truthful with me."

"I…don't know. Just thought…I had a guardian angel."

"A guardian is the last thing you should name your Fallen counterpart. An angel was in your home last night. The man who shifted halfway with wings." He pointed to the painting. "Did he have sex with you?"

She shook her head violently. "Please, let me go."

"Why didn't he? That is his only reason for walking this earth. To find his muse—you—and get you pregnant."

A muse? Why did he name her that?

Yet, she wanted to cooperate. Maybe he'd release her. "There was another…creature. Made of metal. Stopped…the angel. They fought. I ran out."

"The Sinistari demon?"

"A demon?"

"I marvel you know so little."

He showed her a page from her notebook that featured a circle sigil with Y-shaped dashes growing out at four points. "This angel—Zaqiel—died a few months ago. Slain by a Sinistari. If your angel has no desire to have sex with you then I need to summon another. Something must be wrong with the idiot Fallen one. I can use the sigils to summon another, but I also need names."

He paged to the sigil matching the one on her arm and tapped the design Sophia had always thought looked like two sevens butting heads. "Juphiel. That is the angel's name who seeks you."

"No. He said his name was…Cooper."

"Interesting. Did you see the sigil on him?"

Had she seen— Yes, she recalled now that blue mark on his abdomen, riding the tight ridges of his muscles. It had glowed, but at the time she had been frantic to escape so couldn't be sure the design had matched hers.

"And who does this one belong to?" He opened to the next page and held it before her. On it she'd drawn three parallel lines topped by three dots.

"I don't know names," she pleaded. "I had no

idea those images were related to angel sigils. I see them in dreams!"

"I think you're lying."

Perhaps, but she wasn't lying about not knowing the names.

"Yes, well, get comfy, Sophia. If Juphiel has tasted you once, he will want another taste. Did he give you the angelkiss?"

She shook her head, not understanding.

"Lick you somewhere?"

"Yes," she whispered. "My neck." And to confirm that weird act now made the skin on her neck burn. She slapped a palm to it.

"Excellent. We've merely to sit back and wait for him."

He strode away, and Sophia slid to the dais edge. The chain spilled over the edge and clattered heavily to the floor.

"Sit tight, pretty muse," Antonio called.

The door slammed shut, sealing her in the stone cell. Instead of screaming, Sophia fainted.

Pyx wandered the muse's apartment. The living room was a mess. The walls and windows looked as if a wild animal had scratched its talons across them.

She was looking for an address book, something that would lead her to the mother, but then she had the notion that perhaps a daughter would not need to write down her parents' address.

"This isn't going to help me find the muse."

Instincts warned Pyx that the muse was not with her mother. That nothing had been normal for the muse since last night. But how dare she go to Cooper with this worry? He needed to stay as far from the muse as possible.

Unless the Sinistari demon could finally convince him to take his muse.

"No. I don't want him near the muse."

She couldn't kill him last night.

She wouldn't kill him now.

She wanted to make love with him again.

Yes, she'd thought the *L*-word. Because it was fore in her mind. And though she had no experience with it previously, Pyx knew to her very black marrow that love was what pushed her solidly across the line to stand on Cooper's side now.

"I'll take the punishment I deserve. I no longer wish to deny my wants. I make this choice," she said. "I will not kill the Fallen."

"Where's the bitch?" Antonio asked his assistant.

"Sedated."

"I wanted her alert."

"She was strong."

"Leave her to me."

Antonio stalked down the hallway toward the cell where prisoners were kept. It had been months since he'd seen Vinny. She had been his favorite until she'd decided to flee from his tutelage and take up with a mortal.

A *mortal*.

The rebellion cut into his heart. He'd survived this world for three centuries and rarely had he opened his heart to any of his blood children.

As a mortal, Vinny had been feisty and ambitious. Antonio had found her bleeding in an alley after an attack by some of his tribe. The attack had been an anomaly. He did not sanction murder. Vinny had clung to him, fearful, yet near death for she'd been bitten over and over and had lost copious amounts of blood. He'd promised to give her all she asked for if she would take his blood.

He wondered now if she had agreed because the idea of death so young was horrific, or if she had been attracted to him. He'd thought there was an attraction. He had been stupid.

He kicked the metal door and it swung inside the small cell carved out of a vein of granite, which was in abundance beneath the city of Paris. A raised stone slab provided a place to rest, but not at all comfortably.

Vinny was alert and sitting up. Big green eyes assessed him with a look that again made him realize what a fool he had been to believe she could have loved him.

"The strays eventually return to the flock," he said calmly, stepping to the stone slab to loom over her. Her long wavy hair was secured at the back of her head in a ponytail, making her narrow face appear thin, almost skeletal. "You're looking gaunt, Vinny. The boyfriend not taking proper care of you? You decide the best sip is from your master and come to beg my mercy?"

She tucked her head against the inside of her elbow. Not going to play? Antonio used the heel of his boot to shove her arm from her knee, forcing her to look up.

She was frightened of him. As she should be.

He leaned over her and gripped a hank of her hair. "You smell like dirty mortal." He'd kept her from feeding on mortals to keep her as his own. Until the damned halo hunter had arrived on the scene.

"It's the same blood you drink," she whispered viciously. He detected not a hint of fear in her voice. "What do you want from me?"

"Besides contrition?"

"You're not my confessor. I have no god."

"You should, Vinny. We all require something or someone to believe in."

"You're a hypocrite. This has to do with the Fallen, doesn't it?"

"Now we're getting somewhere."

Releasing her hair, he squatted before her. She would be a fool to charge him, but then, he would not put it past her. He was more powerful. And once already he'd held her captive within the cage of light beaming down from the dungeon ceiling. She would not forget her place.

"I'm going to send you on your way to rendez-vous with your insipid mortal lover. And when you return to his side, you will tell him to bring the Fallen to me, or I will hunt you both down and slay him first so you can watch, and then I'll chain you out in the sun. Sound like fun?"

"How are we supposed to get the angel to you? He doesn't trust Michael."

"Isn't your lover some kind of hunter of halos? Doesn't he have halos with which to bait the angel?"

"We've already checked. None of them are the Fallen's."

"That's because I hold the angel's halo."

"You do not."

"Does not the halo glow blue when in the pres-ence of its rightful owner?"

"You have a halo that glows? But if you've not been near the angel…"

"This halo was found in the vicinity of the angel's home."

"Well, if you know where he lives—"

Antonio grabbed her by the throat, pressing his thumb in deep. "Do not argue with me. You want freedom? You bring the angel to me." He released her roughly, and stood. "Don't think you can run from me, Venezia. You know that would be a mistake."

He left her to consider her alliances.

Chapter 21

Cooper paced the quiet rooms of his apartment. The high ceilings gave the rooms a vast, spacious atmosphere without closing him in as he'd been accustomed to while imprisoned in the Ninth Void. This was different. This was real.

Humanity. It was a delicious tease, but only that.

He would miss it.

Weird, but in little over a fortnight he'd already put down roots in this city. He liked this home. He liked this realm. It felt comfortable. It offered everything he'd never had Above, most especially, love.

She does love you. Don't give that up.

Cooper punched a fist into his open palm with a smack. "I love her."

And that was why he had to leave. It wasn't right to expect Pyx to ignore her Sinistari calling over something the demon would be punished severely for. But if he was nowhere near the muse, then Pyx wouldn't have to ignore a thing.

Flicking off the light switch, he trundled toward the front door, combat boots beating the hardwood floor. He needn't carry belongings with him; there was nothing he valued that was tangible and clothing he could assume with ease.

According to research on the internet, the frozen wasteland of northwestern Siberia boasted a small population, and was not welcoming. Nor did it provide optimum living conditions to the few who did live there. Cooper figured no sane muse would live there. He would get used to the cold.

He'd set up in an apartment—maybe an igloo—and then focus on locating his halo. It wouldn't be an easy quest, as it had been for Pyx.

Her halo had glowed. *Not his*. And as far as Cooper knew she couldn't use it. A demon had to make a kill to gain a soul, didn't they?

"Pyx." He stopped at the front door and tilted his head back, closing his eyes. She was the one tangible thing he would miss. Much as he hated leaving her without a word, he knew Siberia wouldn't keep the Sinistari away.

"She'll find me. And when that happens, at least there won't be a muse in the vicinity."

Which could prove good for their relationship. If they hadn't the interference of the muse they could focus on each other.

No, as much as he and the demon got along, and they enjoyed sex together, Cooper suspected Pyx wasn't in it for the long run.

Was he?

He did like the demon, despite, well, that she was a demon. Hell, he could go there. It wasn't just *like*. He loved her. How crazy was that?

Love was a bright and vast feeling that exploded in his chest every time he saw Pyx. And maybe, just maybe, a part of her really did love him.

It was too great to hope for. But he did.

A knock on the door pulled Cooper from his thoughts of the sexy demon. The door opened as he turned the knob. Michael Donovan and his girl-friend Vinny walked through.

"They've got the muse," Donovan said, striding on into the kitchen as if Cooper had invited him.

The vampiress hung back, following Cooper, but he was bothered by her presence. He noticed she didn't look at him and when he arrived in the kitchen Cooper bowed to look at her face. "What happened to you, little one?"

A green-and-violet bruise angered the skin below her left eye.

Michael hugged her about the shoulders. "Antonio and his tribe worked her over. Wanted her to bring a message to you."

"Me? Why?" He eyed Vinny cautiously. "I thought vampires healed fast?"

"Just gives you an idea how badly they hurt her," Michael said.

Vinny glanced toward the window but remained quiet. Something was off with her.

Seriously? She'd taken such an awful beating that she still had not healed. That was remarkable for a vampire. Her kind normally regenerated surface wounds within an hour. Even a mortal wound took less than a day to heal over. Unless it was a holy wound. If baptized, the vampire never healed from a holy wound.

The bruise on Vinny's face did not appear cross-shaped.

"So what's the message?" Cooper asked, folding his arms high over his chest.

The door opened and Pyx barged in, looking fierce and ready for—hell, she always looked ready to kick ass. Cooper smiled broadly, despite the disturbing company. That was his girl.

Pyx wore a long black leather dress that was split hip-high and beneath that wore thigh-high leather boots. Black fingerless gloves glinted with a few rivets and her red hair was pulled into a sleek tight ponytail. She was either in angel-slaying mode or fashion-model meltdown.

Either way, she *owned* that outfit. And Cooper could think only of removing it from her body.

"Pyx," he said on a breath. "Good to see you. That dress is…hot."

"It's actually pretty cool. I'm told leather is what all the fashionable people wear." She crossed her arms, feet squared and chin up. Yeah, she was in angel-hunting mode, Cooper could feel her stealthy focus and it tensed his muscles. She flicked a nod toward the couple. "What do they want?"

"The Anakim tribe has Cooper's muse," Michael said. "They sent the message through Vinny."

Pyx observed the vampiress with a narrow glare. "Why would they send a message via another vampire? Why didn't Stellan tell me? Or heck, Cooper has his own vamp shadow. And so what if they have the muse? Angel boy here isn't interested."

"That's not what I heard," Michael said. He turned a look over his shoulder at Cooper. "Heard you had a go at the muse last night."

"It couldn't be helped," he answered, flexing his fingers in and out of fists. The halo hunter pressed the bounds of respect. He had no right to infer that Cooper was in the wrong. "But it will be. I'm leaving town as soon as I shuffle you sorts out of here."

"Leaving?" Pyx tilted a look at him. It asked

"What's the deal? First you leave me in bed, now you're leaving the country?"

"They've got your halo, too," Vinny shot out. "I saw it."

"My—" Cooper stopped himself from clutching hope. Instead he chuckled as a defensive reply to the wily vampiress.

"They have dozens of halos," Pyx argued. "You have no proof the one you saw is Cooper's."

"It glowed," Vinny said. "Just like yours did, Sinistari."

Cooper caught Pyx's raise of brow. They exchanged silent looks for a tense moment.

Finally Pyx said, "I'll go and check things out. There could be another Fallen in the city we're not aware of. Which would explain why the one in the hotel glowed. It was *not* mine."

Cooper shook his head. "I'm not letting you barge into a lair of vampires by yourself."

"Oh, yeah? You want to go muse hunting, big boy?"

He didn't like her tone. It was as if they'd never shared a night of passion, or whispered things like they could do this forever and wouldn't it be awesome if they both had their souls and could live happily ever after. Pyx was hard today.

Was it because he'd told her about her origins? The news should have endeared him to her. They were two alike. But it could have had an opposite effect. If she hated angels then knowing she had been one would be the ultimate blow.

"They'll kill the muse," Vinny warned.

Pyx approached the vampiress and towered over her, arms still crossed. "Why would the vampires kill a perfectly good muse? If they don't snag Cooper they can use her to catch another Fallen. That's how it works. You, vampire bitch, are lying."

"No, I'm not," Vinny rushed out. "I made a guess about them killing her. I'm sorry. They've got her chained to a wall. She's bleeding."

"Bleeding?" Cooper winced. What had they done to her?

Siberia would have to wait. Sophia was an innocent in all of this, and he would not suffer the bloody vamp who had harmed her.

"Doesn't matter," he said. "We need to get her out of there. Bunch of bloodthirsty animals, is what they are."

He paused to notice Vinny cringe as her boyfriend hugged her. Weird pair.

"Take us there," he commanded Vinny. "Once inside, I can track the muse by the angelkiss I gave her." He avoided looking at Pyx but could feel her disappointment burn through the back of his skull. "And you, Donovan, are going in with me. While I'm looking for the muse, you'll be retrieving my halo."

"What do I get out of it?" Donovan countered.

"You get to live."

"I'm going in, too," Pyx said. "If you get too close to the muse the rescue mission will go cockeyed, and you know that."

Cooper nodded. "You two, meet us outside." The halo hunter nodded and led the vampire out.

Cooper grabbed Pyx and kissed her. She struggled from him and stepped back.

"What's wrong?"

"We are," she said. "We can't do…this."

"Is it because you were once an angel? You do believe me, Pyx."

"I do. I can. I know you wouldn't lie to me. But it doesn't matter what I was, only what I am now. And what I am is a slayer. And I haven't been doing a bang-up job with it lately."

"I thought you were falling on the side of staying here on earth. If that's your halo—"

"You don't know that."

"Kadesch."

"Don't call me that. Wait. I'm sorry, I do believe you, Cooper. What were we like? It wasn't like a boyfriend and girlfriend thing, was it?"

"Not at all. We were friends. We trusted one another. You, Kadesch, gave me hope."

"I wish I could do that for you now."

Cooper sighed. "Let's go."

"I got your back."

He led her out of the apartment. She'd been granted a renewed need to do her job. He wanted Pyx to win a soul. And he wanted the muse safe. Could he manage both tonight?

Vinny and Michael Donovan walked ahead down the narrow alleyway deep in the heart of the Parisian right bank. Pyx sensed Cooper's pace slowed as they neared the vampire lair set up in the old church. He wasn't eager to get near his muse.

She knew Cooper. He was too kind. A gentle warrior. He didn't want to make some woman pregnant with a monster child. The guy simply wanted to live without having to worry about vampires or Sinistari chasing after him.

And she loved that he was that guy. *Liked.*

No, you went there before. Own it now.

Okay, she *loved* him.

Cooper was the one angel who had fallen away from the rest. *An angel who had originally fallen with her.* She couldn't remember her time from Above. But she did believe it.

Kadesch. Yes, she could claim that name.

The halo in Michael's pack had glowed. Could it really be hers? And could she get her mortal soul from the halo and still leave Cooper alive?

Suddenly her shoulders hit the wall. Cooper pressed his palms to her shoulders. The intensity of his nearness shivered through her system. His breaths huffed across her mouth.

Pyx glanced down the alley. Michael and Vinny wandered ahead.

"We'll catch up to them," Cooper said. "I have something I need to say before we do whatever it is we're going to do tonight."

"We're going to kick vampire butt and save the muse."

"Sounds like the perfect ending to a popcorn night. But you know exactly what will happen when I get near my muse."

Yep, and it wouldn't be pretty. "Then don't go inside. I can handle this, Cooper."

"I have to. I want to. Because—" He dropped his forehead onto her shoulder. "Pyx, I need you to be able to do your job tonight. And that's only going to happen if I go after the muse. Don't let me do it, Pyx. When I shift and go after the muse…"

She shook her head, knowing what he was going to say.

"You gotta kill me, Pyx."

She shook her head more vigorously, but didn't speak.

"I know you can do it. You're strong. You're determined. And, blessed Above, you're so gorgeous when you try to deny your feelings."

He gripped her head and kissed her. Hard and determined, he dashed his tongue into her mouth to taste her. The taste of him was warm, urgent and needy. She wanted to give him what he needed. But then she tasted his regret and the subtle warning as he gently bit the edge of her lip.

It was a kiss that should have brought her to her knees in a blissful surrender, but instead it made her straighter, more determined, more…committed to him.

"Promise me?" he whispered breathlessly.

"I won't. No!"

"You have to. I love you, Pyx. I want you to get your mortal soul."

"No, don't say that." She pushed his chest, but he was like a stone statue she couldn't move. Didn't want to move.

Another kiss silenced her protests. He clung to her. His fingers curved against her back, clutching and keeping her. If he pulled her against him, she would stay there, her hard demon heart clanking against his glass angel heart.

Her heart had once been like his; cold, solid, red glass. Now it was black steel. Neither beat.

Yes, they were two alike, in ways she could never have imagined. They wanted freedom from the immense and unforgiving realm of which they'd been born. They desired mortality. Cooper desired humanity.

She desired him.

"I love you so much," he whispered aside her cheek. "But I will not conceive of allowing you to walk this earth one moment longer carrying the burden of the Sinistari. Take your soul tonight, Pyx. If you love me, you must take it."

"I…"

He pressed his mouth to hers again. No movement, just the heat of their lips sealing them together, endlessly. Forever. And yet only for one last night.

Cooper pulled away and pressed his fingers over her mouth to ask for her silence. "I know you can't say it. But I have to know if you feel the same for me."

"If I say it now, the Sinistari could take me— Wait."

Pyx shoved her hand in a pocket and palmed the small metal iPod. She turned it on and clicked to the video section to select the one video she had watched.

"There's no time, Pyx."

"Just be quiet and watch this."

She pressed the play button and turned the small screen toward him. The woman on the video sashayed toward the viewer and said the words Pyx pined to give Cooper. The words that would see her banished to Beneath.

Three simple words. So devastating to her kind.

Cooper grasped the player and searched her eyes.

"I mean it," she offered.

"That's all I needed to hear. Pyx, I love you." He tucked the iPod back in her pocket and kissed her hard. Then softly. Then he brushed his lips over hers and moaned, speaking the language they'd created when making love. "Let's get this done with."

She grabbed his wrist as he turned to walk on. "Don't trust them," she said of the halo hunter and his girlfriend. "The vampire is lying."

"I suspect as much. It would mean a lot to her if a nephilim were created this night. If she's allied with tribe Anakim she could earn the means to walk in daylight."

"Exactly. All right then. You know what's up." She swung her arms, wishing the idea of pulling him in for another kiss would fizzle.

Slapping a hand under her arm, she drew out Joe. "I got your back, angel."

"It had better be my heart, when the time is right."

Michael Donovan called to them, and Cooper took off, leaving Pyx to falter after him. She shoved Joe in the leather sheath, wishing she could toss it away and wash her hands of the impulse to slay.

She'd never felt more conflicted. Save the angel or win her soul?

* * *

The foursome entered the abandoned church through a window from which Cooper had ripped the boards. Inside the building was black; no human could see his hand before him, so Vinny grabbed Michael's hand.

Cooper and Pyx followed, each able to navigate with ease. When they'd gone twenty paces in, Cooper felt Pyx slip her hand in his. He squeezed and drew it to his chest.

The woman in the video had said "I love you." It had been an intimate moment only they had shared, and he still couldn't chase away the giddy flutter humming in his heart.

She loved him. She really did.

Juphiel and Kadesch had once shared the same beliefs. This may be the last time they shared the strange connection they'd been given, a gift, since landing on earth to pursue their respective quests. A reconnection actually.

He didn't want this moment to end. He kissed her knuckles and rubbed her hand.

"There's a six-foot drop ahead," Vinny instructed.

"Into the catacombs?" Michael asked.

"It's not the catacombs proper," the vampire explained. "Antonio del Gado and the entire tribe Anakim occupy some caverns immediately under the Hôtel Solange, a residence the tribe uses. It's not deep, but vast. And there are sun traps all over."

"Sun traps?" Pyx asked.

"We won't have to worry about them tonight," Vinny said.

"We?" Pyx chuckled. "Only you, lady, only you."

Michael and Vinny dropped down first.

Cooper wouldn't let go of Pyx's hand. He pulled her to him and spread a hand down her hip and over her ass, pressing her hips to his. But all the sweet video expressions in the world couldn't erase their truth at this moment. "Where's Joe?"

She slapped the holster at her hip. "Ready to rock. You got your muse mojo on?"

He sighed.

"I'm thinking I can rush in ahead and grab her and take off before you even shift."

That surprised him. She *didn't* want to slay him? "That's not how this is supposed to go down."

"Yeah? Well, it's not how we're supposed to go down either. You did watch the video. We've been pretty spectacular together lately. Hate to see that end because of some stupid compulsion to create your murderous progeny."

The smell of her, bubble-gum innocence and sultry temptress, momentarily weakened his determination. "Did I tell you I love you?"

"Yes. But can you prove it?"

"Ask anything of me."

"Stay here," Pyx said. "Don't go any farther. I'll get the muse and flash her somewhere. It could work."

It wasn't an awful plan, just desperate. "Sooner or later I'll find her, Pyx. She's marked with my angelkiss. That never wears away."

"Isn't the prospect of a few more days with me a little exciting?"

"Guys?" Donovan called from the dark depths below.

"Coming!" Cooper called. "You march ahead. We'll catch up. Not as if we can't flash ahead of them, eh?" he said to Pyx.

"Exactly." She disappeared in a waver of shadows.

He liked that chick's process. But he wasn't about to sit tight and let the girl get all the glory. Though, he did pause. Cooper knew he was endangering the muse simply by walking farther in. He could not control the shift. Could he swallow his pride and stand here?

A rustle around the corner alerted him. A familiar face stepped into view. Bruce grinned and displayed a small silver device held in his hand.

A nasty foreboding poked pinpricks up Cooper's spine, but before he could flash, the fierce electric jolt zapped him in the lower back. It was like being hit with a million volts. His arms straightened.

Legs stiffened, his entire musculature froze from the sudden, excruciating pain.

He managed not to shift. How, he didn't know.

Didn't matter. Cooper blacked out.

Chapter 22

The halo hunter startled at Pyx's sudden appearance in front of him. She laughed when Donovan kept checking behind him as if to discern from where she had materialized.

"I have my talents," Pyx said. She looked beyond the pair, hoping *not* to see a flash of Cooper's white shirt and sexy kilt.

But if she could flash to the end of the tunnel that meant Cooper could flash inside whatever was beyond the medieval pair of doors she stood before. If that's where the angelkiss led him, he may have no choice but to follow.

Don't do it, Cooper. Just stay put. If you love me, you will.

"Where's the Fallen?" Michael asked. "Did he flash with you?"

"It disturbs me a mortal knows so much about us," Pyx said.

"I was baptized by fire, demon. I didn't want the knowledge. It was shoved on me. So where is he?"

"I told him to wait above. I'm going to grab the muse and flash her somewhere Cooper won't be able to find."

The vampiress huffed. "Told you we couldn't trust her."

Pyx stepped before the woman and looked down her nose at the pitiful petite thing. "Don't trust you either, vamp. That's why I had Cooper stay behind. You're not telling the truth, and that lie is going to get Cooper in a lot of trouble."

"Bitch at me all you like. Won't do you any good," Vinny said with equal defiance. "The Fallen is already inside. I just heard him land."

"What?"

Pyx turned and kicked the heavy door. Ramming a shoulder against the studded wood she shoved it until she met a wall.

Not a physical wall. Pyx leaned into the partly open door but her shoulder stopped in midair, crushing against something intangible, as if a wall. She punched a fist toward the door yet it met the same unseen blockade.

The vampire's chuckle stabbed along the back of Pyx's neck. Pyx spun around and swung a fist for the woman, but again she landed her knuckles against an invisible barrier.

The halo hunter took a penlight out of his pocket and flashed the blacklight across the floor. The beam revealed a ward marked in a chalk circle beneath Pyx.

"Demon binding spell," Vinny said with far too much satisfaction. "Had to be done."

The spell was strong. Pyx could feel the invisible walls hum in warning like an electrified fence. Both she and Cooper hadn't trusted the vamp. So how could she have been so stupid now?

"You two were never in this to help Cooper," she said. "You want him to get to his muse."

"Don't you?" Michael flicked the light toward her face. Pyx growled at the annoyance. "Thought you came here to slay the angel."

"What I want is none of your damned business." She hissed through clenched teeth and punched at the barrier with little result beyond making her knuckles sting. Stupid mortal flesh. And trapped inside a binding ring she couldn't shift to demon form. "Release me!"

"Not until after the show."

The vampiress pushed the metal-studded door inside to reveal Cooper lying prone on the floor. Out cold, he lay with arms stretched to the side and shirt torn to reveal his abdomen. The sigil on his side glowed blue.

Pyx couldn't figure how that had happened. Why was he out? If he had flashed inside he would still be conscious.

"The vampires got him," she decided and snapped a look at the grinning vampiress. "I thought you weren't in the tribe?"

"I escaped tribe Anakim months ago. But I owed Antonio one. And I want to walk in the daylight. It's nothing against the angel. We all act for survival. This is my only means to a better life."

Her boyfriend hugged her and nodded in agreement.

"He'll destroy the muse, and not because he wants to—because, damn it, he does not want to—but because he's compelled to."

"The vampires will grab the muse before the Fallen can harm her," Michael offered in what he must have thought a reassuring voice. "They have to keep her alive to give birth to the nephilim. We'll release the binding spell as soon as he's done."

"Done," Pyx said on a gasp.

She peered inside the cavernous room. Done, as in, have his way with the muse against her will.

The binding spell held her imprisoned. She was helpless.

A glance at her lover, lying prone on the floor, ripped at her steel heart. A heart that Cooper had touched. If the damned chunk of metal could beat it would surely beat for him. She clasped a hand over her chest.

The glowing sigil on Cooper's gut pulsed faster. It sensed the muse nearby. And the angel Juphiel's instincts would not allow Cooper to disregard the need to mate.

"Oh, Cooper, please fight it. You can do it, I know you can resist. For us."

Cooper slapped a palm on the icy stone floor. He bent a leg and pulled himself up to a kneeling position. His head ached. How had he been knocked out so easily by the vampires? It had felt like thousands of volts shocking through his system.

It's that damned chip or tracking device or whatever it is they implanted in you. It had reacted to whatever they'd used on him. He felt like a cow must feel after it had been prodded, only to the tenth power.

Now his body hummed minutely. Stirred, actually. Something was not right. He slapped a palm to his abdomen. The sigil burned against his flesh. It was a cold burn. Ethereal. Yet wrong.

Or maybe something was very right.

He scanned the room, walled in cement— no, it was stone, perhaps carved from the very earth? He hadn't thought they'd descended so far underground.

A life-size painting of him was propped against one wall. And on the painting his sigil had been traced over in red. Blood. It had been used in a summoning ritual, he was sure of it. The vampires had brought him to earth to complete the goal of his original fall.

As his eyes tripped over the rough-hewn walls, Cooper's breathing increased and he thought he felt his heart pulse.

He slid a palm over his chest. As hard and adamant as time itself, his heart would never change form or substance—unless he found his halo.

But now he remembered. There was something else he sought. Not purposefully, yet instinctually. In fact, he felt its presence. He had marked it with an angelkiss.

He roved his gaze along the front of a stone dais and tripped over a delicate hand. Cooper's heart dropped to his gut.

The muse clung at the dais edge, kneeling, her eyes frantic at sight of him. A chain ran from one wrist to a bolt on the wall. Her gorgeous ink-black hair hung in tousled waves and one shirtsleeve was torn to reveal her shoulder. Soft, pale flesh that smelled…

Cooper lifted his head and sniffed. Rose perfume. Coffee beans. The heady lure of fear. So sweet. Like nothing he'd ever had before and like everything he must possess.

Do not harm her. You know the vampires want this. Fight it!

Stretching his neck and rolling his head from side to side he momentarily agreed with his conscience—he, Cooper Truhart, would not harm Sophia—but then instinct overwhelmed rationality. The angelkiss screamed to him.

She was his muse. Her name mattered little. Nor did the ridiculous mortal name he'd chosen for himself.

Juphiel the Fallen must have her—now. The urgent sensation crept up his legs, mobilizing him to stand.

Walking forward, every step he took made the muse scramble backward until she was glued to the wall at shoulders and hips. Shaking her head frantically, but unable to speak, her teary brown eyes silently pleaded against his most base and darkest compulsion. Her neck was red, raw where she must have scratched the angelkiss. The beacon called to him.

The angel's footsteps trudged laboriously across the floor as he fought against that compulsion. Muscles stiffening and jaw clenched, Cooper for a moment managed to stop.

Turn around. Walk away.

He could not move his hips, but he could turn his head.

A gorgeous redheaded demon stood in the

doorway to this dismal chamber. Her head shook left to right. Her bright eyes were shadowed.

Why did she simply stand there? He needed her to do her job.

"Do it!" Cooper shouted to the demon. "Stop me!"

Another footstep brought him to the dais. The muse screamed. The agonizing sound echoed in his skull but did not dissuade the Fallen angel, Juphiel.

Where were the vampires? Cooper could smell their greedy observance. They lurked, yet he suspected they would not show themselves until the wicked deed had been accomplished.

He jumped onto the dais. *Want her. Must have her.*

Can't do it in human form.

Every muscle stretching his body began to shiver. The bones from waist up began to shift. Cooper knew transformation would occur without his volition.

He slapped his palms to either side of the muse's head. His body shook, but he controlled the urge to hurt her. It took all his resolve to hiss out, "I do not want to harm you. I cannot control myself. Listen to me. You will have one chance. I will break the chains. Then run! Do you understand?"

She nodded frantically. So pretty. Sophia of the

lush dark hair and wide, wanting eyes. *Don't want to hurt her.*

Take her.

"Resist," he ground between his teeth, tasting bloody spittle.

Wings grew out between his shoulder blades. His flesh hardened. His form grew adamant yet sinuously flexible.

Cooper growled and smashed his glass fist upon the bolt where it connected to the wall. It dropped free. The heavy chain coiled at the muse's feet. "Go!"

The muse stumbled on the chain. She landed on her knees and palms with a painful scream.

Completely shifted, Cooper yowled, stretching out his arms and wings and crying to the heavens above that the wicked pact he'd joined would now claim him in its dark truth.

The muse struggled to clasp the chain and bolt to her chest so she could run.

The angel Juphiel tilted his head, noting her trouble. He stomped a foot on the chain. "Not so fast, pretty."

Chapter 23

The vampiress and halo hunter huddled together in the doorway watching the Fallen go after his muse. Pyx looked away from the dreadful sight. She was helpless to stop her lover from doing the one thing he had never wanted to do.

It wasn't in Cooper to want to harm anyone. Well, anyone innocent. Vampires were not included on that list.

And even if he didn't harm the muse now, and simply had sex with her and pushed her aside, the harm would be mentally implanted, and later, as far as Pyx understood, the muse would never survive giving birth.

She kicked the floor. The damned ward she

stood on acted as a steel-barred prison, keeping Pyx from moving outside of the circle, or flashing.

This was her moment. Her one opportunity as a Sinistari to prove herself to her brethren and claim the task of slaying a Fallen. And she was trapped!

Not that she intended to shove Joe into Cooper's chest and take his life. Perhaps for a second or two she had felt all-powerful and determined to prove herself to her Sinistari brethren.

But that was then. Now she wanted freedom, her own mortality. The ability to choose how to live her life. She wanted to dress like a girl and do girl things, like put on makeup and chatter about lovers with girlfriends. She wanted to make a home with a man and create a family.

Most of all she wanted Cooper. In her arms. In her life. Telling her she was sexy the way she was, goofy attempts at femininity included. And she wanted to answer with "I love you."

A growl from inside the dungeon indicated Cooper fought his vicious innate urge.

She was not holding up her end of the bargain they'd made.

The halo hunter toppled as he shuffled around behind the vampiress in an attempt to get a better view. For one moment, his shoulder and left hip swung over the binding ward—it held no power against him.

That moment was all Pyx needed. She grabbed

the messenger bag slung over his shoulder. He tugged on the leather strap, but Pyx managed to overturn it and the halos spilled out around her feet, *inside* the binding circle. One wobbled and fell against the wall, out of her reach.

"You've had them all along," Pyx said. "You've probably got Cooper's halo here."

Kneeling to gather the halos into her arms, she threaded her hand through them and strung them over her wrist like oversize bracelets. None of them glowed. Where was her halo? She couldn't reach the one by the wall.

"Give them back!" Donovan yelled. He made no move to reach for them. The hunter knew his place. "She's got the halos! The one Antonio gave you."

Ah-ha. So one of these was Cooper's. Pyx took the first from her wrist.

"Too late, the Fallen is moving in on his prey," the vampiress reported.

Prey? Pyx winced. So not Cooper.

She had to help him. She would even if it meant…yes, killing him. But she was yet trapped and too far away to plunge a dagger into his heart.

She held a halo before her. There was one other option.

"You will not harm the muse. I won't let it happen!"

Pyx threw the first halo into the room. It landed

near the dais, far from Cooper's grasp or notice. It didn't glow.

Gripping another halo as if to throw a Frisbee, she sent it flying. Nothing.

She tried three more in rapid succession. One hit Cooper's hard glass abdomen. It bounced to the floor and rolled toward the doorway where the vampiress reclaimed it. It didn't glow, so Pyx wasn't upset about the nab.

The last one she gripped and held above her head. As Cooper clutched the struggling muse's chain to drag her onto the dais, Pyx saw the sigil on his abdomen glow. The design flashed blue, getting brighter and brighter, as if a fresh brand.

"Please let this be the one." Kissing it for luck, she aimed and threw the halo.

The vampiress jumped, her fingertips snagging the center of the halo and upsetting its course. The halo wobbled midair, glowing blue, and landed on the dais but inches from the muse's groping and bloodied fingers.

It glowed. It was the one!

"Get it!" Pyx yelled. She beat fists against her invisible cage. "Sophia! It's the one!"

She was sure the muse did not understand her desperate pleas. And if Cooper did hear, in his state he was focused only on one thing, and that was not claiming his earthbound soul.

"Go in there and get it out of the way," the vampiress urged Donovan. "Hurry!"

The halo hunter dashed inside the chamber, ducking and trying to sneak up behind the Fallen who lifted the muse by a shoulder and turned her over onto her back. The muse was still conscious, but she looked defeated, close to surrender as her eyelids fluttered.

Pyx bit her lower lip and tasted acrid blood. She clenched her fists until it felt as if her adamant bones would tear the human skin. Stepping from foot to foot she beat upon the binding walls. Clawing her nails down them did nothing but bring her own pain. Fine runnels of black blood trickled down the invisible walls before her, unable to permeate the ward.

But what was that?

The muse had the halo in hand. Yes! But she was not in control, and the angel easily moved her about, dragging her close to the edge of the dais. And yet, she was trying to utilize the halo as a weapon, her fingers curling about the innocuous circle of ineffable substance.

The sigils glowed brightly on both the muse's forearm and Cooper's stomach.

Suddenly the muse swept the hand holding the halo through the air before her. The halo's curved edge neatly cut through Cooper's cheek. Blue blood drooled down his jaw and spattered the muse's dirty white shirt.

The Fallen yowled and grabbed the halo, dropping the muse in a sprawl. The muse lifted her hand from the puddle of angel blood and marveled at the odd color.

Noticing the halo hunter creeping up behind him, Cooper set him back with a mere shoving gesture. Donovan hit the wall, spine flat, arms spread and head lolling. He dropped in a heap on the floor.

"Yes," Pyx hissed. "One down." She reached for the vampiress but her knuckles slammed into the blood-spattered invisible wall. "Just take a few steps back, bitch. Come on!"

Vinny remained oblivious to the demon's struggles. She eyed her boyfriend, and the angel who stood, staggering.

Cooper studied the halo, glowing brightly in his clenched grip. Did he know what it was while in his altered state? He must. But did he know how to use it beyond as a weapon?

"Do it, Cooper!" Pyx shouted. "Step away from the muse. Take your freedom. You can make that choice!"

The angel turned a look on her. Their eyes held across the distance.

Pyx's heart boomed. Memory of their lovemaking deepened her conviction, the longing that her

lover have the one thing he desired. Could he remember that desire now? Would it help?

Suddenly, the angel nodded. Pyx didn't know if
it was an "I will do the right thing" nod, or a "this
will serve to cut off someone's head nicely" nod.

She slammed her palms against the warded
walls and gasped down her heartbeats. All she
could do was wait. And hope.

Cooper raised the halo high above his head. The
circle glowed brighter, changing from blue to bold
silver. A bell-like ringing echoed off the walls,
drowning out the muse's cries. And when he let
go of the halo, it hovered and found position above
and behind his head, locking into place.

The room filled with light so bright even Pyx
had to look away. But as she did so, the light forced
the vampiress from her feet, and she collided with
the limestone wall outside Pyx's prison. Her hand
landed a grasp away from the stray halo, but the
vampire didn't notice it in the shadows.

The muse, scrambling along the wall toward the
door, stopped and blocked her eyes with a hand.
The sigil on her forearm glowed bright silver to
match Cooper's halo.

Donovan woke and cowered at the sight, tucking
his head against the wall and tugging up his jacket
to cover his face.

The vampire swore and kicked the door frame.

And Pyx sniffed away a tear. She stepped back,

arms hanging loose at her sides. Sound had ceased. Frustrated anger ceased. Wonder eddied through her veins.

She had never witnessed a sight more eloquent and perfect.

The angel's wings stretched high and flapped a few times as if to take flight. Like a grand peacock, the blue, emerald and violet glass shimmered. The entire angel glowed as if sunlight burst out through his pores. It was an angel complete, shaped as a man, but not human by any means.

Cooper's feet left the ground. Arms and head flung back and chest lifted, he rose two feet from the dais as if being drawn Above by a guiding hand. He closed his eyes as he tilted his head skyward. He'd never been able to look up for his crime of falling.

Tears streamed down Pyx's face. She sputtered and hugged herself. Joy infused her heart and she cried happily for her lover.

And then the stained-glass wings began to crack.

Stretching out his arms and releasing his voice, Cooper shouted at the immense pain as his glass flesh crackled and chipped away. At once the ineffable substance glowed molten red then cool blue.

The wings shattered and shards of glass sprayed the room. Donovan dashed for the muse to protect her, and managed to drag her out from the room.

"What'd you do that for?" his girlfriend asked, eyeing the muse.

"We don't want her dead."

"Yeah? We don't want to stick around here any-more either. I can feel them." She looked around and down the long dark hallway. "They're getting closer."

"The vampires? Then let's go." He grabbed her hand. "We tried, Vinny. There's nothing more we can do now."

"Let me out!" Pyx insisted, beating the invisible barrier.

"You'll kill us," Vinny said.

"I won't. I want to keep the muse safe. I prom-ised Cooper. I can flash her away from him."

Michael stepped on the chalk-drawn sigil and shuffled his feet over it. It broke the circle. Pyx sucked in the air as if she'd been deprived. With that, he grabbed his girlfriend's hand and took off.

Pyx plunged down to scoop the trembling muse into her arms. She glanced up to see Cooper lying amidst a pile of glass shards on the floor, half-naked and not glowing.

"Maybe you're safe now," she said and set the muse down. "I think he's done it."

"No, don't leave me!" The muse grabbed Pyx's leather skirt. "They're coming back!"

Indeed, she smelled the vampires before she saw

them. With a decisive nod, Pyx scooped up the muse and flashed to her apartment. They arrived in the living room. She set the muse down on the green velvet sofa. The stuffing exploded out of one end where Pyxion the Other had stepped on it with her hoof.

"I can't stay. I have to get back to Cooper. You're safe from him now, but not the vampires. I suggest you move away from Paris. Fast."

"Mon Dieu," the muse cried and grabbed Pyx's arm. Tears spattered her neck and chest.

Pyx slapped a hand over her burning flesh. It sizzled. Mortal tears. The agony of contact stretched a scream from her mouth. Each tiny droplet burned through her tender flesh and began to eat away at the metal bone beneath.

Grasping for something—anything—to support her, Pyx blacked out and collapsed on the floor before the stunned muse.

His hand shifted over the rubble of glass shards. The scattered tinging noise sweetened the air and the odd aches and pains in his limbs segued to the background. Even sweeter was the dull, steady thud that sounded so close. Ta-dum. Ta-dum. Thud.

Inside his ears? Where was it coming from?

Pushing onto his forearms, Cooper shook his head and blinked. He lay on a pile of broken glass, but didn't appear to be cut.

Where was here? The room was a huge cavern of stone. To his side an open doorway exposed the dark maw of what must be a hallway.

The *thud, thud* continued. And suddenly he knew.

Cooper slapped a palm to his chest. "Heartbeats?"

He'd only heard the sort when he'd press his ear to a mortal's chest or held them and traced his fingers over the pulsing vein.

"It worked."

He shuffled his palms over the glass shards and found the cold, dull halo. It didn't glow when he picked it up. It didn't have to. It couldn't now.

"I'm human." He savored the word, the meaning of it.

All he had ever wanted—dreamed about for millennia while imprisoned in the Ninth Void—now it was his. He had a soul. And he'd gotten it—

"Sophia?" He scanned the room. The muse was nowhere to be seen. Nor was Pyx. Where was everybody?

"I didn't hurt her." Pray, he had not hurt Sophia.

Pyx had come to the rescue, as promised. Though he'd expected her to plunge Joe into his heart, instead, she'd put his halo in his hands.

He heard footsteps scuffling down the dark hallway. More than one person. Clutching the halo,

Cooper pushed up to sit, but that was all he could manage. He looked down the kilt and over his bare legs. These mortal bones felt as though they'd just run a marathon.

A smear of red dashed his leg below the kilt hem.

"Blood?"

Real, red mortal blood. With a shout of joy tickling his tongue, Cooper's elation was interrupted.

Bruce paused in the doorway, arms outstretched to stop the gang behind him from charging inside. The vampire sneered, revealing fangs.

Cooper cursed. He thrust out his hand, an intuitive move, and wished the vampire away. But the command did not work. It couldn't work.

He was now mortal.

Facing down a gang of hungry vampires. He had no stake. No means to defense.

"What's up?" someone behind Bruce asked.

"I think he's done it," Bruce said. "He's mortal now."

"Where's the muse?"

"They're all gone. Except him."

"What do we do with him?"

Bruce threaded the fingers of both hands together and flexed them out. "Let's take him out!"

This could not end well.

Cooper clutched a shard of glass in one hand. Blood spilled down the edge of it, and even as he braced himself to be pummeled by vampires he couldn't help but marvel.

Red blood. Coming from him!

But now he was mortal, he had to stay alive if he wanted to enjoy that prize.

The first vampire lunged. Cooper lashed out with the glass shard, catching the vamp across the jugular.

Pyx gasped breath. The mortal tears ate at her flesh. She had to get away from Sophia. She flashed outside the cavernous room where she had left her lover upon the heap of shattered wings. Colliding with the wall, she staggered and swept low, almost falling, but caught herself with a hand to the floor.

"Cooper," she managed to say.

Everything hurt. Her skin sizzled. Sophia's tears were eating along her arm and up her shoulder.

A fog of ash dispersed before her eyes, and before she could think *dead vamp,* Cooper knelt before her. A glass shard had been utilized as a stake; it dripped with blood.

"Hey, sweetie. Killin' some vamps."

"I can see that."

"Are you okay? Did one of them get you?"

"No, I'm fine. Just a little weak after flashing the muse away." She sat up against the door frame, and it was easier to breathe. Yet her neck burned now.

She scanned the room. No more vampires. But

plenty of piles of ash, as well as the glass remains of Cooper's wings. "You've been busy. But does that mean…"

"Kiss me." He tugged her to him and embraced her with bloody hands. The glass shard he dropped, the halo she felt crush against her spine. His face was spattered in vamp blood, but she didn't mind as he kissed her.

This kiss felt different than any previous kiss he'd given her. It was warmer, lusher, more urgent, and the blood taste from his lip tasted salty and new.

It would be their goodbye kiss.

"You taste so good," he said. "I love you, Pyx."

She wiped a smear of blood from the corner of his eye. New blood gushed out behind her finger. "Cooper?"

He nodded. The twinkle in his eye confused her. But more so the blood flowing from beside his eye did. "Are you…? Is this your blood?"

"Yep." He kissed her again. "Some vampire blood, too. Those bastards are nasty, but once you ash one of them the others get leery or run away. I toasted three or four."

"Good for you."

His bare shoulders were covered with ash. His skin was red and cut from the glass. And he bled…

…red blood.

"You got your soul?"

"I did," he said. "A bright and shiny mortal soul. My heart is beating. Feel it." He pulled her hand over his chest, where indeed, Pyx felt the insistent heartbeats. "What is this?"

He touched her shoulder gently, but Pyx sucked in a hiss at the painful contact.

"Pyx?"

"Mortal tears," she managed, feeling the burn work at her throat. "Just…kiss me again. Please?"

"Your skin is burning away. Pyx, the tears will kill you. I've got to stop this. How can I?"

Her head lolled to the side, and she saw the flash of a halo sitting in the darkness. Cooper must have seen it too, because he lunged for it. It glowed blue in his hands.

"I'm no longer Fallen," he said, "which means… Pyx, this is yours. It can save you."

"We don't know that."

"But we don't know otherwise. We've got to try it. I wonder how this works." He held it above her head, as it had moved above his for proper position. "Feel anything?"

Only pain creeping under her jaw and up the back of her skull. Pyx nodded lethargically.

"There's gotta be a way to make it work." He touched it to her forehead. Nothing happened. "Maybe if you hold it in your hands?"

"No," she muttered.

"Damn it, Pyx, you're not going to give up!" He slammed it against her chest and suddenly Pyx's entire body stiffened.

The halo heated against the leather dress and it burned far worse than the mortal tears.

"It's glowing brightly," her lover said on a gasp. "Does it hurt, Pyx? I'll stop it—"

"Leave it," she managed.

The burn permeated her skin and breasts and all the way into her heart. Something was wrong. It hurt worse than any pain she had felt since walking earth.

Crying out, Pyx stretched her arms out wide. The halo melted through her dress. Stench of burned flesh filled the air. The ineffable metal sank into her, burning through flesh, muscle and bone. She could not bend her arms to grab it away.

All she could do was scream, until her scream grew to silence.

"Christ," she heard Cooper say as an oath.

She felt it all. The halo clanged against her adamant heart, then curved and began to form about the hideous organ. Black demon blood oozed from the circle entrance wound marking the upper part of her chest.

And then it ceased. The burn grew cold. Her heart, which had felt molten, pulsed once. And then again.

Pyx dropped her head and slapped a hand against the oozing wound on her chest.

A squeezing clutch gripped her heart. She gasped as if her hard, demonic lungs required air. She couldn't breathe. And then she wondered if it was because her lungs really did need air.

Was she becoming mortal?

"Talk to me, Pyx. The burns on your neck and arm are gone. But your chest is healing too slowly. What have I done?"

She reached out blindly and landed her fingers loosely on his chest. *Be still,* she wanted to say, *let it happen.*

And then she felt it—the first pulse of mortality. Sweet. Enormous. *Thud.* And again, *thud, thud, thud.*

Smiling, Pyx dragged Cooper's hand up to place over her chest. The leather dress had a circle burned out of the middle between her breasts, and exposed one to the nipple.

The angel—former angel—chuckled softly and then nuzzled his ear against her breast. "It's beating. Just like mine. You're mortal now, Pyx."

"I know. And I like it."

"I love it," he said.

"Yes." She traced a finger down the side of his face, drawing his beauty in her mind. "Love."

"Pyx." He pulled her close and she closed her

eyes and held on to him tighter than she'd hold a cliff hanging over Beneath. "I love you, Pyx."

"I love you, too." She stroked her fingers through his ash and blood-soaked hair. "We did it," she exclaimed. "We really did it."

"And I didn't have to harm the muse in the process. I didn't harm her, did I?"

"She's fine. I flashed her home and told her to get out of town."

"She's a beacon to any other Fallen who may have been summoned by the insane leader of this vampire tribe." Cooper squatted on his haunches. "We need to go after Antonio del Gado if we want this to stop."

"He wasn't in the gang you slayed?"

"Don't know what he looks like. He could be ash." He turned to inspect the ash piles in the dungeon.

"We'll walk the entire place," Pyx said. "If he's here, we'll find him and stake him."

"Not you, sweetie. You're not going to put yourself in danger now that you're mortal."

"Oh, yeah? I'm feeling much stronger now. A few more minutes and I bet this wound will be completely healed. Besides, you're mortal now, too."

"I can handle a few vamps." He displayed the blood-soaked halo proudly. "This thing works pretty slick when you get them in the jugular. I'll protect you from now on."

She was about to protest, but instead Pyx shrugged and nodded. "Works for me. But before you go off stalking vampires will you do something for me?"

"Anything."

"Come here." She gripped the waist of his kilt, which was shredded and loose thanks to his shift, and tugged him down to straddle her, knees to either side of her thighs. "Kiss me, lover."

"Gladly."

The former angel and former demon kissed amid the vampire ash and Fallen detritus. The room glittered as moonlight sifted across the glass shards, and lifted the fine vampire ash to flutter through the air like fairy dust.

Neither noticed the magical moment, for this kiss was their first mortal connection. And they intended to make it last.

Epilogue

No vampires underground, at least, none that Pyx could sense. But she'd lost her vampire-sensing skills, so they wouldn't know if a vampire was around the next corner or not.

Which is why Cooper held Pyx close and walked ahead, makeshift stake from a chair leg held at the ready.

They were both aware that when a supernatural being claimed a mortal soul, that new mortal being eventually forgot their origins. They didn't know how much time they had, but prayed they would not also forget their love for one another.

Cooper kissed her forehead. "I won't forget

you. And not knowing what I once was will be a blessing."

"I agree."

Now aboveground, they walked the halls and rooms of the rococo mansion. The office had been swept of incriminating evidence. No signs of Antonio del Gado anywhere. They even checked the coffin in the master bedroom. Yes, there was a coffin.

"What do you think?" Pyx leaned against the open coffin, elbows to the red satin edge, as Cooper kicked aside an overturned chair. The room had been cleaned out swiftly.

"He's gone."

"Which means more Fallen may be summoned to earth. And more Sinistari will be dispatched to slay them."

"And more muses in peril," Cooper finished. "I can't let that happen to those innocent women."

"Didn't think so." She spun the stake expertly. "We don't have to be supernatural to chase vampires."

"No, but it would help. Wait. What's this?"

He moved aside a thick black damask curtain, but instead of revealing a window, it showed two paintings of angels. Matches to the life-size painting of Juphiel that had been in the dungeon, these paintings were of two different Fallen.

Cooper stroked a palm over the one that featured

an angel designed of silver. The sigil on its breast was a spiral capped by a boxed line. It had been traced over with blood. "Samandiriel."

"You know this one?" Pyx came to his side.

Cooper turned and squinted at her, as if seeing her for the first time. "Know…what?"

"The angel in the painting. You said Samandiriel? Is that the angel's name?"

He returned his attention to the painting, then stepped back, unsure.

"You've forgotten," she decided. "Cooper? Do you know me?"

"Of course, love. But what are these paintings about? I don't understand them. And who is Samandiriel?"

"He's an angel who fell to earth and may have been summoned by the vampire Antonio del Gado."

Her lover winced at her remarkable statement.

Pyx embraced him and laid her head aside his shoulder. So strong and warm. He'd lost all memory that he'd once been an angel. Good. It would be a horrible burden to bear now he was human.

She kissed him. "Let's walk, and fast."

"Whatever you say, sweetie."

They strode quickly down the halls of the mansion.

"I love you, Cooper Truhart."

"I love you, Pyx." He kissed her on the cheek. "You smell like bubble gum."

"You smell like the man I want to spend the rest of my life with."

They entered the night and it kissed them both with a brisk fall breeze. Pyx tugged Cooper down the steps.

"I think that sounds like a marriage proposal," he said. "The rest of your life?"

"Would you be my hubby?"

"Nothing would make me happier."

Kaylee has one addiction: her boyfriend, Nash.

A banshee like Kaylee, Nash understands her like no one else. Nothing can come between them. Until something does.

Demon breath—a super-addictive paranormal drug that can kill. Kaylee and Nash need to cut off the source and protect their human friends—one of whom is already hooked.

But then Kaylee uncovers another demon breath addict. *Nash.*

Book three in the unmissable Soul Screamers *series.*

www.miraink.co.uk

Join us at facebook.com/miraink

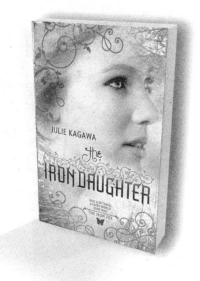

KEEP YOUR HEAD DOWN.
DON'T GET NOTICED.
OR ELSE.

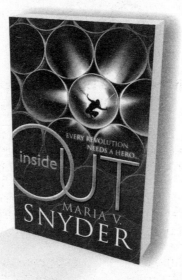

I'm Trella. I'm a scrub. A nobody. One of thousands who work the lower levels, keeping Inside clean for the Uppers. I've got one friend, do my job and try to avoid the Pop Cops. So what if I occasionally use the pipes to sneak around the Upper levels? The only neck at risk is my own. Until I accidentally start a rebellion and become the go-to girl to lead a revolution.

I should have just said no…

www.miraink.co.uk

Discover Pure Reading Pleasure with

MILLS
BOON®

**Visit the Mills & Boon website for all
the latest in romance**

Buy all the latest
releases, backlist
and eBooks

Find out more
about our authors
and their books

Join our community
and chat to authors
and other readers

Free online reads
from your favourite
authors

Win with our
fantastic online
competitions

Sign up for our
free monthly
eNewsletter

Tell us what you
think by signing up to
our reader panel

Rate and review
books with our star
system

www.millsandboon.co.uk

 Follow us at twitter.com/millsandboonuk

 Become a fan at facebook.com/romancehq

FREE BOOK
AND A SURPRISE GIFT

We would like to take this opportunity to thank you for reading this Mills & Boon® book by offering you the chance to take a specially selected book from the Nocturne™ series absolutely FREE! We're also making this offer to introduce you to the benefits of the Mills & Boon® Book Club™—

- **FREE home delivery**
- **FREE gifts and competitions**
- **FREE monthly Newsletter**
- **Exclusive Mills & Boon Book Club offers**
- **Books available before they're in the shops**

Accepting this FREE book and gift places you under no obligation to buy, you may cancel at any time, even after receiving your free book. Simply complete your details below and return the entire page to the address below. You don't even need a stamp!

YES Please send me a free Nocturne book and a surprise gift. I understand that unless you hear from me, I will receive 3 superb new stories every month, two priced at £4.99 and a third larger version priced at £6.99, postage and packing free. I am under no obligation to purchase any books and may cancel my subscription at any time. The free book and gift will be mine to keep in any case.

Ms/Mrs/Miss/Mr _____ Initials _____

Surname _____
Address _____

_____ Postcode _____
E-mail _____

Send this whole page to: Mills & Boon Book Club, Free Book Offer, FREEPOST NAT 10298, Richmond, TW9 1BR